An Uncertain Heart

An Uncertain Heart

JUNE TATE

Allison & Busby Limited
12 Fitzroy Mews
London W1T 6DW
allisonandbusby.com

First published in Great Britain by Allison & Busby in 2017.

A CIP catalogue record for this book is available from
the British Library.

First Edition

ISBN 978-0-7490-2133-7

Typeset in 11/16 pt Sabon by
Allison & Busby Ltd.

The paper used for this Allison & Busby publication
has been produced from trees that have been legally sourced
from well-managed and credibly certified forests.

Printed and bound by
CPI Group (UK) Ltd, Croydon, CR0 4YY

For my dear cousin
Margaret McVickers
with love

Chapter One

Belgium. July, 1917

It was just after dawn at the base hospital at Poperinghe, a few miles from the front line. Wards were made out of wooden huts and tents to house the many patients who had been brought in from the front. A place that was a mud bath underfoot after the heaviest rainfall in thirty years, where drainage systems had all but been destroyed by preliminary bombardments. Where troops faced the enemy, ankle-deep in mud, where the duckboards now failed to give the men a solid footage and where rats scuttled round their feet as the troops stood waiting for the order to go over the top, many of them knowing they might never return to the safety of the trenches.

Gunfire sounded in the far distance as Sister Helen Chalmers climbed out of her camp bed, and washed in a small tin bowl with cold water before donning her uniform and hat. She quickly checked her reflection in the cracked mirror, hanging from a nail in the tent pole, before pulling on a pair of boots and swishing her cape around her shoulders. Taking an extra pair of shoes, she opened the flap of the tent and, lifting her skirts, made her way through the mud, eyes down allowing her to pick her way through the ruts and deep puddles. The sky was grey without a hint of sunlight to follow.

She walked into the large tent that was the operating theatre, took off the boots and changed into her shoes. There were three tables awaiting the injured, with surgeons and staff standing ready, scrubbed up, preparing for another long day of surgery, knowing that soon, ambulances would be arriving, full of injured soldiers in desperate need of their skill. Then the first patient was brought in.

Hours later, Helen looked over her face mask at Captain Richard Carson, the surgeon with whom she worked, as she handed him a scalpel. This was their sixth operation of the day and yet another brave soldier was to go under the knife. As the battle raged on at Ypres, more and more casualties arrived. They were attended to by the medical orderlies and nurses, assessing which patient necessitated the urgent attention of the surgeon, who could wait and who was beyond medical help. It was a desperate choice to have to make, but the medical staff remained as stoic as possible under the strain. Those who could wait were taken to their beds, their uniforms, caked with mud, blood and crawling with lice, were removed and the men given blanket baths.

In the operating theatre, one of the nurses leant forward and wiped the sweat from the surgeon's brow. He nodded his thanks and continued. The day wore on. Limbs were amputated, shrapnel removed from chests, blistering from mustard gas treated, hoping to stave off infection from bacteria. Lives were saved and lives were lost on the operating tables. Bodies removed, the next patient brought in.

Eventually, other medical teams took over, giving those who'd worked time for a break and a meal. They made their way through the lines of washed sheets, pillowcases and bandages hanging out to dry.

Richard Carson lowered his aching body onto a bench at the table in the mess. He stretched his back and let out a deep sigh. Looking across at Helen, he smiled ruefully.

'At least we didn't lose many today.'

'No,' she agreed, 'it could have been so much worse.'

They ate in silence, lost in their own thoughts, almost too weary to make conversation.

'I'm going to get my head down for a couple of hours,' he said. 'I'll see you back in the theatre later. Perhaps after dinner you would like to come to my tent and have a well-earned glass?'

She nodded, rose to her feet and made her way to her own room. Stripping off her uniform, she set her alarm clock and climbed into bed.

Later that night, after completing their second shift, Richard and Helen made their way from the mess to Richard's tent. She sat on the bed whilst the surgeon poured two glasses of whisky, and handing one to her he sat in a chair. 'Bottoms up!'

She smiled and drank, closing her eyes, enjoying the heat from the liquor as it slid down her throat. Her back was painful, her legs ached and she longed to soak in a hot bath with water up to her neck as she lay back, but it wouldn't be until she was on leave that this luxury would be on offer. She rose wearily from the bed.

'I'm off to grab some sleep.'

Richard got to his feet and gathered her into his arms and kissed her.

'God! I don't know what I'd do if you weren't here.'

'Your job – that's why you're here, like the rest of us.'

She kissed him quickly and walked out of the tent, deliberately ignoring the picture of his wife, placed upon his desk.

Alone in her own tent, she undressed. She could still feel the imprint of Richard's mouth on hers and cursed the war. War messed with people's lives. How else would she have become a mistress of such an eminent man and who was married? They had worked together under the most difficult conditions, had faced gunfire, sometimes escaping with their lives by a hair's breadth whilst moving from one hospital to another. Facing death brought people together, lowered the barriers that should have kept them apart and now she was involved with a man who belonged to another!

At the end of July, Sir Douglas Haig ordered another attack on Passchendaele. The infantry attack churned the clay soil and smashed even more of the remaining drainage systems. The mud was now a quagmire, clogging rifles and immobilising tanks. In some parts the mud was so deep that men and horses drowned – and the hospital was full to overloading.

Outside of the hospital, lines of injured men lay on stretchers, waiting to be attended. The death list grew, and in the theatre surgeons and nurses worked non-stop for hours on end. Wards were full of lines of iron beds, moved close together to take as many patients as possible. During the day, the side flaps of the tents were lifted to allow air to flow through the inside, giving at least a modicum of comfort.

Those in pain called out and nurses would scurry over to them to try and relieve their suffering, bathe their fevered brow, try to calm them and give them comfort.

'I ain't never going back to that hellhole again, Nurse!' cried one young soldier to the nurse attending him.

'Indeed you won't, Corporal Greene,' she said with conviction, knowing that the young man had lost a limb and that, due to his fever, he was as yet unaware of this. 'You'll be going home as soon as you're fit enough. Now, be a good lad and try and get some sleep.'

She moved on to the next bed, taking the temperature of the patient, checking his chart, having a few words of cheer, offering a sip of water, then on to the next man to change his dressing, still thinking of her first patient, hoping she wouldn't be the one to eventually tell the poor boy he'd lost a leg. She'd had to do it too many times and had to cope with the distress, sometimes hysteria, other times silence – then shock, followed by the realisation among the married men that they'd be unable to return to their jobs and make a living for their families.

At the front it was strangely quiet, both sides had stopped firing at each other. Tinned mugs, full of tea, were gratefully received, cigarettes were lit, men perched wherever they could or leant against the stacked sacks that made the high wall between them and the enemy. Where the ladders rested, waiting for the men to climb up and over the top at the next excursion in an attempt to gain territory.

It was a soulless scene between the lines. Rolls of barbed wire crossed the landscape, now obliterated by the rain. There were no green fields here, only mud and potholes made by the bombs that had been dropped and holes made from heavy cannon fire. There was no birdsong – no birds. Any trees had been obliterated or left stripped of leaves like wooden sentinels. Battle-worn, like the troops on either side.

Yet there was black humour despite everything. The indomitable spirit surfaced at the oddest moments, a half-buried, raised hand sticking out of the mud. One of the soldiers took off his tin hat to take a rest. He hung it on the fingers of the hand.

'Here, hold this a minute, mate, will you?'

'Should have brought my bloody mother-in-law with me,' said another. 'She'd have frightened the Hun to death with just one look!'

Captain James Havers walked among his men, stopping to chat to them as he made his rounds. He had been sent to the Fifth Army immediately after getting his commission. It had been a baptism of fire in every way, but he was a good officer, mentally attuned to what needed to be done and had a good rapport with his men. He had a natural air of authority about him and his men would have followed him anywhere.

His batman, Bert Higgins, handed him a mug of strong tea.

'Here you are, sir, bet you could murder this right now.'

'Thanks, Higgins. We all needed this break.'

'How long before we go over the top again?'

'I'm just waiting for my orders. Let's hope it's not too soon.'

Higgins walked away and lighting a cigarette muttered to himself, 'Anytime is too bloody soon for me.' He took from a pocket in his uniform a creased picture of his wife and baby. He stared at it, wondering if he'd ever see them again, and fervently prayed that he would.

The orders came through, and a few minutes later James blew his whistle. The men climbed the ladders to go over the top and advance on the enemy once again. Immediately, the opposing guns opened fire, the air full of screams as men were cut down. Cries of 'Medic!' carried in the air.

James crouched low as he advanced. His heart was beating so hard he thought it might burst through his chest. Bullets whizzed past him and every moment he thought would be his last, but he called out encouragement to his men as they advanced.

'Keep down. Stay low!' He and several others dived for cover into a large crater and sank in the mud, water up to their knees. One of the men carried a green canvas bag holding Mills bombs.

'How's your aim, Jenkins?' James asked.

'Played cricket for my county, sir. Was the best bowler on the team.'

'Right, think you can hit that machine-gun post over there?'

'No problem, sir.' The man took out a bomb, lifted his head to quickly glance over the top of the crater to find his target and tossed it towards the enemy lines. Everybody ducked. The sound of the explosion filled the air. They waited . . . the machine gun was silenced.

James shouted his order and they climbed out of the crater, running towards the enemy, but gunfire opened from other positions and James saw Jenkins fall, a look of surprise on his face. He stopped, bent down and shook the man.

'Jenkins! Come on, man, speak to me.'

But there was no expression in the eyes that were still open. No sign of life. Just a bullet hole in his forehead, showing what had transpired. Another man fell beside them, his blood splattering James, but he was still alive.

'Medic!' James called. 'Over here!' But he had to move on.

The onslaught was relentless. Cries of pain could be heard as men were injured. Body parts were strewn over the ground as the troops were battered by gunfire and brought down by flying pieces of shrapnel. The company did their best, but eventually James had no choice but to order a retreat, beaten once again by the strength of the enemy.

He climbed down the ladder with the others, relieved that they were still alive. James waited for all his men that were left to return, the injured carried away on stretchers, then he went to his quarters and poured a hefty measure of Scotch. He was shaking so much he could hardly hold the glass.

Months passed. Several attempts were made to win back ground but little was achieved except for the cost of more lives of the gallant troops and it wasn't until November that what remained of Passchendaele was captured by British and Canadian troops, fighting together. It had taken this long and many lives to cover five miles.

* * *

During the following weeks, the hospital was made redundant and moved. All staff were deployed elsewhere and at last given leave. They were driven to a hotel way behind the lines, where the hotel manager was delighted to still be in business making money from the British government for catering to the troops.

Helen Chalmers leant back in the bath, resting her head on the rim, water up to her neck as she'd dreamt of back in the days, near the fighting. She let out a deep sigh and relaxed, squeezing the soapy water out of the sponge over her arms, watching the water trickle, pondering as to how such a simple thing could mean so much. But then a lump of stale bread given to a starving person would seem like a feast, she mused. She closed her eyes. For the following three days there would be none of the blood and gore of the operating theatre. No smell of ether or stench of rotting flesh. She could rest, eat in the dining room, drink at the bar and feel like a human being once again and at night she could lay in the arms of her lover. His wife could have him back when they returned to England but for now, he was hers.

She reluctantly climbed out of the bath and dressed in a long skirt and a white blouse. It was a joy to wear civilian clothes, a dash of perfume and make-up. Brushing her hair, she looked at her reflection in the mirror, then made her way downstairs to the dining room. Richard was already eating his breakfast. He rose from his seat as she approached.

'Good morning. Sleep well?'

She smiled softly, knowing that he'd shared her bed, and after they'd made love they'd slept entwined in each other's arms until the early hours, when he'd returned to his own room.

'Like a baby,' she answered as she sat down.

She helped herself to a couple of croissants and spread marmalade over one as a waiter came over with a fresh pot of coffee for her.

'Being here, you can almost forget the war,' she remarked and bit into her pastry.

'Fancy a walk round the grounds after?'

'Why not, but not until I've finished eating everything and emptied the coffee pot. It's been so long without such luxuries, it's made me greedy.'

He looked across the table at her and softly said, 'Not only for food, darling.'

She felt her cheeks flush. It was true, away from the battlefront and the hospital, the long hours, which sapped every ounce of her energy, she felt renewed and couldn't get enough of Richard. It was like being on a honeymoon.

'Are you complaining?'

'Don't be ridiculous! I'd happily stay in your bed all day and send for room service when we wanted nourishment and a rest.'

Helen started laughing, which made some of the others in the room look over to see what had amused her so. 'You are outrageous.'

'No, darling, just being truthful.' He sipped his coffee, staring at her over the rim of his cup, his eyes twinkling.

Looking at her lover, Helen was pleased to see that he'd lost the drawn look that so many hours in the operating theatre had caused. His skin was no longer sallow and he was relaxed. She wondered just how much longer they could have carried on without a break.

Drinking the last of her coffee she looked at him.

'Ready for that walk?'

'Indeed I am, let's get some fresh air in our lungs. I'll get my coat.'

An army lorry pulled up outside the hotel and Captain James Havers stepped out, pulling his haversack after him. He thanked the driver and walked into the hotel and up to the reception desk where he was greeted warmly by the owner.

'Good morning, sir, what can I do for you?'

James smiled warmly. 'I'm hoping you have a room free for a few days.'

'I have, sir, once it's been cleaned. Somebody signed out this morning. Let me take you to the dining room for some breakfast while you wait. Leave your bag with me.'

The young captain was only too happy to oblige. He'd been travelling for thirty-six hours and was thirsty and starving – a bath could wait.

Pouring a cup of steaming coffee, James lifted it and breathed in the strong aroma. God! How long had it been since he'd had a decent coffee? He eyed the continental breakfast placed before him. He'd have given anything for bacon and eggs, but nevertheless, he was glad of anything right now. His stomach was empty and he was ready for a welcome break, accepting anything that was on offer. After breakfast he would have a bath and sleep. The thought of a proper bed with clean sheets was now uppermost in his mind and he hoped that his room would soon be ready.

He looked around at the other diners; everyone looked worn out. Not surprising. The battlefront was relentless. Ground won and lost, so many deaths for so little. He knew how lucky he was to still be in one piece and alive.

As he finished his breakfast, the manager walked over to his table and handed him a key. 'Your room is ready now, sir,' he said.

James thanked him, gulped down the last of the coffee, picked up the key and made his way to his room on the first floor. As he took off his uniform jacket, he gazed out of the window overlooking the gardens. Here everything was green – the grass, the many shrubs and some trees – unlike the mud-laden fields he'd so recently left. He ran a bath, soaked in it until the water cooled, then dried himself and climbed into bed after closing the curtains. He lay for a second and listened. It was quiet, strange, no sound of gunfire. He shut his eyes and within minutes was asleep.

Helen and Richard pulled their coats around them as they strolled through the gardens. There was a bitter wind but the skies were clear and the air fresh. They found a bench seat beneath a cedar tree and sat, chatting. Soon they'd receive their orders and Richard was wondering where they'd be sent.

Helen snuggled closer. 'Let's leave the war behind whilst we're here,' she pleaded. 'I'm so sick of it, I want to forget it until we leave.'

Catching hold of her hand, he apologised. 'Sorry, darling, just thinking aloud. Perhaps on our next leave we can pull a few strings and get a few days somewhere really nice.'

They chatted about the possibility and what they'd

like to do if it were possible. They walked further around the grounds until, driven by the cold, they returned to the comfort of the hotel lounge, where they both sat writing letters to their folk back home. Helen, writing to her mother, tried to shut out the fact that Richard would be writing to his wife.

James Havers eventually woke from his sleep and stretched languidly before climbing out of bed. He wandered into the bathroom, swilled his face in cold water to help him wake up, then shaved. He felt like a different man. He dressed and, leaving his room, headed to the bar, where he perched on a stool and ordered a Scotch and soda.

In the lounge, Helen had finished her letters and, seeing Richard was still writing, quietly left her seat and wandered off to the bar. She knew it was wrong of her but she was feeling peeved, knowing to whom Richard was writing. There was a lone figure sitting at the counter. He smiled at her.

'Hello. I hate drinking alone, so can I buy you a drink?'

Helen looked at the young captain and smiled. 'That's a great idea. Thanks.' She held out her hand. 'Helen Chalmers.'

He placed his hand in hers. 'James Havers. What are you doing here?'

'I'm on leave, I'm one of Queen Alexandra's nursing sisters.'

'So what's your poison?' he asked.

'A gin and tonic would go down very well at this moment.'

She studied the stranger whilst he ordered her drink. His

blonde hair, worn short as was required by the military, his blue eyes, wide apart, and a full, sensuous mouth, which parted to smile at her, showing perfect white teeth. Far too good-looking for his own good, she mused, but as he chatted to her, there was no arrogance in his tone. He had a quiet but sharp sense of humour and he soon had her laughing.

Grinning at her he said, 'You are the first woman I've seen in a very long time. I've been surrounded by men and mud for an age, I began to wonder if I was really human! There wasn't anything to enjoy at Passchendaele.'

'I can believe it. We dealt with so many of your casualties. I can't begin to imagine what it must have been like.'

For a moment a frown creased his brow and his smile faded and Helen saw behind the eyes, a brief memory of a man who had been in the midst of the war. Then he smiled again. 'Let's not talk about the war. Where is your home in Blighty?'

'I live in the Cotswolds in the Vale of Evesham – and you?'

'Would you believe, Cheltenham?' He began to laugh. 'I have to come all this way to meet a near neighbour.'

They spent the next half an hour talking about home, the places they both knew and how wonderful it would be to get back to civilisation.

Richard entered the bar and seeing her, walked over. 'So here you are.'

'Richard, this is Captain James Havers, he's also on leave. James this is Captain Richard Carson, the surgeon I work with.'

The two men shook hands.

'He lives in Cheltenham, would you believe? Imagine that!' she said.

With a broad grin, James looked at Richard. 'Small world, isn't it?'

Richard and Helen spent a relaxing day in the hotel, sitting reading, having lunch, neither wanting to do anything but recharge their batteries. They drank cocktails at the bar before dinner and went to bed early, enjoying the fact they could make love leisurely without the fear of interruption or discovery.

Helen stretched, arms above her head, and let out a deep sigh.

'It's easy to forget the war here,' she said. 'No sound of gunfire, a comfortable bed. Log fires in the lounge, a bar, food served on proper plates, not tin ones.'

Richard swung his legs over the side of the bed and lit a cigarette. 'I can't see it going on for much longer,' he said. 'The number of casualties and deaths alone weaken the forces on both sides. Something has to give.'

'Imagine, Richard, being able to go home. To return to normality. Will you go back to the hospital in London?'

'Yes, fortunately for me I do have a job waiting.' He turned to her, his hand caressing her bare breast. 'You could be my theatre sister there too, if you want. I can fix it for you.'

She frowned. 'I don't think that's a good idea.'

He looked surprised. 'Why on earth not?'

'Because things will be different. You'll be back with your wife, leading a normal life. It would be awkward after our relationship.'

His hand slipped to her inner thighs. 'That doesn't have to change,' he said.

Helen caught hold of his hand and pushed it away. 'I can't believe you said that!' She sat up, pulling the sheet around her.

'I don't understand,' he exclaimed, 'you knew I was married, I never pretended to be anything else.'

'True. But when we do go home, I'm certainly not playing the part of your mistress, waiting for you to spare a few hours when you can. Let's face it, it was only the war that brought us together. Had we met and worked back at home, it wouldn't have happened – but it did. Be honest, we both knew it wasn't going to last.'

'God, that sounds so cold! Is that all I mean to you?'

'No, of course not,' she said softly. 'If you were free, then it would be wonderful.' She paused. 'Let me ask you a question and I want you to promise to give me an honest answer.'

He looked at her and saw she was deadly serious. 'I promise.'

'Are you prepared to divorce your wife for me?'

He didn't answer but continued to look at her.

'There, your silence speaks volumes.'

He rose to his feet. 'I don't know what's got into you tonight.'

Helen turned back the covers on her side and, getting out of bed, put on a dressing gown. 'Let's face it, Richard, in the hospital, surrounded by death and war, we clung together for comfort, affection, mutual respect and desire, but sometime we'll have to face up to the future. I realised that one day you would no longer be in my life. I'd got so used to you – to us – and there is no us . . . only now.'

Richard dressed hurriedly. 'I can't cope with you in this mood; I'm going to the bar for a nightcap.'

She watched him dress and walk out of the room, then wandered over to the French windows, opened them and walked outside, lit a cigarette and gazed out over the garden now bathed in moonlight. Men! She couldn't believe that Richard thought they could continue their relationship when they returned home. What was he thinking? Of course they couldn't! In wartime it was different. Things happened. Men and women found comfort where they could, not knowing if every day would be their last. That was acceptable in a strange way, but after . . . well that was a different thing entirely. You had to try to return to normality. Perhaps it was time to prepare for the future – without Richard.

Chapter Two

When Helen walked into the dining room the following morning, the waiter told her that Captain Carson had already eaten. She was somewhat relieved. After their confrontation the previous night she hadn't been looking forward to facing him. She sat at a table set for two just as James Havers walked into the room. Seeing her sitting alone, he wandered over to her.

'Do you mind if I join you?'

'Not at all. Please, sit down.'

The waiter came over with two pots of coffee. They both immediately poured a cup of the steaming liquid with great haste.

James chuckled. 'It's easy to see just how long we've been without the real stuff, isn't it?'

She smiled as she said, 'I know. I've learnt to enjoy coffee even more than tea. Perhaps it's the tin mugs that change the taste? Served in a cup, tea tastes differently.'

'You know, my men used to chat about the things they were looking forward to when they got home. Food was one of the main things. Roast beef and Yorkshire pudding was the favourite, as I recall, and an English breakfast was a close second – or fish and chips.'

'Mine was a hot bath with water up to the waste pipe, followed by roast pork with lots of crackling and a glass of champagne,' Helen volunteered.

He thought for a moment. 'Yes, I wanted a good meal and a bath, but even more I wanted to ride out among the English countryside on my beloved horse, Cleo.'

She looked amused. 'Cleo?'

'Short for Cleopatra because she's a bit of a strumpet with a mind of her own.'

'Where do you keep her?'

He reached for some toast. 'At home. We have stables as my parents ride. I started off with a small pony when I was four. Do you ride, Helen?'

'No, I've never had the opportunity.'

He beamed at her. 'Then when we eventually return home, I'll teach you . . . that's if you want to?'

'I'd like that, although it would have to be on a horse that was gentle, because I'm sure I'd be somewhat nervous.'

He looked steadily at her. 'Don't worry, I'd take care of you, make sure you came to no harm.'

She stared back at him. Although there was a strength about his bearing, there was also a gentleness in his expression, and she felt with him she would be safe should they ever keep that appointment. She became curious about the stranger.

'Surely you must have a girlfriend waiting for you back in Cheltenham?'

'Not much time for courting, I'm afraid. I was training for the army, taking exams, working for my commission.

Besides, in wartime anything can happen, it didn't seem right to ask anyone to wait, unless you were married, of course. What about you? After all, Helen, you are a very attractive woman. I can't imagine you are without your admirers?'

She laughed. 'I've had my moments, but that's about it.' She poured another coffee thinking that Richard was indeed her moment, but James didn't need to know that.

They eventually finished their breakfast and James suggested they walk down to the village together.

'I've no idea what it's like or if there is anything standing. But looking at this building, perhaps they missed being a victim of the fighting. Want to go and find out?'

'Why not? I'll go and get my coat. I'll meet you in the foyer in ten minutes.'

When she returned, James greeted her. 'Can you ride a bike?' he asked.

'Yes – well, I used to. I haven't done so in a while. Why?'

He led her outside. Leaning against the wall were two bicycles.

'I borrowed them from the staff. Come on, let's give it a go. It'll save walking. Look, try it out on the drive first.'

Helen climbed on the bike and started pedalling. At first she was a bit unbalanced but was soon back in control and they set off, laughing like a couple of teenagers on an adventure.

Cycling along the country lane, they saw only a few signs of the war. Some fields had been torn up by what they imagined might have been artillery fire, and one or two houses were in ruins, but on the whole this little corner seemed to have escaped the destruction of war and soon they came to the main street where there were signs of life. Among the houses was a parade of shops that were open. They parked their bikes and wandered around.

A couple of food shops were poorly stocked, they noticed, a small cafe was open with a few elderly gentlemen inside playing cards and drinking coffee, small glasses of alcohol beside them. There was another shop selling fancy goods and Helen saw a beautiful turquoise silk scarf displayed in the window.

'Oh, that's just lovely!' she exclaimed.

James took her hand. 'Come on,' he said. 'Let's go in and I'll buy it for you.'

'No, I'll buy it myself,' she argued.

He wouldn't hear of it and insisted it was a gift from him to repay her for her company. He wouldn't let the girl wrap it and picking it up, he put it round Helen's neck.

'There. It brings out the colour of your eyes,' he said and stood back to admire her.

She put her hand to feel the softness of it and the assistant held up a mirror so she could see for herself just how it looked.

'Thank you, James, it's really beautiful.'

He looked pleased. 'My pleasure entirely.'

They made their way to the coffee shop where they ordered a coffee and liqueur, sitting quietly at a corner table.

James picked up his glass. 'Cheers, Helen. May this be the first of our many meetings.'

Picking up her glass she touched his with it. 'Cheers.'

It was easy to forget about the war and what they'd both been through, sitting quietly in the shop with the only noises made by the chatter from the other customers. They sat talking, getting to know one another. Their conversation flowed easily as they laughed and enjoyed each other's company, but eventually they had to return to reality.

'Have you any idea where you are to be sent?' James asked.

'No, Richard and I are waiting for our orders. We should hear today as our leave is up tomorrow. How about you?'

'I'm waiting too. I'm being seconded to another regiment but as yet I don't know which. No doubt in some war zone or other.'

'Surely it can't go on for much longer,' she said, a note of desperation in her voice. 'The losses have been horrendous – and the casualties.'

He saw the sadness in her eyes. 'Yes, you've seen as much death as I have. We just have to do our best until the end and then try and put it to the back of our minds when it's over.'

Thinking of her patients, Helen said, 'I don't have to tell you, that's not going to be easy, and for some, they'll live with the aftermath all their lives.'

He reached for her hand. 'We have to be strong for those who can't be. We are both in a position where we have no choice.' He ordered another liqueur. 'Let's drink to the day when we can go home and I take you riding.'

Shortly after, they climbed on the borrowed bikes and rode back to the hotel. They parked them against the hotel wall and entered the foyer. Richard was there, waiting.

'Where on earth have you been?' he demanded. 'I've been looking everywhere for you.'

'Morning!' James greeted him.

Richard ignored him. 'Our orders have come through. A car is coming for us in an hour's time to take us to the General Hospital number 10 at Rouen. At least we'll have a proper hospital to work in with better facilities – at last! You'd better get your stuff together, we've a long drive ahead of us.' He nodded to James and walked to the reception desk.

James smiled wryly. 'Not exactly a bundle of laughs, is he? Go and pack and I'll wait here and see you on your way.'

It was with great sadness that Helen changed back into her uniform and packed her case. It had been a wonderful few days and she knew it would be some time before she'd enjoy such luxury again. She'd be sorry to say goodbye to James, he'd been so much fun, and she did hope that she'd see him again back in her beloved Cotswolds. Taking one last look around the room, she picked up her case and made her way to reception.

James came over immediately. 'As soon as I know where I'm to be posted, I'll write to you. I'd like to keep in touch, if that's alright?'

'Yes, of course it's alright but I don't know the address,' she protested.

'Your boss said it was the General Hospital number 10 in Rouen. I'll find out.' He smiled at her. 'I must say you look very efficient in your uniform, Sister!'

'You make sure you keep your head down wherever you're sent. I don't want to find you being carried into the hospital on a stretcher.'

Before he could answer, Richard arrived. 'The car is

here,' he said. 'We must be on our way.' Turning to James he said, 'Good luck,' and walked outside.

James carried Helen's case for her and handed it to the driver, then he held her gently by the shoulders. 'You keep out of trouble, because I'm determined to see you again.' He pulled her nearer and kissed her. It was much more than a kiss from an acquaintance, it was more a kiss with a promise – and when he released her, he stared into her eyes and said softly, 'Keep safe.'

'You too,' she answered, feeling unexpectedly emotional, then she climbed into the car. As it drove away, she waved to the solitary figure standing on the steps of the hotel.

During the drive, Helen sat in the back of the car, looking out of the window at the passing scenery. Richard was sitting in the front, chatting to the driver. The journey was not without its problems: damaged roadways; tanks that had become useless, bogged down in the mud; troops on the move, walking slowly, too tired and weary to march in a smart military fashion, some wearing bandages around their heads, beneath their caps, others with arms in slings, some on crutches, others propped up on horse-driven carts. Her heart went out to them, but what really upset her was seeing the bloated, rotting remains of the horses that had perished. Those brave animals, ridden during gunfire and with an ignominious ending. James would hate to see this, she thought, then realised he probably had done so.

The journey seemed endless. They stayed overnight in an army camp, ate a quick breakfast to sustain them and hours later they reached their destination and were ushered into the office of the chief medical officer. He greeted them warmly.

'Please sit down. I can't tell you how pleased I am that you're here. We are inundated with casualties, as you can imagine, and are greatly in need of another surgeon and theatre sister. I'll send you quickly round the hospital to familiarise yourself with the layout before you have a rest and a meal, but you will be on duty in the morning.' He rose to his feet and shook hands with them both. 'My sergeant will show you round,' he said and pressed a bell on his desk. There was a knock on the door and a sergeant entered.

'Take Captain Carson and Sister Chalmers around the wards and the theatre, will you? But first make them a cup of tea, I'm sure they need it after their journey.'

'Yes, sir,' he replied. Turning to Richard and Helen he said, 'If you'll follow me, please.' In the outer office, Helen and Richard drank the tea, needing the comfort of the beverage after such a long time in the car, and then made their way, following their guide.

They toured the wards, talking to the matron and one of the surgeons in each one, being appraised of the patients' treatment, who were all dressed in their 'convalescent blues', as their hospital wear had been christened. Richard nodded to the soldier in each bed, picked up the chart at the end of some to check on their recovery, asked a question now and then and talked to one or two of the casualties.

Helen glanced across the ward and saw a soldier sitting on the side of his bed. She saw that he was distressed and walked over, picked up the chart at the end and read it. He was suffering from facial burns from an explosion, she noted. Returning the chart, she sat beside him.

'Hello, Private Barnes, how are you feeling?'

As the young man turned to her, she saw the dreadful puckered and burnt skin on his face and she reached out and held his hand as she saw the tears gather in his eyes.

'Look at me, Sister. No woman is going to fancy a man who looks like this. I'm nineteen and my life is over.'

'It may seem that way now, Barnes, but in time the scars will fade a lot and yes, you will never be the same physically when you see your reflection, but believe me, your life isn't over. I'm not saying there won't be women who will reject you, because life and people can be cruel, but you have to have the courage to rise above such ignorance. One day, one young lady will come along and see beyond your battle scars, see the man behind them. You just have to be patient.'

'What do *you* see when you look at me, tell me that!'

'I see someone who is suffering at the moment. I see a man who has lived through hell, but has come through it, albeit with injuries, but I see a man with nice eyes, a kind heart – and a life ahead of him. A life that won't be without its difficulties, but a life that could be fulfilled as long as you don't become bitter. Look around you, Private. Look at those who've lost their limbs, some that will leave the hospital in a body bag, who won't have a future at all.'

He looked around the ward as he thought of her words, then back at her.

'Do you honestly think I stand a chance?'

She smiled softly. 'That's mainly up to you and how you handle your situation, but yes, I do believe you have every chance.'

She rose from the bed. 'I'll look in on you again and see how you're doing.'

'Thank you, Sister,' he said. 'It was kind of you to take the trouble.'

'I can assure you it was no trouble at all. I'll see you soon.'

Helen rejoined Richard and the matron on their rounds. Several patients were on the road to recovery, others would be in the hospital for some time and a few wouldn't make it. Eventually they were taken to one of the operating theatres, which was empty. Both Richard and Helen were pleased with the facilities.

'It will be a joy working here after the base hospital,' he said to her. 'Thank God for that!' It was the first time he'd spoken to her since they'd left the hotel.

She agreed. 'It will be better for the patients, that's for sure,' she said.

The sergeant showed them the mess hall and said dinner would be served in half an hour, then he took them to their quarters where their bags were already installed.

'I'll meet you in the mess after you've unpacked,' Richard said and walked away.

Nurse Jenny Palmer had watched them leave the ward. Good-looking man, she thought as she gazed at Richard's retreating figure. She'd been pleased to see the sister stop and talk to Private Barnes, one of her favourite patients. The boy needed encouragement and it was obvious, watching the two of them, that the sister had been a help. She picked up several dressings and walked over to her next patient, an army sergeant who had lost his left leg just below the knee.

'Right, Sergeant, are you ready? I have to change your dressing.' She knew this caused her patient a lot of pain but the man was brave and seldom complained. He covered his discomfort with humour.

'You know, Nurse, if anyone looked at you, they'd think you were a gentle young lady – they would have no idea that you could be a past mistress of torture!'

She grinned broadly at him. 'Honestly! You go on like that, you'll ruin my chances of meeting a nice young man. You'll scare them all away.' She started removing the bloodstained dressings as gently as she could but she felt him flinch beneath her fingers.

'Nearly finished,' she said softly.

She bathed the stump with a carbolic lotion, then after soaking clean gauzes in the same solution, she dressed his wound, pleased to see that it was clean, without infection, but it would be a while before the man would be well enough to go home.

'There you go,' she said as she finished binding the leg. 'I'll leave you in peace.'

'Got a minute for a chat, Nurse?'

Jenny was surprised at the request as the sergeant had not said a lot to her other than to chide her over her treatment.

'I've always got time for my patients,' she said as she sat beside the bed. 'What's on your mind, Sergeant?'

He lowered his voice. 'How's my wife going to react to my stump, Nurse Palmer? I mean, imagine when we get into bed together and I get undressed and my injury is there in front of her. Won't she find it gruesome? Won't she go off me as a man?'

Jenny took hold of his hand. 'Does your wife love you, Sergeant?'

He looked embarrassed. 'Well, yes, she does. We don't often put it into words, like, but yes . . . as I do her.'

'Have you written and told her about your injury?'

Frowning, he said, 'Well, I've told her I was injured and had to have an operation but, no – not exactly.' His voice chocked in his throat. 'I couldn't find the words.'

'You have to write and tell her; you can't suddenly turn up without giving her a warning of what to expect.' Her heart ached at his expression as he faced the fact.

'I can't bring myself to do it, Nurse.' His eyes filled with tears, which made her feel even worse, seeing this strong individual trying to cope with his dilemma.

'Would you like me to write to her and put her in the picture?'

She would never forget the look of relief on the man's face.

'Would you, Nurse? Would you really do this for me?'

'Of course. If you give me her address I'll write tonight when I'm off duty. You see, Sergeant, when you get home she'll be more prepared, and loving you as she does, you'll work it out together, I'm sure.'

'If I wasn't a married man I'd kiss you, Nurse Palmer!'

Laughing, Jenny got to her feet. 'Now that would ruin my reputation. Write the address and I'll come and collect it before I go off duty.'

He clasped her hand and said very quietly, 'Thank you.'

Giving his hand a quick squeeze, she walked away, battling with her own emotions after their conversation, cursing the war that had affected so many lives and messed with their future, which would never be the same and which would produce so many problems. She would try and prepare the sergeant's wife for his homecoming and advise her how to manage him until they worked out their own routine. It was the least she could do for such a brave man. After that, it would be up to the couple to find their own way, which she hoped fervently they would be able to do. At least she wasn't having to write and inform the family that their son or husband had passed away; others had that task. Those were the hardest letters to write.

Chapter Three

Helen made her way to her quarters and was grateful for a proper room as opposed to a tent and eyed the bed with pleasure. A camp bed hadn't been the most comfortable of places to try and sleep after a heavy day in the theatre, and there was also a wardrobe for her clothes.

Walking over to the small hand basin she turned on the tap. The water was hot! No more washing in a tin bowl of cold water, and there was a shared bathroom where she'd be able to immerse herself in hot water. But as she told herself, those days near the battlefield made her more appreciative of what was now on offer.

Once unpacked, she made her way to the mess hall. It was a fair size and busy. She saw Richard standing in the queue for food, he waved and called her over, handing her a tray.

'I don't know about you, but I'm starving and I have to say the food smells appetising.'

They were served a healthy portion of beef stew, mashed potatoes, various vegetables and a portion of sponge pudding and custard, which they carried over to a table after helping themselves to cutlery. On the table was a jug of water and glasses. They sat down.

Richard tasted the beef. 'It's alright,' he said. 'Thank goodness for some decent cooks. By the way, in my room is the list for the morning,' he told her. 'We start at eight-thirty and tonight we meet the rest of my team. The break was good, but now we must get back to business.'

'Well, at least we've had a rest and lived like a human again, even if it was only for a few days,' she said.

'You seemed to enjoy yourself with Captain Havers. That scene as we left was *very* touching.'

The irony in his voice didn't escape her, but she ignored it. 'Yes, it was ages since I'd ridden a bike and the village was quite picturesque, without much damage.'

'Will you be seeing him again?'

'I've no idea, he's being seconded to another regiment, but after the war – if we are spared – yes, I'll probably see him when I get home. He lives in Cheltenham.'

'Yes, so you said. Very convenient!'

'Stop this, Richard! You haven't the right to be jealous, and certainly not over my meeting a young officer I might never see again.'

He looked disgruntled. 'If you say so,' he snapped.

The meal was finished in silence.

After they'd eaten he explained to her where his office was situated and told her to be there in an hour's time.

'The rest of the team will be there and we can run through tomorrow's list together.'

She caught hold of his arm. 'Richard, we have to work together, so please, don't let there be any bad feeling between us.'

'Of course not. We are both professionals and we have a job to do. I'll see you in my office.'

The nurses and an orderly sat with Helen and Richard in his office shortly afterwards, and after introducing themselves they set about planning the following day's list. They seemed a friendly bunch, all looking a bit jaded, in need of a break, but mindful of what lay before them, and when they'd left, Richard said they seemed well trained, which was a great relief to him as he was a stickler for precision in his theatre.

The following weeks soon fell into a routine as the team coped with the influx of patients and the rounds in the wards after, checking on their patients' recovery. It wasn't always easy when recovery meant a return home because an injury meant the man was no longer fit for duty, but could return to his family. For some it meant facing hardship, perhaps because of a loss of a limb, and that was a cause for concern as to how they would be able to earn a living. Despite this, it was a great relief for the men, knowing that at least they wouldn't have to return to the fighting.

Some of the patients suffered from shell shock. Their road to recovery would take much longer and, with others, they would never be the same again and despite being professional, Helen was deeply moved by their predicament, which sometimes caused her many sleepless nights. She visited Private Barnes regularly and was pleased to see he seemed to be recovering mentally and was beginning to cope with his injuries.

'I've written to my mum,' he told her. 'Thought it best to warn her what I look like, otherwise it would be too much of a shock.'

'That's very wise of you,' Helen said. 'Expect tears, Private, you know what mothers are like, then after, she'll be making such a fuss of you, you won't be able to breathe.'

He smiled. 'That sounds like heaven to me, Sister.'

A month later, to her delight, Helen received a letter from James. She sat in her room reading it. He had been sent to Cambrai where there had been fighting, but he was fine. He wrote of their time together and the trip to the village, he told her stories about his troops that were hilarious and made her smile. She was pleased that he'd retained his sense of humour, but was aware he'd written nothing about the fighting.

Write to me, Helen. You know how important letters are to us poor soldiers. If I thought I could end up in your hospital, I could feign an injury so you could take care of me, but I'll just have to wait until we get home.

I hope that old misery isn't working you too hard! You tell him I said he'll have me to answer to if he doesn't look after you.

Take care, keep safe and write soon.

Love,

James

She got out her writing pad and answered his letter immediately.

It was almost Christmas and the hospital staff had managed to purchase decorations for the wards in an effort to cheer the troops. Paper chains were being hung. Helen had climbed a stepladder and was trying to pin the end of a paper chain to the ceiling. One of the patients was holding the bottom of the ladder so it wouldn't slip, one leg in plaster, a crutch under his free arm.

'You be careful up there, Sister,' he said. 'I don't want you falling off the ladder, you might break my other leg, then where would I be?'

She looked down and grinned at him. 'Back in bed and at my mercy!'

'Can't I be at your mercy, anyway, without any more injuries?'

'You, Private Ellis, are far too cheeky for your own good.'

'Well, I've been told that before,' he said, laughing.

She climbed down and looked at him, eyes twinkling. 'I don't doubt that for a minute. Now away with you before I decide to give you an injection for your cheek.'

Someone had found a phonograph on which to play records, and after someone wound it up Christmas carols filled the air. It certainly lifted the atmosphere. Some of the patients joined in, taking their mind away from their injuries and pain.

'Make sure Father Christmas stops at my bed, Sister,' called one. 'I didn't send him a letter this year.'

'Don't you worry, young man, he has a list of all the patients,' she said as she left the ward.

That evening after dinner, she and Richard were in his office going over the plans for the morrow and, after they'd finished, Helen was saying how the Christmas spirit was helping the patients. He agreed with her.

'Yes, I noticed that when I made my rounds. I must say the place does look very festive, it helps us all to feel cheerful. Fancy a drink?' He poured two glasses of whisky.

'Thanks,' said Helen. She looked across the desk at him. They hadn't slept together ever since they'd moved into the hospital, or had any physical contact. It was as if James Havers had come between them despite not being in the vicinity. Yet they had maintained their closeness professionally in the theatre.

Richard returned her gaze. 'I miss you, you know,' he said quietly.

Completely surprised by his comment she asked, 'What do you mean?'

'Do I really have to spell it out, Helen? We have been lovers for a long time until we moved here and I miss that closeness. Don't you?'

She thought for a moment and had to admit that she did. 'Yes, I suppose I do. It was always comforting to have a cuddle after a bad day in the theatre, we both needed that, I believe.'

'Is that all?' There was a definite challenge in his voice and his eyes.

Despite everything – his wife, James – there had always been a chemistry between her and Richard from the moment they'd met and as she looked at him now and saw the invitation in his eyes, she knew it hadn't entirely diminished. They had been close for so long and he had been an important part of her life despite their recent differences and she could still feel that affinity.

'No, that's not all.'

He gave an enigmatic smile. 'I can't tell you how happy that makes me, Helen. God, there have been times these past weeks when I've ached for you so much, I've wanted to drag you off to my quarters!'

She found this amusing and started to laugh. 'My goodness, that would have caused a scandal!'

He rose from his chair and walking round the desk, pulled her to her feet. Catching hold of the back of her head, he held her and covered her lips with his. His kisses were full of passion as his mouth explored hers. She found herself responding. It had been a while and the needs of both of them surfaced. They lost themselves in the moment.

He released her and staring into her eyes said, 'Your quarters or mine?'

'Mine,' she said, 'it's quieter and there is less chance of us being seen.'

'You go now and I'll come along in a few minutes.'

Helen walked to her quarters and began to undress with a mounting need for the promised intimacy and soon she heard footsteps. There was a gentle tap on the door and she opened it. Richard stepped inside. He was carrying a file, which he held up for her to see.

With a grin he said, 'Well, at least this looks official.' He put it down on the chair and reached for her, caressing her as he rained kisses on her bare body. Then he too undressed after carefully locking the door.

'We don't want to be interrupted, do we?'

Eyes twinkling, Helen said, 'Absolutely not,' as she threw back the bedcovers.

They were so used to each other, they knew how to please, but it had been so long since they'd been together, there was a hunger about their lovemaking. Like a starving man, suddenly faced with a feast.

Eventually they lay together, entwined and exhausted. Richard wiped the perspiration from his brow.

'Oh my God, Helen, I needed that!'

'So it would seem,' she said, chuckling softly, then she let out a deep sigh.

Pulling her to him he asked, 'Was that a sigh of satisfaction?'

She gently chided him. 'What is it with you men? You always want a reference after making love!'

He raised his eyebrows in surprise. 'How many men have you known that makes you such an expert?'

Removing his arm, she got out of bed and started dressing. 'That, Richard, is none of your business. Now, I suggest you get dressed and leave before someone comes along.'

He did so, reluctantly. 'We need to book into a hotel so we can really relax without any worries, then we can really take our time and enjoy each other.'

When dressed, he leant forward and kissed her. 'See you tomorrow.' Picking up the file, he left.

It was Christmas Eve and a vicar with his choir from a nearby church arrived at the hospital. The patients who were mobile sat in chairs in the main entrance to the hospital, which had been prepared and where an altar had been placed. Those who were bedridden and wanted to attend had been wheeled in and placed around the room, while others were in wheelchairs. There had been very few who were unable to attend the service and everyone joined the choir in singing carols. The atmosphere was filled with emotion that was palpable as patients and medical staff thought of home and families and prayers were said. But the final carol, 'While Shepherds Watched Their Flocks by Night', lifted the spirits and was sung with gusto.

The patients were returned to their wards and laughter

could be heard as beds were wheeled and wheelchairs pushed. One of the doctors, dressed as Father Christmas, toured the wards, dispensing small gifts to each patient. Paper hats were worn and the banter among the patients and the staff caused much merriment.

'Where's the mistletoe, Sister?' called out one of the patients. 'I was hoping for a Christmas kiss!'

Helen laughed and shook her finger at him. 'Now, don't be naughty – you a married man, too.'

'I won't tell if you don't!' he called out.

Helen walked on shaking her head, but she was delighted by the happy atmosphere because these men had been through so much and many still had very difficult days ahead of them and, for some, the rest of their lives would be severely impaired.

In the mess the medical staff who were not on duty gathered for their Christmas fare. Silly hats were worn, the odd bottle of beer and bottle of wine procured from unknown sources as is always the way during wartime, where some bright spark would discover someone with a secret hoard willing to sell for a price. After the meal, tables and chairs were moved to make room for dancing, all arranged by the female staff who were determined to make the most of the holiday.

Helen was dancing with Richard, who was saying how well the church service went and how great it was for the patients, when suddenly he felt a tap on his shoulder.

'Sorry, old man, but I'm cutting in!' James Havers neatly took Helen into his arms and danced her away.

'James! How marvellous to see you,' she exclaimed. 'What on earth are you doing here?'

'What a ridiculous question, I've come to see you, of course!' He drew her closer. 'God, Helen, you feel good, I'm so relieved to have found you all in one piece.'

She started laughing. 'You are an extraordinary man. You turn up out of the blue without any warning. Why didn't you let me know you were coming?'

'I couldn't because I wasn't sure I could make it, but in the end I managed to get some leave and here I am.' He looked at her with a sudden frown. 'I do hope you're pleased to see me? I don't want to barge in at the wrong time.'

Shaking her head she smiled at him. 'Oh, James, I couldn't have wished for a nicer Christmas gift.'

He beamed with delight. 'Let's get out of here.'

Before she knew what was happening, James had rushed her outside, taken her into his arms and kissed her. His hands held her firmly, but tenderly, against him.

Helen, carried away by the surprise and so happy to see he was still alive, just relaxed in his arms and returned his kisses, until they were both breathless.

He gazed at her in the shaft of light from the moon. 'You have no idea, Sister Helen Chalmers, just how I've longed for this moment.'

Eventually the cold air drove them back inside and leading Helen onto the dance floor, James held her close, his head against hers as they danced to a waltz, and when the music stopped he led her to a quiet corner.

'There were times when I thought I would never see you again,' he confessed, 'but thankfully we have both been spared and you look wonderful.'

Helen could see from the dark circles under his eyes, the loss of weight and the drawn expression that would occasionally cross his features, that her friend had been through hell. 'Was it really bad at Cambrai?' she asked.

'Well, it was never good, but this time we were able to make use of the tanks, which made a deal of difference. I didn't lose so many men and that was a relief, as you can imagine, but it certainly wasn't a bed of roses. How's it been for you?'

'Busy, there are still too many casualties, but at least here we have better facilities to cope with and that makes a huge difference.'

'How's the captain treating you?'

Helen felt her cheeks flush. 'Fine. Richard is a good surgeon and we have a good team working with us.'

'Any chance of you being shipped home in the near future?'

Shaking her head she said, 'Not as far as I know.'

He stroked her hair. 'Pity. I would feel so much better if I knew you were safe and sound.'

'You shouldn't worry about me, James. I'm not your responsibility,' she said jokingly.

'I know, but I'd like you to be.'

She gazed at him and saw that he was being serious. Seeing her consternation, he spoke again.

'Ever since we said goodbye I haven't been able to get you out of my mind. The fact that you might be in danger from the enemy is a constant worry to me. You see, Helen, I do believe I'm falling in love with you.'

'But, James, you hardly know me!'

He held her hand. 'I know. Crazy, isn't it, but I've never been more certain about anything in my life.'

Helen was completely nonplussed and speechless. She had been delighted to see James and was attracted to him, but this was a complete surprise. 'I don't know what to say.'

His eyes twinkled. 'But tell me honestly, do you have any feelings for me at all? Am I barking up the wrong tree altogether or is there some hope that you could possibly love me . . . just a little bit?' He held up his thumb and first finger, showing a small measure. 'Even just that much?'

She couldn't help but laugh. 'You really are outrageous.' But she knew beneath the banter he meant it. 'I do like you very much, James, but we don't know one another. I would need time spent with you, to get to know you, away from the war. You know as well as I do, wars can muddy the waters when it comes down to relationships. In civilian life it's very different.'

He looked pleased at her response. 'Well at least you haven't kicked me out and that's a hell of a relief.'

She rose to her feet. 'Come on, we'd better dance or people will begin to talk.'

As they walked onto the floor, James said, 'I'm staying nearby at a small hotel I've found that's still open, albeit in reduced circumstances, but I'm here for four more days before I have to start back. Can you get any time off?'

Knowing that this wasn't possible, she said, 'Only between shifts, I would think – an afternoon, maybe, if I'm on duty early, and in the evenings when I've finished, but that's all.'

'I'll take what I can get,' he said as they arrived back and joined the throng.

Across the room, Helen saw Richard looking over towards them with a thunderous expression on his face. He turned sharply away.

Chapter Four

The following morning in the operating theatre, the atmosphere was decidedly frosty. The rest of the team, not knowing of the relationship between the surgeon and theatre sister, were puzzled. Richard was abrupt with everyone and when eventually the shift was over, it was with a certain feeling of relief for all, especially Helen.

As the last patient was wheeled away to a ward, Richard was writing up his notes and giving instructions to Helen about the patient's medication and further treatment. She picked up the file and went to walk away.

'So, your boyfriend looks well,' he said with a note of sarcasm.

'He's not my boyfriend,' she protested, 'just a friend.'

'Really? It looked more than that to me when you finally emerged from your sudden exit. You were very quick to leave my arms and go to his!'

Helen was embarrassed because he spoke the truth, but it angered her too, because he made her sound like a loose woman and she wasn't. She'd only kissed James, that was all. She glared at him and walked away, her mind in a whirl.

It had been a hard day for Nurse Jenny Palmer. So many patients to care for in a full ward where the metal beds were lined up in three rows, to allow for as many patients as possible, but in one corner lay a soldier who had been in a gas attack. Jenny had to give him oxygen every hour for five minutes to help him breathe and then spray his throat. He was drenched in perspiration as he fought for breath and he could hardly speak. She would be as gentle as she could, talking softly to him as she cared for his needs, but it upset her to see him suffer so. She knew he had but a number of hours before the end.

He would plead with the nurses to sit with him and they all did when they could find a minute to do so as it was obvious the man was scared of being alone. It was really the only other thing they could do for him. Jenny had vowed the man would not die without someone to comfort him and that night instead of going off duty, she sat with him, holding his hand, talking softly to him until he drew his last breath. Then she went to her room and cried.

She sobbed until she was exhausted. All her pent-up feelings had at last come to the fore. Despite being professional, she could only take so much. She railed to herself about the futility of war. She'd seen so many good men maimed and for what? Lives had been lost unnecessarily . . . and for what? She put on her cape, left her room and walked outside to get some air. Air that didn't smell of ether and disinfectant.

It was a cold, crisp night with a clear sky. She gazed up, looking at the stars.

'You alright, Jenny?'

She spun round and saw Corporal Harry Gibbs, one of the orderlies, standing next to her.

Shaking her head she said, 'Frankly, no!' Her voice choked with emotion she asked, 'How much longer can the war go on?'

He lit a cigarette. 'I wish I knew, love, I wish I knew. Here, have a fag, you'll feel better.'

They stood together silently, neither speaking until she said, 'I don't know just how much more I can take, Harry.'

'I ask myself that daily, Jenny, but I go back to my ward because those poor buggers need me. They need you and everyone else. We have a duty to care for them, you know that as well as I do and because you do, you'll be on duty until it's all over. Then we'll really have something to celebrate.'

Stubbing out her cigarette she said, 'You're right, of course. I was just having a bad moment.'

'You're allowed, love, you're allowed. It helps to get it out of the system now and again, that's what keeps us sane. Come on, I'll walk you back to your quarters.'

Jenny thanked him when they reached her room.

'It's alright, love. Try and get some sleep, you'll feel better in the morning.'

She undressed and climbed into bed, feeling mentally and physically drained.

The next morning she was back on duty, doing the rounds as usual, remembering Harry's comment. He was right, of course, they had a duty to care for their patients, that was their job, and if she was honest it was a lot better than being on the battlefield as her patients had been.

Harry walked past her, wheeling a patient back to his bed. He smiled and winked at her. 'You alright, Nurse Palmer?'

'Yes, Harry, fine thanks.'

'That's the ticket,' he said and carried on.

Later that morning she accompanied Richard as he did his rounds, checking on his patients. She was a little in awe of him. He had an air of superiority about him, but she knew he was a brilliant surgeon – she'd seen the results of his work and so was full of admiration too. She was surprised when at the end of his rounds he stopped her as she was about to walk away.

'I hear you spent last night with the young man who was gassed, that was kind of you.'

She looked at him in surprise.

He smiled softly. 'Nothing is hidden in a hospital, Nurse, but I want to thank you for being with him until the end. No one wants to die alone.' He walked away before she could speak.

That evening after her shift, Helen met James and they found a small cafe where they sat and chatted whilst eating an acceptable meal and drinking wine.

He grinned as he picked up his glass.

'The French would die rather than be without any of this . . . thank heavens. How's your day been?'

'Much as any other,' she replied. 'Every day is the same, really, that's why we're here. I just wish the war was over, that for once the men at the top on both sides would realise it was all a waste of time and lives.'

'We can only hope that doesn't take too long,' he said. 'I've lost too many good men.'

After their meal, they took a walk along the harbour. Even here, they couldn't escape the war. A ship had just docked and soldiers were making their way down the gangway. None of them looked happy. On many a face Helen saw the fear she recognised so well, the uncertainty, and the male ego, which was trying to cover such feelings, men desperately trying to be brave in front of their comrades. Behind them, cargo was being unloaded, cranes lifting heavy crates from the hold. Lorries waited to take the goods away. But at least here, there was no sound of gunfire.

'You know what upsets me as much as anything?' James suddenly asked.

'No, what's that?'

'The bloated corpses of the dead horses. It makes me think of home and Cleo, my own horse. So many officers brought their own mounts to the battlefield, they must have been devastated to lose their friend, because that's what your mount becomes. They do everything you ask of them and it breaks my heart to see them abandoned.'

Helen remembered seeing such things and how upset she had been. 'They don't have time to dispose of them,' she said. 'If they fall in fighting their rider has to move on.'

'I know, but often they have to put a bullet in the head of the animal to put them out of their suffering. I hate it!'

She didn't have the words to comfort him and they slowly walked back to the hospital.

'I'm off duty for a couple of hours only, tomorrow

afternoon,' Helen told James, 'not long enough to do anything I'm afraid, so feel free to go off somewhere.'

He declined. 'I'll still come over. I'll try and rustle up some sandwiches and we can perhaps get a cup of tea in the mess, if you like, of course?'

'That'll be fine. I'll meet you there at four o'clock.'

James leant forward and kissed her. 'Take care, Helen – until tomorrow, then.'

As he walked away, James sighed. Today had been so good, just walking and talking. He hoped and prayed that he would survive the war so that he and Helen could continue to meet, which would give him time and opportunity to convince her that a life with him would be happy and one she was willing to share, but he knew that it was all in the lap of the gods. It was the only thing that kept him going during his worst moments. He saw a bar and walked in and ordered a drink.

The last day of James's leave arrived, and although the time seemed to have flown and the two had only been able to be together for a few hours each day, they had enjoyed each other's company. For Helen, to get away from the hospital and all things medical had been therapeutic: James was so easy to talk to and she was growing fond of him.

They had just four hours in the final afternoon before she had to go back on duty and James had to return to his regiment. Both in their own way dreaded the moment they had to say goodbye, knowing that there was no certainty of any further meetings. James would again be involved in the fighting, which meant his life would be in danger once again. It was no surprise, therefore, that the time spent together was somewhat subdued.

Inside a small cafe, they sat drinking coffee, both trying to be cheerful, both failing dismally. Eventually Helen took his hand.

'For goodness' sake keep your head down when you go back!' She battled with the tears that threatened.

Squeezing her hand, he tried to lighten the mood.

'Sister Chalmers, I do believe you care for me a little!'

She gave a wry smile. 'Of course I do. I want to learn to ride.' But as the silent tears trickled down her cheeks, she added, 'I couldn't bear it if anything happened to you, James. I need you to come back, preferably in one piece.'

He took her other hand and lifting both to his lips, he kissed them.

'Nothing – and I mean *nothing* – will stop me. We have a relationship to build between us. This is only the beginning, you have to believe that. I knew it when I first bought you a drink in the bar that day.'

She saw the intensity in his eyes and knew he meant every word, and now she knew she wanted the chance to really get to know this man.

He removed a signet ring from his little finger and held it up. 'Will you wear this until I get back as a good luck charm?'

Without hesitation she said, 'Yes, I will.'

He put the ring on her finger on her right hand, then leaning forward, gave her a lingering kiss, oblivious of the others in the cafe.

They walked around the town, arms round each other until they reached the hospital. James drew her into his arms and kissed her as if he'd never let her go. Then staring into her eyes he said, 'Write often and I'll do the same. I don't have to tell you about my mail being held up sometimes, but when that happens, you're not to worry. I have a very good reason now to survive, and believe me I will.'

They clasped each other tightly and then Helen broke away.

'I have to go, James.'

'I know. Just take care of yourself until next we meet.'

She caressed his face. 'I will,' she whispered. She ran up the stairs to the entrance without looking back because she couldn't bear to.

Chapter Five

Helen walked into the surgery and stood beside Richard to scrub up. She took off the ring James had given her and put it into her pocket. Neither spoke until the next patient arrived and Richard gave his instructions to his team. They worked hard during their shift, trying to repair the broken bodies before them.

Helen watched Richard work and as usual was full of admiration for his skills, thinking how very fortunate the patients were who came to the table to have this man operate on them. At long last, they had finished the list.

Helen removed her surgical gloves, throwing them into the receptacle, and taking the ring James had given her, put it back on her finger. Richard came over as she did so and took her hand in his to look at the ring. He saw the initials on it and gazed at her.

'Not on the left hand, I see?'

'No,' she said and walked out of the surgery. There was no way she was going to get into an argument with him, she really wasn't in the mood and she craved solitude.

Richard washed his hands, his anger rising. 'Young

upstart!' he muttered as he thought about the young officer who had suddenly appeared and had upset his relationship with Helen, just as they had repaired their earlier spat. He was fond of her, of course, but Helen was aware he'd return to the marital bed when the war was over and she'd made it very clear that would be the end of their relationship; nevertheless, he felt as if his territory had been invaded and he was not happy about it.

Helen walked around the grounds of the hospital, wondering just how far James had travelled, wondering, too, just how soon he'd be back among the fighting, and asking herself, would he come through it unscathed? Would she ever see him again, and if she did, would their relationship grow into something permanent? Her thoughts were driving her mad so she made her way to the mess hall, collected her meal and sat alone at a table.

Jenny Palmer queued for her food and saw Helen sitting on her own. Walking over she asked, 'Do you mind if I join you?'

'Of course not,' Helen said, 'I'd be pleased with the company,' thinking that Richard would leave her alone if she was sitting with someone. 'How's Private Barnes?'

'He's going home tomorrow,' Jenny told her, 'and he's worried sick, wondering how his mother will handle his injuries. You wouldn't like to have a chat with him, I suppose? I know he enjoys talking to you.'

'No, of course not, I'll pop into the ward when I leave here.' Helen noticed the dark circles under the girl's eyes. 'Are you alright, Nurse?'

Jenny gave a wry smile. 'Better than my patients, but . . .'

'But?' Helen encouraged.

'We lost two more men last night. So much suffering shouldn't be allowed. If this war continues we'll lose even more. I know we are supposed to be professional and not get close to the patient emotionally, but how can you help it?'

'You can't, it's not possible, but you learn to cope with it, you haven't a choice. A good cry in private helps, I find,' she said.

Jenny looked surprised.

'Oh yes, Nurse Palmer, we all suffer at times – we are human beings, after all.'

After they'd finished eating, they walked back together to the ward and Helen went over to Private Barnes and sat on his bed.

'I hear you're off to Blighty tomorrow. How marvellous!'

He looked somewhat disconcerted. 'Well, in one way I can't wait, but in another I'm real scared,' he said.

'I expect your mum feels just the same.' She saw his look. 'Why are you surprised? She can't wait for her son to be safe within her four walls and she'll be worried about your injuries. I told you, she'll be shocked and that's natural. Don't blame her when she is, but after that she'll be fine. You, my boy, will thrive, smothered in motherly love!'

He couldn't help but smile at the thought. 'She didn't want me to join up,' he said. 'I was a fool to do so, really, and I lied about my age.' He paused and looked down at his tightly clasped hands. 'People will stare at me, I know that, and I don't think I can bear anyone looking at me, Sister.'

'Now you listen to me, Barnes, don't you dare stay inside your four walls hiding away, not after the surgeons worked for hours to repair your face, and yes, at the moment it looks bad, but in time the angry scars will fade. All your other faculties are fine. You can walk, you have the use of your arms, unlike that poor man over there. He lost a leg and an arm, and the man next to him has shrapnel in his brain and has no memory at the moment and no one knows if he'll ever get it back. You, young man, in comparison are very lucky!'

'Well, Sister, when you put it like that, I suppose I am.'

She rose from his bed. 'Good luck, Private Barnes. Learn a little patience with people, forgive their ignorance. They have *no* idea what it's like on the battlefield, they only know what they read in the papers, and let's hope they never have to find out.' She shook his hand and he held on to it.

'Thanks, Sister Chalmers. I won't forget your kindness.'

'Don't let me down now,' she chided. Then she walked away.

The following morning Helen joined Richard on his rounds with the matron, looking at his patients, checking on their recovery, changing medication where necessary, looking at wounds as they were redressed. He talked to the men, giving reassurance where necessary. As they walked away, he glanced over to see if Helen was still wearing the ring James had given to her.

He gestured towards her hand.

'Does that mean it's all over between us?' he asked abruptly.

She was taken aback momentarily, then she looked at him. She had to admit that there was no future with Richard, he'd made that very clear, and now she'd met

James, who wanted to build one with her. In her heart she was unsure about this, but she was drawn to him, loved being with him, and even if in time their relationship came to nothing, he was a free man, whereas Richard never would be, so why continue down this path?

'Yes, Richard, it does, I'm sorry.'

'Are you really?' There was such a note of sarcasm in his voice, she felt her hackles rise.

He continued: 'It didn't take much for you to change your mind, did it? I mean Havers sweeps in like a knight without his horse and you are swept away . . . just like that.'

'I'm not getting into an argument over this,' she said sharply. 'After all, our relationship had to end sometime, it was just earlier than we expected and for a reason other than the war was over and you were going home to your wife.'

'What are you saying, Helen, that I was just using you?'

'Not at all. We were drawn together because of the war and circumstances. Now it's over. If you'll excuse me I have some paperwork to catch up on.'

The next day, just as the last patient had been wheeled out of the theatre, an emergency case was rushed in and as the nurses started to cut away the uniform of the injured man, Helen walked over to assist and let out a gasp of horror as she saw that it was James who had been brought in, covered in blood.

According to the medics, the car James had been travelling in had been caught in crossfire. The driver had been killed, but James had been pulled from the car before it caught fire.

Richard looked up and glared at her. 'Are you alright to continue, Sister?'

'Yes,' she replied, 'let's get these clothes off so we can see what we have to do.' Her professionalism kicked in, knowing that time was critical and not knowing as yet how serious were the injuries James had sustained.

His leg was broken, shrapnel had peppered his body and he had superficial cuts on his face. One or two only just missed damaging his eyes.

Richard barked out his orders and they began. The shrapnel had fortunately missed his heart but had damaged his liver and a piece of it had to be removed. Helen held her breath as Richard proceeded. The patient lost a lot of blood during this part of the operation and needed several transfusions. Not knowing the type of blood needed, Richard asked for type O Rh negative, which was compatible with most. He didn't have a choice.

Some of the shrapnel was deeply imbedded in other parts of the patient's body and it took great skill and delicacy to remove it without causing great damage to the muscles and nerves.

Helen walked behind the patient as he was wheeled into a small recovery room, then she sat beside him and tried to fight the tears that threatened.

She held his hand, willing him to recover. She turned as Richard entered.

'Is he going to be alright?' she asked.

'He's strong, healthy, the next few days will be critical, but I expect him to pull through as long as there is no complication from the loss of a piece of his liver, but we'll have to see just how well he recovers and if any nerves were damaged.' He looked at her and frowned. 'Are you alright?'

She was deeply touched at his concern, after all he'd just saved the life of the man who'd come between them.

'Not really. I was so shocked when I saw who the medics had brought in.'

'That's understandable,' he said gruffly. 'Take the next twenty-four hours off, but I need you back on duty after.'

'Thank you, Richard, and thank you for saving James. I know it was down to your skill that he survived.'

'I was just doing my job. Now I'm off to eat. You make sure you do too. I can't have you passing out through lack of food in the theatre. I need to be able to rely on you.' He hurried away.

A few moments later Jenny Palmer entered and stood beside Helen.

'I believe the patient is someone you know,' she said quietly.

Helen nodded, unable to speak.

'I'll sit with him while you go to the mess and eat,' the nurse said.

Helen was about to refuse when Jenny interrupted. 'The surgeon insisted that you do so, Sister, and it's more than my job's worth not to carry out his orders. Besides,' she placed a comforting hand on Helen's shoulder, 'it'll be some time before he comes round from the anaesthetic and you need to keep up your strength, you don't need me to tell you that.'

Helen nodded and rose to her feet. 'Thanks,' she said and left, but instead of going to the mess she went outside and, finding a quiet corner, she wept.

Eventually she made her way to the mess and had a light

meal followed by a cup of strong coffee, sitting quietly, trying to compose herself for her return to James's bedside.

It seemed an eternity before James began to stir, but as soon as she realised he was coming round, Helen stood up and spoke softly. 'Hello, James.'

He opened his eyes slowly, still muzzy from the anaesthetic. It took a moment before he looked at her clearly.

'Helen?' he muttered.

'Yes, James, it's me. You are in my hospital. You were caught in the crossfire in a car.'

He was dazed and it was obvious at this moment he didn't remember.

'You have a broken leg and other minor injuries, but you're going to be fine.' She took his hand and held it, but didn't say more, allowing her patient to come to in his own time.

Eventually, when he was more compos mentis, she smiled at him and spoke:

'I know you said you'd like to come here and have me look after you, but this is a bit extreme, James.'

He gave a wan smile. His voice was weak but he had still retained his sense of humour.

'Yes, well it wasn't meant to be quite as bad as this.' He frowned and paused. 'We were driving along and suddenly there was this tremendous noise of gunfire. I don't remember anything else . . . my driver?'

'He didn't make it, I'm afraid.'

'Poor devil. How did I manage to survive, then?'

'You were pulled free from the car and brought here.

You were very lucky that there was a company nearby.'

Jenny Palmer came into the room and she and Helen gently hoisted the patient up a little higher in his bed. James saw the splint on his leg and grimaced. 'Will this interfere with my ability to ride?'

'We'll have to wait and see but I don't want you worrying about anything. We have to get you fit and it will take time. Richard operated on you and he's a fine surgeon, the best, so you were lucky in that respect.'

At that moment, Richard entered.

'I heard you were awake, Havers. How do you feel?' he asked as he took James's wrist and felt his pulse.

'As if I've been hit by a tank, but I believe I have you to thank for my survival.'

'Just doing my job. Now you must rest and I'll look in again tomorrow.' He turned to Helen. 'You get some rest too, the patient will be fine. The nurse will watch him and I'll see him again in the morning.'

'Man of few words is your surgeon,' said James. 'Is he always so abrupt?'

'No, not always.' She could hardly explain how she knew. 'I'll leave you to sleep and I'll come back this evening.' She kissed his forehead and left somewhat reluctantly. She would have liked to stay but Richard was right, she too needed to sleep and if she remained beside James, the last thing she would do was close her eyes.

As she undressed in her room, she thought how strange life was. She had been in love with Richard, or so she imagined, then James came into her life and not for one moment did she consider their relationship would be anything but a meeting in wartime – people come and go – and then he'd turned up at Christmas and things had changed. But was she in love with James? She was attracted to him – who wouldn't be? – but she knew she wanted him in her life. She supposed she was wary of committing herself again and so soon.

One day at a time, that was the way to go. Firstly they must get James fit. Life would sort itself out after that. If only the damned war was over, it would be less complicated. Then they could get back to reality and things would be clearer.

Chapter Six

It was now late March and the war still raged on different fronts. Nothing seemed to change in the life of the hospital. Patients were still brought in, others shipped home to their families, some returned to the fighting, all scared of what was before them, having already faced the enemy.

James Havers was slowly recovering. He was up and about, walking gingerly with two sticks until he recovered from the operation on his liver and his injured leg, but he suffered traumatic dreams that would leave him trembling when he woke. Like many patients, their experiences would stay with them, one way or another and no one knew for how long.

He was on the list for the next repatriation and Helen, due for some leave, had managed to get it at the same time so she could accompany him home to Cheltenham. Her own home in Evesham was but a few miles away, so she could see her family too.

The train was full as they left Rouen for Calais, then across the Channel in a hospital ship heading for England. When at last the sight of the white cliffs of home were to be seen, for many of the men it was an emotional moment after all they'd been through and many shed tears.

Helen, standing by the ship's rails with James, felt her eyes fill with tears too. James gently put an arm around her and pulled her close.

'I did wonder many times if ever I would see this,' he said quietly. 'I cannot tell you how very thankful and relieved I am to do so. So many good men didn't.'

'I know, but war is so destructive. It made me so angry to see those who arrived in the hospital so badly injured. Fortunately, many will be able to live reasonable lives once they finish their recovery, but mentally they will carry their scars for ever. Their family life will never be the same again. Marriages will suffer.'

'Well, Helen, you and all the medical staff did the best you could. Just think of those who did get home because of you. Me for one.'

She smiled up at him. 'Yes, I'm really pleased about that. Now, come on, let's rest a while before we get to Southampton as the disembarkation will be tiring and we have more travelling ahead of us before we get home.'

The ensuing journey seemed endless. After leaving the ship and being taken by ambulance to the train station, they had to change trains once and James became tired. Although his leg was healing, he still hadn't recovered fully from the operation on his liver and the wounds from the shrapnel. Helen made sure he slept as much as possible. She had his medication and gave it to him throughout the journey until eventually they pulled into Cheltenham.

There they were met by James's father who was waiting anxiously on the platform for his son's arrival. As he saw them alight, he rushed over to help, clasping his son in his arms, being careful not to knock him off his walking sticks. 'Good to see you, my boy,' he said, his voice choked with emotion.

'Hello, Dad. This is Helen Chalmers.'

Seeing Helen's nurse's uniform, Edward Havers assumed she was travelling with James to look after his needs.

'Thank you, my dear, for looking after my son. Let's get him into the car and then home. How long will you be staying to look after him?'

James caught his father by the arm and grinned broadly.

'The army didn't send a nurse to care for me, Dad. Helen is a friend of mine and she's on leave. She lives in Evesham and has been looking after me in hospital, but we met before that.'

Edward looked totally confused.

Helen came to his rescue. 'I think we should get James home and in bed first, explanations can wait.'

Outside the station stood a car and, to Helen's surprise, Edward carried the baggage over to it.

'Good heavens, Dad, when did you buy the Rover?' asked James.

'A few months ago,' he said with a note of male pride. 'Let me help you in. The roads are not always kind to motors but in time, of course, as more are built, then they will have to do something about it. This is the future, James.'

Helen sat in the back and breathed in the air. Home! How long she'd thought of being here. She gazed at the passing houses built in the stone so prevalent in the Cotswolds and was content. She closed her mind to the conversation between the two men and just mentally soaked up the passing country scenes before her. It was so therapeutic. She felt herself beginning to relax and just enjoy the journey until she felt the vehicle slow and Edward turned into a long driveway, situated behind open iron gates.

She sat higher in her seat as they drove towards a splendid-looking manor house. James came from a wealthy background, which was now obvious. Standing at the top of the steps leading to the large, carved front door stood a woman, dressed elegantly with a long coat draped round her shoulders, whom Helen assumed was the mother of James. She walked down the steps to greet them.

Edward got out of the driving seat and picked up the two suitcases as Helen helped James. His mother embraced him immediately.

'James, darling, I can't tell you how good it is to see you home, safe and sound.'

Kissing his mother he said, 'It's good to be back. Mother, this is Helen, a friend of mine, also my nurse when I was in hospital. She did a great deal to help with my recovery.'

Frances Havers saw the look of affection that her son bestowed on the nurse. She smiled at Helen. 'Welcome to Gately Manor, I'm so happy to meet you and be able to thank you personally.'

'Helen will be staying a couple of days, Mother, then she's off to her own parents in Evesham. She's on leave, you see. Unlike me, she has to return to France.'

'We need to get James settled, Mrs Havers,' said Helen. 'We've been travelling for two days and he really needs to rest.'

'Of course,' said Frances. 'Would you like something to eat first?'

James looked at Helen. 'That sounds like a good idea. I don't know about you, but I'm starving.'

'Now you mention it, I'm hungry too.' Turning to

Frances she said, 'But could it be something light for now?'

'Of course. Let's go into the living room; I'll send for a pot of tea and have a word with the cook. Follow me, please.'

The hallway was large and full of light from the big windows. A long table stood alongside the stairway and a couple of easy chairs were placed next to a bookcase. It had a warm, cosy feel to it. The drawing room was elegant but welcoming with its log fire burning in the open grate. Two comfortable settees were placed opposite each other with a long coffee table between them.

'Come near the fire and get warm,' Frances suggested, 'and I'll go and see the cook.'

James settled down and looked round the room, then at Helen. 'You will understand just how wonderful it is to sit here and see everything that is familiar and safe, but for me the nicest thing of all is to see you here as well.'

'It's a lovely house,' she said, gazing out of the French doors at the garden. 'Now you'll soon recover.'

'Doctor Coombs is calling to see you in the morning,' Edward said as he joined them. Turning to Helen he added, 'It's a bonus that you're here, my dear, as you can give him vital information about my son's condition.'

'I'll be happy to,' she said.

Frances returned with a tray of tea. 'Here, a cup of tea cures all, or so we are led to believe,' she said, smiling.

A while later, James and Helen sat in the dining room and enjoyed a meal of fish, mashed potatoes and mixed vegetables, followed by home-made Bakewell tart. It was like a banquet, they were so hungry. But after, Helen insisted that James should rest.

Mrs Havers had thoughtfully prepared a room for her son downstairs; knowing that he'd had a broken leg, she thought it would save him having to go up and down the stairs each day, until the leg was completely healed.

Helen helped him get out of his uniform, seeing how weary he now looked, and got him settled. It was a pleasant room with a big window overlooking the garden and as Helen made him comfortable, she felt him slowly relax.

'Try and sleep, James. It's been a devil of a journey and we don't want you to do too much as soon as you're home.'

'Tomorrow I'll take you to meet Chloe,' he said. 'I can't wait to see the old girl.'

'I'm sure she'll be as happy to see you. Now get some sleep. When you wake, then you can get up and sit with your parents. I'll go and get changed out of these clothes and if possible I'll have a bath. I feel decidedly scruffy and dirty.'

He caught her by the hand. 'You look good to me, Helen.'

Laughing she said, 'Ah yes, but you're biased. I'll see you later.'

Mrs Havers met Helen in the hallway. 'I'll show you to your room upstairs,' she said. 'The bathroom is opposite and there's plenty of hot water if you need to bathe. There are towels on the bed.'

Helen thanked her. 'The thing I want to do more than anything right now is to sink into a bath of hot water.'

'If you want to rest after your journey, please do,' her hostess said. 'We'll be in the drawing room until dinner. Please make yourself at home.'

The room was reasonably large, with twin beds, a wardrobe, dressing table and mirror, and a small, comfortable easy chair with a side table. Walking to the window, Helen saw that this room also overlooked the well-kept garden. Evergreen shrubs filled the beds, the deciduous trees were as yet without their leaves, but Helen recognised a couple of beds filled with rose bushes and could imagine how beautiful it would look when they were in bloom.

She undressed, put on a dressing gown and made her way to the bathroom. After turning on the taps, she found bath cubes and crumbed a couple in the running water, then disrobed and climbed into the bath. She just lay there as the bath filled with water, closed her eyes and relaxed. The last time she'd done this was in the hotel when she was on leave with Richard – when they were still lovers. Strange how life could change so quickly. It was at the same hotel that she'd met James and now here she was in his home, and he convalescing after his injuries. She sat up, remembering the shock she had when she realised who was on the operating table. It had been one of the worst moments of her life, but thanks to Richard's skill, he had saved James, which was ironic to say the least.

She eventually stepped out of the bath, dried herself and returned to her room, looked longingly at the bed for a moment and then climbed in, pulling the sheets and blankets around her.

Two hours later Helen woke. For a moment she was confused as to where she was, then she remembered. Stifling a yawn, she climbed out of bed, quickly remade it and dressed. She walked downstairs and tapping gently on the door of James's room, entered. The bed was empty.

As she left the room she heard voices coming from what she imagined was the drawing room and she made her way over towards the noise. The door was open and she saw James, in a dressing gown, sitting near the fire, talking to his parents.

'Come in, my dear,' Edward Havers said as he saw her.

'It seems you needed that rest more than I did,' James remarked. 'Come and sit beside me.' He moved along the settee. 'It's lovely to see you out of uniform.'

'Dinner will be in half an hour,' said Frances Havers. 'James has passed on a sherry, but can I get one for you?'

'How lovely, thank you.'

James held her hand. 'Isn't it marvellous to be in an English household again. It makes me realise how lucky we are to have survived.'

'I'm sure Helen doesn't want to talk about the war, James.' His mother's tone was sharp as she admonished him.

Helen frowned. She could understand the mother talking like this, after all her son had been injured and was now home, but as a nurse she knew that to be able to talk about the war and their experiences went a long way to healing the patient. It was those who kept everything inside who suffered the most and although James was very good at being hearty and happy, she remembered him in his sleep when he'd been having the dreadful nightmares. He was some way from recovery, mentally. This she would explain to his doctor when he came in the morning.

They went into the dining room for dinner shortly after, but by the end of the meal James was flagging and for the first time his parents were able to see that he was not yet as recovered as first they had thought, and when Helen suggested he should retire, they agreed.

When James reached his bedroom, he sat in an easy chair. 'Stay and talk to me, Helen,' he said.

She pulled up another chair and sat beside him.

'I'll be here tomorrow, James, but then I'm going home to my parents. I want you to promise me you'll take it easy. Please don't try and do too much too soon, or you'll undo all the good nursing and care you've received and I would not be pleased.'

He grinned broadly. 'So speaks the nurse.'

'I'm serious, James! Richard worked hard for your recovery, it's through his skill that you are on your feet. Don't undo it all by being stupid.'

'Ah, the brilliant Captain Carson. I know I owe him everything and your brilliant nursing, of course.' He looked thoughtful. 'Is there anything between you and the good surgeon, other than working together?'

This took Helen by surprise. 'Whatever do you mean?'

'Mm, I've seen the way he looks at you sometimes and I know for sure he didn't like having me turn up at Christmas. I wondered if I was stepping on his toes?'

Helen quickly recovered. 'We've worked together in the field for a year now and we've been through a lot. I don't have to tell you what it's like rushing from one place to another amidst gunfire. We have been a team, and through that I suppose you become close in many ways. You learn to lean on your partner.'

'Are you in love with him?'

She quickly denied it. 'Good heavens, no. He's married.'

'Ah, I didn't know that.'

Helen wanted to stop this line of questioning.

'Come along, now, it's time for you to rest, so let's get you into bed. I'll get your medicine. Do you want me to find you a book to read or anything?'

He yawned. 'No thanks, I do feel tired, but tomorrow we go to the stables.'

She smiled at him as she said, 'Oh indeed. I can't go home until I've met the famous Cleo. Here, take your medicine.'

Helen eventually tucked James into bed and, leaning forward, kissed him.

'It's been lovely to bring you home and to meet your parents. I know you'll be well looked after when I'm gone.'

He grabbed hold of her hand and held it tightly. 'If anything happened to you, darling Helen, I don't know what I'd do. Strange, I was the one who wished you were safely back in England when I was out there, but it's me that's safe and you're the one going back to the fighting.'

She sat on the bed. 'That's not quite true. Yes, I'm going back to France, but I'm well away from the fighting so you've nothing to worry about. Now stop fretting and rest. I'll have some breakfast sent into you in the morning. After, we'll go to the stables.'

When she was in her own room, she sat in the chair and took a deep breath. James had surprised her, questioning her relationship with Richard. He wasn't a fool and had picked up on Richard's possessive nature. It had been an uncomfortable moment, but thankfully she'd managed to talk her way out of it. Her leave had come at the right time, she thought. It would really break the thread that had held them together.

Tomorrow, she'd have a word with the doctor, giving him the full picture of James's recovery. She was relieved to be able to do so, then she'd feel better about leaving him.

Tomorrow she would meet the infamous Cleo.

Chapter Seven

The following morning, Helen found the dining room and arranged for breakfast to be taken to James, then she sat and had hers, with Edward, who explained his wife always ate her breakfast in bed.

'I'm pleased we're alone, Helen, because I want you to be truthful about James and his state of health. I need to understand how I can be of help to my son.'

This was a great relief to her. 'James has had an operation on his liver to remove some shrapnel and several other pieces that were in his body, which fortunately missed his vital organs,' she explained. 'The surgeon doesn't think this will be a problem unless some of his nerves or muscles were damaged in the process. He has to recover from the operation on his liver too and this will take some time. He must have plenty of bed rest, especially after our journey to get home, but the one thing that does worry me is his nightmares.'

'Nightmares?' Edward looked concerned.

'Sadly, all of our patients have been through hell and have seen things we can only imagine. They are unforgettable and will stay with them for ever. Each man has his own way of coping, but many get flashbacks of such things – some in their dreams at night and this happens to your son.'

'How long will he suffer this way?'

'There's no way of telling. When he wakes, he's wet with perspiration and his body trembles until he calms down and realises he's safe. If you should be there when it happens, just hold him, talk to him and comfort him when he wakes. I intend to give all this information to the doctor when he visits this morning.'

Edward let out a deep sigh. 'We had no idea, he looks so chipper.'

'Well, you know your son, he wouldn't want to worry you, but there is another thing you can do for him.'

'Tell me, please.'

'Let him talk to you about his war. I understand his mother wants to shut that away, but it would help James to talk about it to you – but only if he wants to. Don't push him, just make him understand that he can.'

Edward looked at her and said, 'I can see you're a fine nurse, Helen. I can't thank you enough for the care you've given him.'

'Well, he was my patient but also my friend. We met several months earlier when we were on leave. You can imagine the shock I had when he was brought into the surgery.'

He frowned. 'That couldn't have been easy for you.'

'No, it wasn't.'

They were interrupted at that moment by the arrival of the doctor. Edward introduced him to Helen, explaining who she was, and they sat together drinking coffee as

Helen gave him all the information she had about James, explaining what medication had been prescribed and about his nightmares.

Doctor Coombs was making notes as Helen spoke, but after hearing about the bad dreams he looked over at Edward.

'Many of the poor devils returning from the battlefield suffer this way. There is no way of knowing how long it will continue or if indeed this condition will ever leave them. We usually get a psychiatrist in to see them but that's all we can do. Right,' he said getting to his feet, 'let's go and see the patient.'

Watching the doctor as he spoke to James and examined him, noting that the long scar down the front of James's torso where the operation on the liver had been done had healed well, Helen was impressed. Here was a man she could leave to look after James and feel that he was in safe hands. She stood back and waited until he'd finished.

The doctor smiled at her as he closed his bag. 'Thank you, Sister, you've been a great help. We'll keep a sharp eye on your patient so there's no need for you to fret.'

'I can see that he'll be well looked after,' she said.

James spoke up. 'Now that you two have discussed my body, I think it's time to get dressed and go and see Cleo!'

Helen grinned broadly and turning to the doctor said, 'The only woman in the life of my patient.'

'Now, Helen, you know that isn't true,' James declared, making her blush.

Doctor Coombs chuckled. 'That's all very well. Yes, of course you can see Cleo but I must impress upon you that you need to rest. I will call again the day after tomorrow to check up on you.' He walked to the door. 'Take things quietly, young James. No rushing about, I mean it!'

'Oh good heavens, you're as bad as the lovely sister, who rules me with a rod of iron.'

Laughing, the doctor took his leave. 'Nice to meet you, Helen.'

Turning to James she said, 'I'll go and get a coat whilst you get dressed. It's cold outside so wrap up warm.'

'Yes, miss!' He turned back the bedcovers. 'Don't take for ever, I've waited a long time for this moment.'

Half an hour later, wrapped up against the cold, they walked to the stables after James had called into the kitchen and begged the cook for some carrots. Helen had been pleased to see how the cook greeted him. James was obviously a favourite of hers.

As they entered the small stable block, James called out, 'Cleo, I'm here at last. How are you, my girl?'

To Helen's great surprise, there was a loud neighing from one of the horseboxes and the sound of movement. Over the doorway a head appeared, the nostrils of the animal snorting with pleasure.

James walked slowly up to the stall and put his sticks against the wall whilst talking softly to Cleo, stroking her nose and handing out his carrot. It was a delightful sight to behold. James buried his head in the horse's neck, his voice choked with emotion as he spoke softly to the creature. Helen stood back, allowing him his moment alone. When he eventually looked at her, she saw the tears on his face.

She then walked over. 'So this is Cleo. She's quite beautiful, James.'

'There you are, Cleo, a woman with great taste.' He handed Helen a carrot. 'Here give this to her.' Seeing her nervous expression, he showed her how to hold the carrot before feeding the horse. 'Now stroke her head, she won't bite, I promise.'

With some trepidation Helen did so and was thrilled when the horse didn't flinch.

'She looks so big,' she remarked.

'Fifteen hands. I can't wait to ride her again.'

'In time, James!' Helen said sharply. 'Not yet.'

Ignoring her, James talked to his mount. 'Did you hear that, Cleo? She's jealous of you, that's why.' Before Helen could say anything James looked at her and said, 'I know I have to wait. I won't do anything stupid, I promise.'

Eventually he walked round the other stalls. Two of them housed horses that his parents rode and in the furthest box a smaller filly, the one that James intended she would ride, he told her.

'This is Miss Millie; she's quiet and by the time you get home for good, she will be well trained and as gentle as a lamb.' He led Helen to a bale of hay and they sat talking.

'I really wish you didn't have to return to France, but let's hope everyone will be home for good soon. I'm really going to miss you, my very dear Helen.' He placed his arm around her shoulder and kissed her cheek.

Tipping up her chin so she was looking into his eyes he said, 'You know I want you to share my life, for us to be together.'

'James, please. Let's get the war over first before we make any plans for a future.'

He lifted her right hand to his lips and kissed it. 'At least you are still wearing my ring. That's a good sign.'

'It's my lucky charm,' she laughed.

'I was hoping it meant more than that,' he chided softly, and she could see he was disappointed.

'Of course it does,' she tried to reassure him. 'You are important to me and I care about you.'

'About me – not for me? What is it, Helen, that makes you so reticent?'

'Just the war, James, that's all. You've seen what can happen in a second. This is not the time to plan a future, surely you can understand after all you've been through?'

He let out a sigh of resignation. 'You're right, of course, but I am impatient now I'm home.'

'That's my biggest concern,' she said.

'You are definitely not to worry, darling. Honestly, I do know how lucky I've been to come through all the surgery, and I do know I've a while to go. You think I don't know I'm not recovered? Of course I do – I'm not an idiot!'

She had to laugh at his indignation. 'Alright, calm down. Now, I saw a bench in the garden. It's sheltered under a tree; let's go and sit there for a while, get some fresh English air into our lungs.'

'Sounds good to me,' he said as he got to his feet with the aid of his sticks, but Helen saw him wince as he did so.

'You alright?' she asked.

'Yes, you know, a few aches and pains here and there, but nothing to worry about. I do honestly know I've a way to go as yet.'

'Come on, then, I'll stop nagging.'

They sat in a sheltered spot beneath an elm tree and looked over the neat lawns and weed-free flower beds. It was quiet and peaceful, apart from the twittering of the birds.

'You know, sitting here like this,' said James, 'one can hardly believe what is going on across the Channel. It's like a bad dream. If only it were so.'

Helen took his hand in hers and squeezed it. 'But you came through it, James. You laid your life down for your country and you came through. You earned the right to sit here.'

'Maybe, but I know so many who didn't, it doesn't seem fair somehow.'

'There's no need for you to feel guilty that you survived. Everyone stands the same chance when they sign up. Some will die, some will live. It sounds harsh put like that but it's the stark truth. You must celebrate your good fortune, not be ashamed of it.'

She turned his face towards hers and kissed him slowly. 'I would have been devastated if you hadn't made it.'

He took her into his arms and held her close. He didn't speak and Helen understood he was fighting with his emotions and let him be. It was all part of his healing, which as a nurse, she understood so well.

In the morning after breakfast, Edward insisted driving Helen to the station to catch her train.

She'd had her breakfast with James in his bedroom so they could have those last few private moments together.

This time it was James handing out the orders.

'Now you make sure you have enough rest, Helen. Remember, I've seen the hours you work, and for goodness' sake, keep safe.'

'Yes, sir, will do, sir!'

'Don't mock me, woman, I want you home in one piece. I don't want to have had Miss Millie trained up for no good reason.' He swung his legs out of bed, put on a dressing gown, and taking Helen by the hand, walked her over to the window. He stood her in front of him and encircled her within his arms, his lips brushing the nape of her neck.

'There will come a day when we'll do this in our own home.'

Helen was about to speak when he turned her round. His gaze was penetrating. 'I know this, darling, we were meant to meet, to be together. I told you I knew it when I met you at the bar in the hotel and I bought you a drink. I thought, here is the woman I'm going to marry.' He leant forward and kissed her slowly at first, but then with a mounting passion that couldn't be ignored.

Helen returned his kisses with a fervour, knowing she was leaving and not knowing when she would see him again. She was suddenly so reluctant to go.

A tap on the door interrupted them. It was Edward, ready to take Helen to the station.

James walked with her to the front door, kissed her goodbye again and watched until the car was out of sight before returning to his room. He felt bereft.

As they drove, Edward spoke. 'I can see that my son adores you, Helen, and I can see why. I also noticed you are wearing his signet ring on your right hand. Does that mean we may see a ring on your other hand in the future?'

Helen faltered for a moment. How was she to answer this delightful man whose love for his son was so apparent?

'Right now, I have no idea,' she told him. 'As I said to

James, we have to finish with this damned war first. We all hope for a future but I've seen it snatched away from so many in a second and so I think it's safer to live for the moment.'

The station loomed before them and Edward parked the car, then carried Helen's case onto the platform.

'Thank you for taking the time from your leave to come home with James, but now, go and enjoy your own family. I just want you to know you will always be welcome in our home in whatever capacity.' He leant forward, kissed her cheek, and with a wave walked out of the station.

What a lovely man, thought Helen. She could see where James had inherited his charm from, but now she was going home to her family and suddenly she felt tearful at the thought. It had been over a year since she'd last seen them, just before she was sent over to Belgium. It was going to be emotional, that was certain, but now she couldn't wait to see her parents.

Chapter Eight

Edward had kindly telephoned Helen's father to inform him of his daughter's imminent arrival, so when the train pulled into Evesham Station, Henry Chalmers was waiting.

Helen ran into his arms and hugged him.

'Oh, Dad, it's so good to see you.'

'And you, my dear,' he said, then held her away from him. 'Let me take a look at you.' He studied her face and smiled. 'Considering where you've been and what you've been doing, you look pretty good to me!' Picking up her case he said, 'I needn't tell you how anxious your mother is to see you. She's at home preparing our lunch.'

'Is she well?' asked Helen.

'Yes, very. You know your mother, her feet never touch the ground. I've never met a woman with so much energy!'

As Helen walked up the path to her front door, it was flung open and a slim woman came rushing out to greet her. Clasped in a warm embrace, Helen smelt lavender, her mother's favourite perfume, and felt her eyes filling with tears at this familiar reminder.

Margaret Chalmers was fighting with her own emotions

as she held on to her daughter. So many times she'd feared for her safety and to be able to hold her close was almost too much for her. Taking a deep breath she spoke:

'How lovely to see you, darling, come on in. We must have a sherry to celebrate.'

Helen walked into the living room, looking around, drinking in every piece of furniture, every ornament, those things that for her meant home. It seemed as if years had passed since last she'd seen them. She looked across the room at her mother.

'I can't tell you just how great it is to be home.'

Margaret smiled softly. 'I know, I feel the same about seeing you standing there. Come on, let's have a drink. I think we all need one.'

A delicious aroma was coming from the kitchen.

'Gosh, that smells good,' Helen remarked.

'The butcher saved me a nice leg of lamb for the occasion,' Margaret told her. 'He knew it was your favourite. He said we must take care of you whilst you're here.'

As they sat drinking the sherry, Helen told them about James, how they met and his being injured and how she'd nursed him and brought him home.

'I was able to give his doctor all his details, which should help in his recovery.'

'Will he recover completely?' Henry asked.

With a shrug Helen said, 'That remains to be seen. He was lucky to survive. Richard Carson did a magnificent job trying to repair the damage to his body. It will take time, though.'

'How is our brilliant surgeon?' asked Margaret.

'Fine, but there are so many casualties coming in every day, it's heartbreaking to see.'

'Do you really have to go back?' asked Margaret.

'You know that I do, Mum. Me and those like me are needed badly until this war comes to an end. I wouldn't feel right staying behind.'

Margaret changed the subject. 'I thought I might have a small party and invite some of the neighbours and your friends round for a few drinks, what do you think?'

'I'd rather you didn't, if you don't mind. All they'll do is ask about the war and they really don't want to know how bad it is and I don't want to talk about it. I'd much rather spend my few days with you and Dad, go for walks, have a quiet time.'

Henry immediately chipped in. 'Of course, we understand completely, don't we, dear?' he said pointedly, looking at his wife, daring her to argue, knowing she'd been baking in preparation for such a do.

'Yes,' she said hurriedly. 'These few days are precious to you and you must do exactly as you please.'

Helen looked relieved. 'I'd like to go shopping one day. I desperately need new underwear, and new boots as the mud can be dreadful if we have more rain, and I need another extra uniform. There's a shop in the town that stocks them and I've already written to them and ordered one.'

After the meal when Margaret refused to let her help clear the dishes, Helen wandered into the back garden and sat on a bench that her father had installed and where he liked to sit in the evenings. She listened to the bird songs, remembering how few there were in a war zone. It was like being in a different world – it was a different world! The air was fresh – no smell of ether or disinfectant here. No cries of pain. No calls of 'Nurse!' No rattling of trolleys carting patients to and fro. No dead bodies. Here there was just . . . peace. The tears slowly trickled down her cheeks.

In the kitchen, Henry looked out of the window and watched his daughter as Margaret dried her hands on a tea towel.

'There, that's done. I'll go into the garden and join Helen.'

He reached out to stop her. 'No, leave her with her thoughts. She needs to be alone at this moment.' As his wife started to argue, he looked at her. 'Margaret, she's crying. Leave her alone!'

Helen slowly started to sob and buried her head in her hands. All her pent-up emotions came pouring out. The war, her patients, the ones they'd been unable to save. Those who were severely injured. The shock of seeing James on the table, covered in blood – and Richard, masked, working, fighting to save him.

Her parents watched. Her mother was distraught to see Helen so distressed.

'Margaret, she needs to get whatever is on her mind out of her system,' said Henry. 'Trust me, she'll feel better afterwards.'

It was painful to watch, but in time Helen stopped crying. They watched her take a deep breath, wipe her eyes, blow her nose and relax against the bench.

'There,' her father said, 'now she'll feel better. Tears are a great safety valve. It's always so much better to let go than try to keep everything buried inside. She'll be fine. She'll come inside when she's ready. Come and sit by the fire, she mustn't know we've been watching.'

* * *

Half an hour later, Helen came back through the kitchen and into the living room.

'The garden's looking lovely,' she said. 'I've been sitting on your bench, Dad. I'm so pleased it's still there.'

Henry cast a quick glance at his wife and smiled before answering:

'Yes, well you know it's my favourite spot after a busy day at the bank. I sit and forget all the awkward customers I've had that day.'

Helen laughed. Her father was the manager of one of the local banks and was well liked. 'You don't have any, Dad. Everyone admires you.'

'Rubbish! Would you like a coffee and a brandy? It's getting cooler now the sun's gone in.'

'That'd be lovely,' she said and sat beside her mother on the settee. 'It's so good to be home,' she said giving Margaret a hug.

The remaining days of Helen's leave seemed to fly by and once again she was standing on a station platform waiting to travel, her parents there to see her on her way.

As the train drew in spilling out its steam, Margaret hugged her.

'Take care, now. The war can't go on for ever, and before you know it, you'll be home for good.'

Henry kissed her goodbye and helped her on board with her luggage.

'You are doing a wonderful job, Helen, and I'm immensely proud of you.' He kissed her cheek. 'Take care.'

Helen leant out of the carriage window and waved to her parents as the train left the station, then she sat down.

She'd have to change trains once to get to Southampton where she had an overnight passage on a hospital ship returning to France.

Although being at home was wonderful and therapeutic, she was now feeling rested and restless to return to work, knowing just how much she'd be needed. Medicine was her life, and without it for too long, she felt lost. She had spoken to James on the telephone and he assured her he was doing fine, being a model patient, and that he'd be writing, urging her to write back to him, or his sanity would be impaired if he didn't hear. He made her laugh as usual.

'Cleo sends her love and Miss Millie too. I'm allowed to visit them once a day for a chat,' he told her, 'and we miss you already.'

She chuckled to herself as she remembered their conversation. How long before she saw him again, she wondered, but at least he was safe and out of the war. That was a great comfort.

Chapter Nine

When eventually Helen arrived back in Rouen, she was exhausted and went straight to her room, unpacked, and had a quick bath. She would be on duty early the next morning and needed to be ready, mentally and physically.

The next morning, she woke to the sound of the bell, got dressed and hurried to the mess to have breakfast, knowing she needed that fuel to sustain her during the following hours in the operating theatre. She'd only just sat down with her tray of food when Richard entered. Seeing her, he collected his meal and walked over to the table and sat down.

'Have a good leave?' he asked abruptly.

'Yes thanks, it was lovely to see the family again and lead a normal life for a few days.'

'Did Havers get home all right?'

'Yes, he was very weary after the journey, of course, but I made sure he rested and took his medication. I was able to meet his doctor the next morning so I filled him in with all the medical details. He seemed a very able man.'

'So there didn't seem to be any undue problems after such a long journey?'

'No, Richard, he was fine, and his doctor made it very clear he was to rest.'

'Good. Did you stay with him for very long?'

'Only twenty-four hours after we arrived to get him settled, then I went to see my people.'

'Good, good. I'm very pleased to see you back. I'm so used to working with you I hate it when you're replaced. It's not the same. Nothing is quite as smooth.'

'How's it been, as busy as ever?'

'I'm afraid so, maybe a little less frantic, but far too many casualties. We have a full list this morning.' Looking at his watch he said, 'We have half an hour, at least it gives us time to enjoy our coffee for a change.'

Before long, Helen was back in the theatre where she belonged, beside Richard who nodded his welcome to normality and smiled across at her as they started to work.

It had been a good shift, there were no fatalities today. Every patient had survived the surgery and been taken off to a ward to recover. The theatre staff felt tired but uplifted at the result as they left the theatre and headed for a well-earned meal and rest. They all sat at the same table, discussing the cases put before them that morning.

One of the nurses sat beside Helen and, leaning towards her so no one could overhear them, spoke: 'Thank goodness you're back, Sister. Captain Carson has been like a bear with a sore head whilst you were on leave.'

'Oh, why?'

'No one could please him because he's so used to having you by his side. I'm not sure you realise but you've worked with him so long, you anticipate his moves and are always ready with the instruments he needs next. We are not so in tune as you are and so were much slower. It drove him crazy.'

Helen started laughing. 'Oh my! I do know those moods. When I started out with him, I was the new girl and, believe me, for a long time I certainly didn't meet his standards. He put me through it for a while.'

When the meal was over, they all departed to rest before the next shift later that evening. Some of them took a quick nap, others filled their time in different ways. Reading, writing home, or walking round the grounds, which was what Richard invited Helen to do.

'Fancy getting a bit of fresh air?'

She looked at him in surprise. 'Yes, if you like.'

The hospital grounds were large and in the past must have been a picture, but were now somewhat battle-scarred and neglected. The gardeners had probably been conscripted into the army. The grass had been cut, but what had once been flower beds were very overgrown and full of weeds.

They walked for a while, then sat on a low wall for a rest.

Richard looked at her for a moment. 'It's so good to have you back,' he said softly. 'I missed you more than I expected to.'

'Ah, that's because you didn't have me in the theatre anticipating your every move. I hear you were not happy.'

He chuckled softly. 'Yes, I'm afraid I was difficult to work with, but you know me, Helen. It makes a great deal of difference.'

'Although I loved being home with my parents,' she confessed, 'after a while, and when I was rested, I was anxious to return. That surprised me.'

Looking at her hand and the signet ring James had given her, he asked, 'Even if it meant leaving your soldier behind?'

'Yes. James has a long journey of recovery ahead of him and the war isn't over. The future is yet to be decided for everyone.' She rose to her feet. 'I need to freshen up and rest before the next shift. I'll see you in the theatre.'

As she walked back to her quarters, she wondered just how James was getting on and hoped that he was getting the rest he needed, but she was even more concerned about his nightmares. Had they ceased? She hoped that being at home in peaceful surroundings might help to settle his mental state.

Sadly, this was not the case, as the parents of James soon discovered a few days after Helen had returned to France.

James had been suffering with a headache and gone to bed early. His mother had looked in on him to make sure he was settled and later she and Edward had retired for the night.

It was in the early hours of the morning that Edward was disturbed. He sat up in bed and listened. He could hear someone shouting and immediately got out of bed and walked onto the landing. The noise was coming from his son's room. He rushed down the stairs and flung open the door.

James was tossing around in his bed shouting orders. 'Take cover! Keep your heads down!' He covered his head with his hands and ducked as if trying to avoid something, then, 'Christ! Medic, over here! He's lost his leg.'

Edward was shocked but quickly remembering what Helen had told him, he rushed over to his son and holding him firmly by his shoulders started talking to him.

'James, it's me, your father. You are safe now.'

James struggled but Edward held him firmly. 'James. That's enough!'

The note of authority seemed to get through the terrifying scenes in his son's head and he stopped shouting. Edward climbed on the bed, and taking James in his arms he continued to talk to him:

'There, son, you're home in Cheltenham with your mother and me. You're away from the war. Tomorrow we'll go and see Cleo.'

'Cleo. My lovely Cleo. Glad she didn't have to go to war. All those bloated bodies of horseflesh Cruel! Cruel!'

'Cleo is fine, we'll go to the stables and see her in the morning. We'll steal some of Cook's carrots. Cleo loves carrots.'

James became still and the wild expression had gone from his eyes. Somewhat stunned he looked up at his father.

'Dad?'

'Yes, James, it's me. You had a bad dream – look, your pyjamas are soaked, let me get you some dry ones.' He walked over to a chest of drawers and searched until he found some. Then, finding a towel, he stripped the soaked pyjamas off his son, wiped him down, and helped him put on his clean clothes. After, he found a clean sheet in the linen cupboard and changed the bedding. Once he'd seen James settled back into bed, he sat beside him.

'Are you alright now?' he asked anxiously, seeing the ashen face of his son.

'I feel a bit shaky, if I'm truthful, Dad. I'm sorry about this.'

'Don't be ridiculous! You can't help it. Look, James, I can't imagine what you've been through but if you ever need to talk about it, I'm willing to listen. Sometimes it helps.'

James looked fondly at his father, a man he loved and admired. 'One day, maybe, but not right now.'

'Can I get you anything, James?'

'No thanks, to be honest I feel drained. All I need is sleep.'

Edward rose to his feet. 'I'll look in on the morning on my way to breakfast.'

'Thanks, Dad. Sleep well.'

Once alone, James sat up and took a long drink of water from the glass beside his bed. He felt dreadful. These nightmares drained him completely. He remembered them clearly. It had been at Passchendaele on one particular attempt to gain ground. The guns had mown his men down. One man lost his leg in front of him. Flesh and blood rained down on him and he yelled for a medic. Another man, caught up on the barbed wire, was bleeding profusely. It had been a carnage and James was certain he was going to die too as he and his men retreated. Running – waiting to be hit by a bullet. Then he would wake in a bath of perspiration, with a feeling of loss and despair. Would they ever stop, he wondered, or was he to be plagued with them for the rest of his life? If that was the case, could he retain his sanity? That was his main concern. How could he expect to ask Helen to share his life if this continued? She'd had enough of caring for the sick, and he felt he couldn't ask her to take on an invalid for life. He sighed and turned over.

The following morning, Edward rang Dr Coombs and told him what had happened.

'I'll come over after my morning surgery,' the doctor said.

James had a bath when he woke, ate some breakfast,

then walked to the stables and straight over to Cleo's stall. He'd taken some sugar lumps with him. It was here every morning that he unburdened himself to his beloved steed. It was like therapy and he swore to himself that the horse understood every word. He stroked Cleo's nose, then buried his head into her neck.

'I had another nightmare last night, Cleo. Dad came down to my room so he must have heard something. What am I going to do if they don't stop, girl?'

The horse whinnied and shook her head from side to side.

'I don't know either. Oh, if only we could go for a ride over the hills like we used to do, but I'm not allowed as yet.' He picked up a curry comb and brushed her, talking all the time. 'How can I ask Helen to marry me when I'm like this? It wouldn't be fair, would it?' The horse pawed the ground as footsteps sounded, and turning round James saw Doctor Coombs approaching.

'Morning, Doc! I suppose Dad called you after last night?'

The doctor leant on the half-open door. 'Yes, James, he did. How are you feeling?'

With a wry smile James said, 'A bath and breakfast is a great healer, you know.' He put down the comb and walked outside the box. 'Will these nightmares ever stop?'

'I wish I had the answer, my boy, but alas no one knows. We know this condition has been brought on by war, of course, but other than that, we have yet to find a way to treat it. I could send you to see a psychiatrist in the hope that he could help in some way.'

'You know what I'd like to do more than anything right now?'

The doctor looked wary. 'No, but I'm sure you're going to tell me.'

'I would like to saddle up my trusty steed here and go for a gentle hack.'

Doctor Coombs pondered on this for a moment. 'Do you think you could manage to do so safely?'

'Oh yes. My leg is all but healed. I'd be very careful, just a gentle trot, nothing more than that, I promise.'

Seeing the longing in the young man's eyes and thinking it may help him mentally, the doctor agreed. 'Only a gentle trot, no more – and not for too long. An hour at the most.'

James's face lit up with joy. 'Oh, thank you so much. You have no idea what this means to me, honestly.' He went back inside the stall, put a halter on the horse and led her outside. He tethered her to the wall and went in search of a saddle in the tack room, returning with one shortly.

The doctor watched as James saddled his horse, then giving him a leg up, he again gave his instructions:

'A gentle hack, no more than a trot and no longer than an hour!'

James grinned broadly, saluted and said, 'Yes, sir!' He dug his heels into the animal and trotted out of the yard.

The doctor smiled to himself. It was the least he could do for the boy; he'd been to hell and back, he was sure. The dreams were a testimony to that, but he'd no way of knowing how long they would continue and how they would affect his recuperation. It was a concern.

James was in heaven. He sat on Cleo's back, walking along the country lane, looking around at the scenery and talking to his friend.

'Oh, Cleo, it's been far too long since we did this, eh girl?' He leant forward and patted her. 'I'm so glad you didn't have to go to war because I might well have lost you and that would be unbearable.' He came to a private path, which led to an open field belonging to his father. 'Come on, girl, let's trot.' His heels gave the orders into the animal's flank and off they went. The field was large and they did several circuits before stopping. James just sat looking around, remembering how he used to ride with the local hunt, jumping fences, chasing their prey. He looked longingly at the hedge between the fields, so wanting to jump it, but knowing he couldn't. Well, not today, anyway. He patted Cleo's neck.

'In time, my girl, in time. We'll take it easy for now.'

He rode up and down the field, and changing direction, did so again several times, then reluctantly rode back to the stables, taking the long way home. Climbing down carefully, he took the saddle off the horse, and returning her to her stall, he gave her a drink of water and wiped her down.

'You have no idea, Cleo, just how long I yearned to do that. But we'll go again tomorrow.' He took some sugar lumps from his pocket and held them out to her. Then after stroking her head, he left.

James made his way to the living room and was surprised to see the doctor sitting having a cup of tea with his mother. He glanced at his wristwatch and was relieved to see he had only taken the allotted hour for his ride.

Doctor Coombs hid a smile as he saw this action but ignored it.

'Enjoy the ride?' he asked.

With a broad grin James answered, 'You have no idea just how therapeutic that was, Doc! I feel a new man.'

'That's good to hear. You have my permission to take a daily ride until you feel well and able enough to at least canter. But small steps, James, and certainly no jumping as yet!' He rose from the chair.

'Must be on my way, just waited to see you were in one piece, my boy.'

Laughing, James assured him that he was fine. He walked with the doctor to the door.

'You have no idea what you did for me today. Thank you.'

'I can see by your expression how much it meant to you. Now, just take care. You still have a way to go, but you know that.'

'I do, believe me.' He shook hands with the man and closed the door. Making his way into the study, he sat down and started a letter to Helen, wanting to tell her about the morning.

His mother peered around the door. 'I'm off to do some shopping, do you need anything?'

'No, Mum, I'm fine thanks, just writing to Helen.'

'Then I'll see you later,' she said and left him alone.

Chapter Ten

Helen was delighted to hear from James, especially when she read he'd been riding, knowing how much it meant to him. He made no mention of his nightmares, but knowing the man as she did, she knew he'd keep such difficulties to himself. Not for a moment did she believe they had stopped. She knew better, after seeing so many young soldiers with the same problem.

Richard and she had settled into a more comfortable relationship. He realised finally that Helen no longer wanted to share his bed and eventually resigned himself to the fact. He occasionally asked after James, but purely from a medical point of view, hoping his surgery had been successful, however there was no longer any bitterness between them.

The months passed by. As one of the interns was heard to say, 'Same shit, different day.' That just about summed up the life in the hospital until the end of July when there was a flu epidemic, which crippled the troops and some of the hospital staff. It was as if there was a lull in the war for about a month, until the epidemic seemed to have passed.

But the hospital had been rushed off its feet, tending to those who'd been struck down, caring for them until they either recovered or died.

But by August, the Germans seemed to be losing and folk began to hope that there was at last an end to the war in sight as the German army retreated on the Western Front. Then in October they appealed for an armistice.

As the news filtered through, the medical staff in the hospital and the patients were euphoric. There were tears amidst the laughter. Men who had been through hell now knew for certain they wouldn't be returning to the trenches – but home to their families.

On hearing the news, Nurse Jenny Palmer flung her arms around Harry Gibbs, the male orderly, with tears streaming down her cheeks.

'Harry, it'll soon be over! Isn't that wonderful news?'

He looked at her fondly and taking out a handkerchief from his pocket, wiped her tears. 'Indeed it is, love. Didn't I tell you we had a duty until the end and then we'd have something to celebrate?'

'Oh yes, you did. I remember that night – I was very down.'

'Now you don't need to be. Look, girl, we're off duty in an hour. I've got a couple of bottles of beer in my room. How about we meet in the garden and have our own celebration?'

Jenny hugged him. 'Can't think of anything I'd like better.' She leant forward and kissed him, then she ran off.

'Bloody 'ell!' he muttered. 'Wasn't expecting that, Harry boy, this might be your lucky night!' He went in search of his beer wearing a broad grin.

* * *

Richard called a meeting of all the surgeons and theatre staff that evening.

'The news is great,' he said, 'but the war isn't over yet and, when it is, we'll still have patients to care for until they are at least well enough to be shipped home. Until then, we'll still be working, but at least, ladies and gentlemen, finally the end is in sight.'

'Well, I feel sorry for any poor devil who meets his maker now. That would be just so sad,' one of the other surgeons remarked.

'Or any poor sod who gets seriously injured,' added another.

'Then we'll do our best for them,' Richard said, 'as we've done all along. I'd like to take this opportunity to thank all of you for your work and dedication. At least we know we've done the best that we could for those we've treated. Now I suggest you get some rest, we still have work to do.'

Helen walked over to him. 'I can't quite believe the news,' she said.

'That's because we've waited so long. It's been a terrible time, so many brave men lost, unnecessarily in my opinion, and that's the saddest thing of all.'

'It'll seem very strange when eventually we do go home. It'll take some time to settle into a new routine after so long.'

'After my leave I'll be back working in a London hospital, as you know, but what about you? Will you keep working?'

She knew he was thinking of James.

'I'm waiting until I get home before making any plans. At this moment we don't know how much longer we'll be here. When I'm on British soil for good, then I'll make my decision.'

As she walked back to her quarters, Helen wondered just what the future held for her. She was worried about James and hoped he was recovering mentally as well as physically. If he was riding, that was a good sign that physically things were going well, but the other was an unknown quantity. She'd just have to wait and see, and how long that would be she'd no idea.

The news of the armistice was uppermost in everybody's mind in Britain. The war, which had been supposed would be over that first Christmas, had seemed endless, and now it was all but signed and sealed. For so many it was remembered with deep sadness. Their brother, husband or son, buried somewhere in a foreign country. No grave to visit . . . no closure.

The Havers family sat down to dinner that night to celebrate the news.

'Only a few more days,' said Edward 'and the war will be officially over. I often wondered just how long we would have to wait for it.'

James was quiet during the meal. In truth, sometimes he felt almost removed from it all having been home for a while, but on the odd occasion when he was alone, he had to admit he missed the camaraderie that wartime produced among the men and that night, unable to sleep, he made his way to the library.

Edward had been working late on his papers and as he made for the stairs he saw a light under the doorway of the library and quietly opened the door. James was standing by the window, looking out at the garden bathed in moonlight. He walked over to him.

'Everything alright, son?'

'Everything is so quiet always, it keeps me awake,' said James. 'On the front line it was so noisy. The sound of artillery, the rattle of machine guns. Explosions. Here, nothing.'

'What was it like, James?'

'A mud bath most of the time. Up to your knees, in some dugouts. Rats running over your feet if you were standing, your body if you were sleeping. Uniforms riddled with lice.' He paused. 'The silence as you waited to go over the top. The waiting seemed endless, and when the time came and I blew my whistle, I knew I was taking some good men to their deaths.' He paused and lit a cigarette. 'Men have been killed when they were just beside me. A shot and they dropped – an explosion and their body parts covered you with blood as they were blasted into smithereens. They were *my* men. Men who fought beside me – who followed my orders to the letter . . . who died!'

'That wasn't your fault, James. You were following orders just like your men.'

'But for what? In months we only covered five miles. Hundreds died for five *bloody* miles!'

Edward was at a loss for words, but it was the first time James had spoken about the war and Helen had told him it would be good for him to open up about his experience, so he said nothing more.

'You should have seen the dead horses, Dad. Lying by the roadside, bodies bloated, discarded . . . forgotten.' His voice choked in his throat and Edward rested a hand on his son's shoulder.

James took a breath. 'It was a living hell, if I'm honest, and I am lucky to survive.'

'But survive you did! Now we have to get you back to full health.'

James paused then looked at his father.

'I'm not at all sure I'll ever be back to full health, Dad. These nightmares could be part of the rest of my life. True, I've not lost a limb and I'm more than grateful for that, but how can I ask Helen to share my life if they continue? It wouldn't be fair.'

'It's early days yet, James. You have to give it time. Anyway, you don't know how long it will be before she comes home.'

'That's true. I imagine the hospital staff will have to stay on until all their patients are sent home. But it is a dilemma.'

'Come along now. Let's both try and get some rest. It's very late.'

But as Edward climbed into bed, he was concerned. It was obvious that James had suffered, as had all men who were sent to the battlefield, and the things he'd heard that night would live with his son for the rest of his life, to some degree, but if he was forever to be plagued with nightmares they surely would be injurious to his health, physically – and mentally. That was his main worry.

For the men still fighting, it was a strange existence. They had only eleven days before the armistice was signed and the war ended, but the guns still fired, the Germans were still the enemy, and the soldiers were frustrated.

'Don't they know about the fucking armistice?' one soldier asked loudly from the trenches. 'It's insane to keep on fighting, killing each other when soon we'll all be going home.'

'You just keep your bloody head down, or it'll be you!' he was told by his commanding officer. 'I want to take all you miserable buggers home in one piece.'

An exploding shell had them ducking as fragments flew in the air.

'Keep those guns firing!' the officer yelled. 'We don't want to have to haul them home. Send the shells to the bloody Boche. Make *them* keep their heads down!'

But at last at eleven o'clock on the eleventh of November, the guns were finally silent. Men cheered, many shed tears. The officers were overcome with relief knowing that at long last they wouldn't have to take men over the top to face their last moments. The rum ration was handed round. The sound of singing could be heard: 'There'll Always be an England', and from the German trenches, their national anthem.

In Rouen at the hospital, they too celebrated. Lists were made of those who were fit enough to be sent home as soon as arrangements could be made, another of those who would have to wait a while, but alas casualties were still arriving by ambulance. The final hours of the war were still claiming lives.

Richard was reading his list of names of the lucky men who would be the first to be repatriated. He talked to them all that evening, telling those who were on the list the good news and commiserating with the others, but promising they wouldn't have to wait too long before being sent to hospitals in England – when they were fit enough to travel, to finish their recovery and convalescence, but at least they'd be on home soil and maybe in a place where their family could visit.

He sat back in his chair and drank a glass of whisky. He'd soon be home too, returning to his house and wife. He lit a cigar someone had given him and, blowing out smoke circles, contemplated living a more normal life as a husband *in situ*. His last leave was six months ago. It had seemed very strange, going to the club, meeting old friends, sleeping with his wife whilst having an affair with Helen. But that was over now. Helen would also be going home . . . to James Havers. Although he had used every bit of knowledge and skill he had to save the man's life, he was still irritated to think that James had been the one to come between them.

Sitting back, he closed his eyes, remembering how it had been with Helen. He could still feel the softness of her flesh, the rise of her breasts, the way she kissed and her cries of delight and passion as he made love to her. He felt himself harden at his memories. God, he wished she were here at this moment!

A tap on his door brought him back to the present.

'Enter!'

A sergeant handed him a file. 'Here are the dates and train times plus the list of men to be sent home, sir.'

'Thanks, Sergeant, put them on the table, please.' He took another swig from the glass and picked up the file.

Chapter Eleven

In London the end of the war brought thousands out onto the streets. Lloyd George appeared on the steps of 10 Downing Street to talk to the public who'd gathered there. King George V and Queen Mary appeared on the balcony of Buckingham Palace, waving to the crowds. There was dancing in the streets. Church bells rang out. Folk laughed and cried and the sense of relief was palpable.

In Cheltenham at Gately Manor, friends of the Havers gathered to celebrate in the living room.

Edward picked up a bottle of champagne and handed another to a friend to open, but as the corks exploded, James let out a cry and flung himself upon the floor, curling up in the foetal position, covering his head with his hands – to the astonishment of the guests. There was immediate silence.

Edward rushed forward and held his son.

'James, it's alright. It isn't the guns, only champagne corks. You're quite safe.'

Frances stood rigid with shock as James was helped

to his feet. He looked around, muttered an apology and walked out of the room.

Edward looked at his guests. 'It's the war, you see.' Then he went in search of his son.

James was sitting on his bed, hands held to his head.

'Are you alright, my boy?' asked his father.

'God, Dad! How embarrassing. I'm so sorry.'

Edward dismissed his words. 'Nonsense! Not one man in that room has seen what you have, but they'll understand. I'm not in the least embarrassed and neither should you be.'

James just shook his head. 'But that could happen at any time, anywhere.' He looked at his father. 'How am I going to cope with that?'

Edward sat beside him. 'You are expecting too much too soon, James. It's early days yet. Just be patient.'

'Go back to your guests, Dad. I'm fine now, honestly. I just need to be on my own for a bit.'

His father left him, somewhat reluctantly.

Getting to his feet, James slipped out of the house and wandered over to the stables and over to Cleo's stall. He stroked the horse's nose.

'Well that was a bloody mess,' he said. 'I can't imagine what those people will have thought. I felt such a fool, Cleo. They'll think I've lost my mind.'

The horse nestled her head against him as if sensing his distress.

'Fancy a ride out? I need to get away, so I'll get a saddle and we'll escape together.'

Glancing out of the living-room window, Edward saw James riding out of the gate and smiled softly. Thank God for that bloody horse, he thought. It was the only thing at the moment that seemed to give his son some peace of mind.

It was a further two months before the last of the patients in the hospital were shipped home, with their medical files to hand over to the hospital in England where they would continue their treatment. A few of the staff stayed behind to pack other files and equipment until they too were finally ready to leave the following morning.

Richard had invited Helen to go out to a nearby hotel for a final meal together and she'd accepted. She changed out of her uniform and put on a gown, wondering if she would decide to continue with her career or become a civilian in the near future. Nursing had been her life but the war had affected her. She was sick of blood, injuries and death and felt the need for a change. After her leave she would have to make a decision, but for this evening, she'd put such thoughts aside.

The meal was good and the wine palatable. It seemed that, for once, Richard had put aside his thoughts of work too. He was as charming as she remembered when first they had met, outside of the operating theatre. Here before her was the man who she'd taken to her bed and she could see why that had happened as they talked about the old days.

'I hope you don't have any regrets about our relationship, Helen?'

'No, of course not, why would I? I knew what I was doing. I didn't feel that I was encroaching on your marriage, it was of the moment and that was all. At the time, Richard, we needed each other in that way as well as professionally. No, I'll never regret it.'

He smiled softly at her. 'That makes me very happy. I don't have any regrets either, and I thank you from my heart for those intimate moments.'

She looked into his eyes, knowing that all she'd have to do was invite him back into her bed for the last time, but that was in the past as far as she was concerned and she changed the subject.

'I can't wait to be back in the Cotswolds with my family. Then I'll have to make a decision whether to stay in nursing or leave to do something else.'

This surprised him. 'You'd give up nursing?'

'I've given it some thought. Oh, Richard, I am so sick of seeing broken bodies, I feel I want to do something entirely different.'

'You may change your mind after some leave. You're a brilliant theatre sister, it would be a pity to waste that talent.'

They then talked about travelling home with other staff members, first by train and then by sea across the English Channel. It would seem a strange journey leaving a battered war zone now at peace, for a quiet English countryside. It would be with mixed emotions for all.

After dinner they walked back to the hospital and Richard escorted her to her room and waited for her to unlock the door.

She did so and turned to him. 'I still have a few things to pack, so I'll see you in the morning.' She saw the disappointment in his eyes.

He caught hold of her and pulled her close. 'Take care, Helen. I hope you find what you're seeking.' Then he kissed her hard and long before letting her go and walking away.

*　*　*

Thirty-six hours later, Helen arrived at Evesham Station and took a taxi to her home. She'd not told her parents of her impending arrival, being uncertain of the time. She knocked on the door and waited.

Her mother opened the door and let out a cry of surprise when she saw who was standing there.

'Helen! Darling, how wonderful. Come in. Henry! It's Helen, she's home.'

Her father came hurrying down the hall and embraced her.

'Why didn't you let us know?' he asked.

'I wasn't sure of any times so I thought I'd just turn up.'

She was ushered into the living room, hugged and kissed and then Margaret disappeared to make a cup of tea.

'How are you, my dear?' asked her father.

'Tired, but so pleased to be home, Dad. You look well.'

'Oh, I'm alright. How long are you home for?'

'I have a month's leave and I'm going to enjoy every minute.'

'And then what?'

'Then? Well I don't know. I have a few decisions to make.'

Her mother came bustling in with a tray of tea and some home-made scones.

'Here, this will freshen you after such a tedious journey.'

They sat chatting and then Helen said she wanted to unpack, take a bath, put on some fresh clothes and call James. Her parents left her alone to do so.

Two hours later, Helen dialled the number of Gately Manor and asked to speak to James.

'Helen! Is that really you?' asked an excited voice on the other end of the line.

'Yes, it's me. I arrived home a couple of hours ago. How are you?'

'I'm fine. Oh my God! It's so good to hear your voice. When can I see you?'

'Give me a couple of days and I'll call you and arrange a meet then.'

'That'll be wonderful but please don't leave it any longer or I may have a relapse and it'll be your fault!'

Laughing she said, 'I promise.'

'Come for a couple of days, why don't you? It will give us time to catch up.'

She agreed.

Two days later, Helen alighted from her train at Cheltenham station to see James standing on the platform waiting. Grinning broadly as she climbed down, he gathered her into his arms and kissed her.

'Oh my God! You don't know how good that felt!'

She looked up at him and said, 'Well I enjoyed it too.'

'Then let's do it again,' he said and kissed her passionately, not caring about the other passengers on the platform. Then he walked her outside to the car.

'You're driving this now?' she asked.

'Oh yes. Dad lets me use it when I need to.'

As they drove, Helen looked at the man beside her. She was delighted to see that he looked well and she'd noticed he was now walking properly too.

James caught her by the hand and squeezed it. 'You have no idea how happy it makes me to see you here beside me.'

'I'm happy to see you too, but don't you think two hands on the wheel would be safer?' she teased.

'Oh, you're no fun,' he retorted as he let go.

'How's Cleo?' she asked.

'Cleo is the only thing keeping me sane,' he said. 'If I didn't have her to ride out on I think I'd go quietly mad, and Miss Millie is just waiting for you to take your first ride on her. I've been breaking her in and now she's ready.'

'Well, let's not rush things,' Helen said hastily.

'Don't worry, darling, I won't push you until you're ready. Ah, here we are. My parents are anxious to see you again.'

Edward and Frances greeted her warmly as she entered the living room.

'How are you, Helen?' Edward asked. 'You look well enough.'

'I'm just a bit tired after packing up the hospital and getting home, but a good meal and a couple of nights' sleep does wonders.'

They chatted for a short while, then James stated that he was taking Helen to the stables and for a walk round the garden as they had some catching up to do.

It was a bright, crisp January day with still a layer of snow left from a downfall a week ago. But the air was fresh, the skies clear as they made their way to the stables, and it pleased Helen to see that James was no longer in need of walking sticks.

'Your leg has healed well by the way you're walking,' she remarked.

'Yes, thanks to Richard. How is he, by the way?'

'Fine, he'll be at home by now with his wife. He's on leave too.'

As they reached the stables, James called out to Cleo

and immediately her head appeared over the half-door of the stall.

'You'll have to take a back seat now, Cleo, my best girl is home!'

The horse gave a snort and whinnied.

'It's almost as if she knows what you're saying,' laughed Helen.

'But of course she does, although nobody believes me.' He stroked the animal's nose and mane. 'I ride her every day now and I've been allowed to jump once again, so we work in the practice ring sometimes.'

James led her to a bale of hay and they sat. He put an arm around her.

'You've been away far too long, Helen. But now you're home and I can't tell you how much that fills me with joy.'

Looking at the man beside her, Helen was filled with emotion, remembering the day James had come into the hospital, not knowing how seriously hurt he was and even if he was going to live or die, realising that she loved him – and now – here he was beside her looking completely recovered.

'I'm happy too, James. Your leg is healed, but what about your nightmares, do you still have those?'

Frowning he said, 'Yes, I'm afraid I do. Maybe not quite so frequently as when I first came home, but yes, they still happen.' There was something in the tone of his voice that made Helen feel there was more to tell.

'Any other symptoms that worry you?'

'Unexpected loud noises. I automatically duck, thinking it's a shell or a bomb. It can be most embarrassing . . . and I'm a bit claustrophobic. Confined spaces tend to freak me out.' His bonhomie had disappeared. 'I'm really a bit of a mess, my dear Helen.'

'No you're not, James! You're still suffering from the war. You and many others. It just takes time, that's all.'

She then saw the fear in his eyes. 'But what if time doesn't change anything. What then?'

'We will deal with it.'

'Darling Helen, there will be no we! No way can I ask you to share my life, suffering with all this. It wouldn't be right.'

'I'll be the judge of that, James Havers! Now, come on, let's go in search of a cup of tea, I'm parched.'

'But you haven't seen Miss Millie!'

'Tomorrow. How about now you drive me into Cheltenham, take me shopping and out for lunch? I have some money I've saved and I want to spend it. It's been a long time since I've been able to wander around the shops and it will do you good to get out and about.'

'Are you sure about this?'

Helen stood up. 'Come on, I'm starving, for a start.' She held out her hand. 'Be brave, James. Shopping with a woman is a dangerous situation for any man.' To her relief, he chuckled and, standing up, followed her out of the stables.

Whilst Helen was off to enjoy her shopping, Richard Carson was sitting in his club in London, reading *The Times* and sipping a Scotch and soda. He was feeling restless, unable to settle to living a normal existence. Hospital life had been so busy, with not much time to relax, and now there was little to do. It was driving him mad.

Ann, his wife, didn't know how to handle the situation. If she tried to talk to him about it, he quickly became irritable and snapped at her, and although he'd been away for so long, as yet, despite sharing a bed, Richard had just kissed her goodnight and turned away.

Sitting alone in her kitchen with a glass of wine, she tried to convince herself it would only be a matter of time before he was able to put the war behind him and return to normal. She'd just have to be patient and wait. It wasn't easy for her either. With an absent husband, she'd made her own life. She spent time with friends, met new ones and belonged to various charitable organisations to fill her days.

Looking at her watch, she rose from her chair and, picking up her coat and bag, left the house and hailed a taxi. She was going to a committee meeting of a charity to help families who had either lost men in the war or whose husbands were injured and were suffering financially. The organisation helped with clothing and food parcels. She felt it was worthwhile and enjoyed being a part of it.

Arriving at her destination in Bayswater, she paid the driver and walked into the building to the rented rooms used by the charity. Everyone asked after her husband.

'He's fine,' she said, 'just trying to get used to being home. It's not easy for any of the men, they need time to adjust.'

Clive Bradshaw, the chairman, looked at her and saw the concern mirrored in her eyes but he didn't say anything until the end of the meeting, when he stopped her as she was about to leave.

'Are you in a hurry to get home, Ann?'

'No, as a matter of fact. Richard said he wouldn't be home until early evening, in time for dinner.'

'Good, let me buy you lunch, there's something I want to discuss with you.'

Puzzled, she agreed.

Once settled in a restaurant and having ordered she turned to him:

'What did you want to discuss, I thought we covered everything this morning?'

'Oh, this isn't business, my dear. I just felt that when you were talking about Richard something was amiss. What's the problem?'

Ann was taken aback at his perception. He was a man she'd now known since Richard was sent abroad. They had become friends and she liked and admired him. Letting out a deep sigh she told him.

'Richard can't settle. If I try to talk to him about it and his homecoming, he snaps my head off and won't discuss it. It's like being with a stranger, and if I'm honest, one I don't like very much.'

'Well you can understand it, really. None of us know what the men have been through, what they've seen and had to endure. Just be patient. After all, out there, you weren't with him to give him comfort and make a fuss of him after a difficult day. He'll settle soon.'

As she walked home, Ann thought over Clive's words. Of course he was right. Time is a great healer, perhaps all Richard needed was a bit of tender care.

Over dinner, Ann told her husband about the charity and how they were helping families of servicemen, of the hardships they faced and how difficult it was for many to manage.

He listened intently and praised her for being a part of it.

'If you saw the state some men were in who returned to their families, you'd understand even better. Some poor devils, especially those who'd lost limbs, were worried out of their minds as to how they would be able to keep their families as they wouldn't be able to work. Well done, darling.'

She was delighted. These were the first kind words he'd said since he came home. So pleased was she that when they climbed into bed that night, she reached for him, putting her arms around him, but he stopped her.

'I'm tired, Ann,' he said and turned away.

Tears welled in her eyes at his rejection and she pulled the sheet up to her neck, then used the corner to wipe her eyes.

Laid beside her, pretending to be asleep, Richard was feeling guilty. He knew his wife was concerned and trying her best to help him back to normality, but he couldn't help himself. Ever since he'd kissed Helen when he'd taken her back to her room after their final dinner together, he was wondering if she was with young Havers. It was her he wanted in his arms, not his wife! Every day he wondered if Helen and her soldier were being intimate as he had been when they were together. He couldn't get the image of them making love out of his mind. He knew he was being not only ridiculous but unfair to Ann. Perhaps when he was back working, he could finally put the past behind him.

He slept fitfully that night, tossing and turning, calling out as he did so.

Ann, disturbed by her husband's restlessness, wondered just who was Helen, the name that her husband was calling for. Whoever she was, it was the reason that he turned away from her. Now she really had a problem.

Chapter Twelve

Back in Cheltenham, Helen's shopping trip was not without its problems. If she and James entered a shop and it was busy, she felt him stiffen and saw the panic in his eyes at the number of shoppers. She put her arm through his.

'Take a deep breath,' she told him. 'You're fine, you're with me. If you feel you have to go, just say so and we'll leave.'

Eventually he seemed to relax and when she went into a cubicle to try on clothes, she made sure he wasn't enclosed in a small space. But it was an ordeal for both of them and she decided that a busy restaurant was not a good idea today. To this end, she bought bread, cheese and tomatoes and let James drive to a quiet spot where they had a picnic on the back seat of the car, cutting the cheese and tomatoes with a penknife that James carried.

'I'm sorry I've spoilt your day, darling,' he said.

'Rubbish! I've bought some clothes, a pair of shoes and some underwear. Now we're having a picnic. What's wrong with that?'

He leant forward and kissed her on the forehead.

'You are an angel, you know that?'

'Of course I do, I'm surprised it took you so long to discover it!' But now she realised how badly the war had affected him, mentally. It was going to be a long journey before James would feel safe enough to do the normal, everyday things that others took for granted.

'Tomorrow, you can introduce me to Miss Millie.'

His face was a joy to behold. Here, he was secure. When he was with his horses he was relaxed and unworried and, despite her reluctance to learn to ride, Helen knew she would have to do so, to make James feel a normal man again.

After breakfast the following morning, Helen, now wearing a pair of James's trousers, belted so as not to lose them, was taken out to the stables. Today the tables were reversed. Today it was James who was trying to dispel Helen's fears.

After talking and feeding carrots to Cleo, James saddled Miss Millie, then calling Helen over he gave her a carrot to feed to the animal.

'Stroke her, darling, honestly she's as docile as can be.'

At last Helen felt able to climb into the saddle with the help of a mounting block.

'It's very high up here,' she said nervously. 'The ground looks a long way down, James!'

'You'll be fine, just don't look down.' He showed her how to hold the reins and then he led the horse out to a practice ring.

'Now just relax into the saddle and stop worrying.' He walked the horse slowly around the ring on a lunge rein and Helen began to enjoy herself.

Seeing her relax at last, James grinned broadly.

'There you are! Didn't I tell you it was easy? Now, we are going into a trot, just move with the horse and then I'll show you how to rise with her.' Seeing her look of consternation he said, 'Now, remember what you told me yesterday? If you want to stop just say so. Alright?'

She just nodded.

Two hours later, Helen had almost mastered the rising trot and was absolutely delighted. As she was led back to the stables she was all smiles.

'Oh, James! I can see why you love riding so much. That was great.'

He helped her down and giving her another carrot he said, 'Now reward Miss Millie, because she was such a good girl.'

This time, Helen had no fear of the horse. She fed it, buried her head into the horse's neck – and thanked her profusely.

'Next time we go shopping, madam, it will be to buy you a pair of trousers and some riding boots.'

'Next time?' Helen laughed. 'So yesterday didn't put you off, then?'

Putting his arm around her he said, 'I have to get used to it, Helen, if I want to lead a normal life.'

She leant forward and kissed him. 'And you will do so . . . in time. I promise.'

That evening, the Havers were out with friends and so James and Helen had dined alone, then moved into the drawing room, to the settee by the fire.

James was in a good mood and was his usual entertaining self. He asked Helen if she'd thought about the immediate future, now she was home.

'To be honest, I haven't. I've just been enjoying being away from everything to do with the war. Loving the peace and quiet.'

'I know, strange isn't it? I can't get used to it, sometimes the quiet keeps me awake.'

'And you, James. What plans have you?'

He leant back. 'Oh, I had it all planned. I would continue in the army, ask you to marry me and live happily ever after, just like a fairy story, but now I can't do these things.'

She frowned. 'What do you mean?'

'I wouldn't pass the medical now, so I'll have to resign my commission and try and find another way to earn a living and, my darling, there is no way I'd expect you to take me on. You've had enough of caring for the sick.'

Helen was at a loss for words. She could hardly tell him now that she was thinking of giving up nursing for that very reason. What was she to say?

'I can understand you leaving the army, but in time you'll get better and be able to live a normal life.'

'But that's not strictly true, Helen. The doctor told me that there's no way of knowing if I'll fully recover. *That* is my dilemma.'

'Well you will just have to take one day at a time, but knowing you'll eventually recover. Be positive! Negative thoughts bring negative things, James. If you convince yourself you'll never get better, then you won't. Your recovery depends so much on your mental attitude. It can make or break you.'

'Oh, feisty! I like a woman with spirit.'

'Don't jest, it's true, every word, and if you're honest, you know I'm right.'

'Darling Helen, I do know you're right, I'm just scared, that's all.'

She enfolded him in her arms to comfort him.

'You were scared every time you blew your whistle and took your men over the top to face the enemy, but you still did it! That took courage and so does this. But at least you came back alive.'

He gazed at her. 'You really do care, don't you? This time you care *for* me not just *about* me.'

'Of course, you stupid man! How could you doubt it? When you were brought into the operating theatre covered in blood I knew just how much I cared. So don't you *ever* do that to me again.' She felt the tears glisten in her eyes.

'Oh, Helen darling, don't cry. I'm sorry to have worried you, but I didn't have a lot of choice at the time. I only remember opening my eyes and there you were. I thought for a moment I'd died and gone to heaven. But sadly, I won't see much of you when you start nursing again.'

She turned to him. 'To be honest, I'd made up my mind to give up nursing. I want a change.'

'Doing what?'

She stared into his eyes. 'How could you forget? You said we would spend our future together . . . or have you changed your mind?'

He was speechless for a moment. 'You still would marry me, knowing my mental state?'

She caressed his face. 'For heaven's sake, James, listen to yourself! The way you talk, anyone who didn't know you would think you're a raving lunatic. You are suffering the same as many others after being involved in the war. You will get better, all you have to do is *believe* it.'

He took her right hand and touched the ring he gave her. 'You would be willing to change this for a wedding ring?'

'Well, I'd like an engagement ring first, if you don't mind. A girl likes that sort of thing.'

Shaking his head he said, 'You are incorrigible!'

Snuggling into him she said, 'Yes, and I'm available.'

'Then, tomorrow, I'd better take you home and ask your father's permission to marry you. Do you think there's a chance he might say no?'

'Absolutely not! He can't wait to get rid of me.'

'Do you want time to think about this? I mean, I don't want you to rush into something you might later regret.'

'James! Haven't you heard a word I've said?'

He laughed at her feigned outrage. 'I can see living with you is going to be quite a challenge.'

'Check with Dad, he'll agree with you. Now, let's go to bed.'

'Is that an invitation, by any chance?'

She held out her left hand. 'When I have an engagement ring on this finger, ask me again. But not tonight. You could have your wicked way with me, then change your mind and my reputation would be ruined.'

He rose and took her hand, chuckling softly. 'I'll remember what you said, young lady.' They walked up the stairs together and at her bedroom door Helen kissed him goodnight and, holding up her left hand, wiggled her fingers at him and laughed as she closed the door.

'You are a minx and a tease, Helen Chalmers!' he called

through the woodwork, then he walked to his own room, grinning broadly.

But as he undressed, he began to think of the future, which to him seemed an enigma. Helen wasn't afraid to face the uncertainty with him, but he was still scared that he could make a mess of it all and that would be unforgivable. But as she had pointed out so passionately, he needed to be positive, so that's what he would do. In fact it was all he could do. He prayed it would be enough.

Chapter Thirteen

The following morning after breakfast, James and Helen drove to her home. They didn't tell Edward of their plans as James insisted they wait until he'd spoken to Henry.

'After all, darling, they've never met me, and your father may think I'm entirely unsuitable.'

Helen grinned at him. 'Don't be ridiculous. You know you can charm the birds from the trees if you want to. After all, I fell for your charms and if you can fool me, my father's a pushover.'

'Maybe, but to be truthful, I'm decidedly nervous. After all, I'm not sure what stability I can offer you, after I give up my commission.'

'Why don't you open a small riding school? You're a good teacher. You have Miss Millie. I can attest to the fact she's docile enough for a beginner.'

He was thoughtful for a moment.

'You know, I've never thought of that. Yes, I kind of like the idea. But first let's get "meeting the parents" over!'

* * *

To say that Henry and Margaret were surprised to meet James would be an understatement, but they made him very welcome. Henry avoided talking about the war, which was a relief. James told them about Helen's progress riding Miss Millie, which was met with some hilarity.

'But Helen doesn't like horses much,' Margaret remarked.

'She does now,' James told them with a broad grin. 'She's a natural. You should see her rising trot after only a couple of hours' tuition. But to be honest, I've come on a mission, Mr Chalmers. I've come to ask for your daughter's hand in marriage.'

'Have you? Well, young man, I'm not at all sure that you know what you'd be taking on. Helen has a mind of her own and she can be stubborn, you know.'

'Dad!' Helen looked horrified.

Margaret started to laugh. 'Henry! How could you?'

'Yes, Dad, how could you?'

'Oh, I've already discovered this in her, but I'm prepared to overlook it,' James replied, trying to keep a straight face.

'Then you must really love her, my boy.'

'Yes, sir, I do. Luckily for me, she feels the same and I'd very much like to walk her down the aisle, if it's alright with you?'

'What do you think, Margaret? Time to cut the apron strings?'

Margaret was grinning broadly at her daughter, who was getting more het up by the minute at this extraordinary exchange.

'Oh yes, I think so,' she said.

'Then that's settled. Welcome to the family, James.' He stood up and shook James by the hand and then he kissed Helen, as did her mother.

James walked over to Helen, took her in his arms and kissed her.

'It would seem that we are engaged, darling.'

'I'll open a bottle of champagne to celebrate,' Henry said. 'I've one left over from New Year. Congratulations, my dear daughter,' he said.

This time James was prepared for the opening of the bottle and allowed himself a feeling of quiet satisfaction.

Margaret insisted they stay for lunch as she had a fish pie in the oven that was enough for all of them and they sat drinking champagne and celebrating.

James explained that he would be leaving the army and that Helen had suggested he open a small riding school and that he was going to give it some considerable thought.

Helen said she was going to give up nursing and settle down to married life.

Her mother asked had they yet thought about the wedding.

'Not yet,' James said. 'It was only yesterday that we decided to get married. There's plenty of time. We have to find somewhere to live first and I have to resign my commission, which means a trip to London.'

Helen immediately realised this would be an ordeal for him, travelling by train and a busy city.

'I'll come with you if you like, we could go shopping after,' she suggested.

James gave her a look of relief but passed it off.

'You didn't warn me that Helen loved to shop, Mr Chalmers.'

'Henry, please. No, I didn't, but she's a woman so why would that surprise you?'

Later that afternoon, James went home. Helen had brought her weekend case home with her and James suggested they go shopping for a ring that weekend.

'Then I'll take you home to show your future in-laws. If it's alright with you, darling, I'll tell the parents our good news when I get home.'

She agreed and walked him to the car, threw her arms round him and kissed him soundly.

'Don't let's wait too long before we get married, James.'

'We'll talk about it later, darling.' He got into the car and drove away.

Henry was sitting in the living room when she returned, her mother in the kitchen.

'Sit down, Helen, I want to talk to you,' he said.

She noted his serious expression and sat beside him.

'James is a lovely young man and I couldn't wish for a nicer son-in-law, but he isn't yet fully recovered, is he?'

'No, Dad. I'm well aware that he has a long way to go yet, but I want to be there to help him.'

'That's very loyal of you, Helen, but it does concern me. Will you be able to cope – and how will it affect your marriage?'

'We will just have to take it one day at a time. I love him and he loves me. Together we will overcome whatever is before us.'

'If you have any doubts, Helen, now is the time to address them, not when it's too late.'

'I know and thank you for looking after me as you have always done, but my mind's made up.'

'Then we'll say no more about it. Come and give your old dad a kiss. It isn't every day one's only daughter gets engaged.'

Things were not so happy in the Carson household. Richard was still restless and had refused the suggestion of Ann's that they go away for a week's holiday to the West Country.

'It's the wrong time of year,' he said, 'it'll be cold and miserable. Let's wait at least until the spring.'

'But you'll be back working then!'

Her protest was ignored.

'In any case,' he said, 'I need to go away for a couple of days on business.'

'Really? That's a bit sudden, isn't it?'

'I need to get some things settled before I start back at the hospital. I'll be leaving in the morning.' He left the room without another word.

Ann was at a loss to understand this turn of events. There had been no mail for Richard, no phone calls that could have propelled his having to leave. Was he going to visit this woman – this Helen, whoever she was? As yet she'd decided not to mention his calling for the stranger in his sleep. She was frightened of making waves that might endanger her marriage even more and had kept silent. She decided to wait and see how Richard reacted on his return. Then who knew, it might be legitimate and all her fears would have been unfounded.

Upstairs in the bedroom, Richard put some fresh underwear, a couple of clean shirts and his shaving gear into an overnight bag, checked his wallet, left the house and made his way to the station, where he bought himself a return ticket to Cheltenham.

Helen was having dinner with her family when the telephone rang.

'I'll get it,' she said, 'it might be James.' She walked into the hallway and picked up the phone, lifting the receiver from its holder.

'Hello.'

'Helen, is that you? It's Richard.'

'Richard?' She couldn't keep the note of surprise from her voice. 'Where are you?'

'I've just arrived in Cheltenham. Could we meet for coffee tomorrow morning at my hotel?'

'Is everything alright? You sound a bit strange.'

'No, I'm fine. I just need to talk to you before I return to duty. About eleven o'clock? Please say you'll come. It's important.'

'But of course I'll come. Where are you staying?'

'The Carleton. I'll meet you in the residents' lounge. See you then.' He hung up.

As she returned to the dining room, she was puzzled. What on earth could bring him to Cheltenham that was so important?

'Was that James?' Henry asked.

'No. It was Richard. He's in Cheltenham and wants to meet me tomorrow at his hotel. I can't imagine why.'

'Perhaps it's about working with him,' suggested her mother.

'Oh well, I'll find out tomorrow. I'll enquire about the time of the trains after dinner.' But she couldn't get out of her mind the tenseness in Richard's tone. Was something wrong?

* * *

It was just after eleven o'clock the next day that Helen walked into the Carleton Hotel and made her way to the residents' lounge, where she saw Richard waiting. He immediately rose to his feet.

Walking over to him she said, 'Hello, this is a surprise.'

He kissed her cheek, helped her off with her coat, then they sat down and he called the waiter over to order coffee and biscuits.

'I don't have to ask how you are, my dear Helen. You look wonderful. The rest has done you the world of good.'

She looked at him and smiled. 'I must say you look so different out of uniform. Most elegant and City of London.' She gazed around. 'No bowler hat?'

'Can't stand them,' he laughed. 'It's good to divest oneself from the army for a while.'

The waiter placed a tray with cups, saucers, a large pot of coffee, a jug of milk and a plate of biscuits before them, then left.

'Shall I be mother?' Richard asked with a grin.

'Carry on, do.'

Once he had done so, Helen looked at him and asked, 'What has brought you to Cheltenham to talk to me? You said it was important.'

Frowning, he said, 'I don't really know where to begin.' He sipped his coffee. 'I was thrilled as we all were that the war was over and at last we could come home, but to be honest, I'm damned if I can settle. I'm like a cat on hot bricks.'

'But that's understandable, Richard. We all found it hard.'

Gazing at her he said, 'But for me it's more than that. I find I can no longer fulfil my role as a husband.'

'I don't understand,' she said, surprised at his remark, and puzzled.

He took a deep drink of his coffee and putting down the cup he said, 'I no longer wish to be with my wife. I don't love her. I feel as guilty as hell because she's a good woman and doesn't deserve this.'

Helen was shocked. 'But that's awful! Don't you think it's just having been away for so long? The things we've been through, the war. Peacetime is so different. I'm sure all you need is time.'

'No, Helen – all I need is you! That's why I'm here.'

Stunned by his declaration, she was speechless.

He continued. 'You once asked me if I would divorce my wife for you and I was silent. Now if you ask me, I'll say yes.'

Oh my God, she thought, this is a terrible situation. What on earth am I going to say? After all, here was the man she admired as a surgeon, a man she'd taken to her bed and with whom she'd enjoyed a long and passionate affair. A man she would have married if, at that time during the war, he had said he would leave his wife for her, but now she would have to be careful how she let him down. Already it was obvious he was in a bad place, she didn't want to completely destroy him.

'Oh, dear Richard. It's not me you want, what you want is time to return to normality. If a soldier came to you and said the same, you would tell him to go home and give it time. You say your wife is a good woman, well she too must be going through it, not understanding you in this state of mind. You have to try, Richard, you have at least to try.'

He looked at her hands. 'I see you are still wearing

Havers' signet ring on your right hand, but I don't see a ring on the other. Does that mean you're just friends still?'

What was she to say? She couldn't lie.

'As a matter of fact, we became engaged yesterday.'

His eyes narrowed. 'Where's your ring, then?'

'We're going to buy one on Saturday.'

'I see.' He leant back in his chair and lit a cigarette. 'How is your soldier, health-wise?'

Helen took a deep breath. 'His leg and other injuries have healed, thanks to your surgery, but he does suffer with nightmares still, but he'll be fine in time.'

Richard sat up and leant forward. 'You're not marrying him to look after him, are you? You don't have to marry him to nurse him, you know. Don't get your emotions jumbled, Helen, you could be making a huge mistake.'

'No, Richard, really I'm not. From the moment I saw James laid out in the operating theatre in Rouen, I knew I wanted to be with him. We love each other.'

He looked shattered. 'I don't know about you, Helen, but I need a drink.' He called the waiter over and ordered two brandies and more coffee.

'Are you absolutely sure you're doing the right thing? You're not confusing love for a need to nurse another injured soul?'

She shook her head. 'No, Richard, honestly. I do love James.'

When his order arrived, he picked up the brandy goblet and held it up.

'To you, my very dear lady. I missed my chance, but at least we did have some time together as lovers, and those I'll treasure.'

137

'Please when you go home, Richard, do try and repair your marriage. It might sound hypocritical coming from me, but as I once told you, when it was obvious you wouldn't leave your wife, what we had was of the moment, it was never meant to be the future. Please try. You say your wife is a good woman, so don't ruin her life. You owe it to her to try and get back to normal.'

He gave a wry smile. 'Helen, my dear, none of us will ever be able to be really normal, not after being involved in a war and what we've been through. Yes, in the end the memories will fade, but they'll never ever be completely forgotten.'

'But think of the many lives you saved, Richard. Think of the men who survived because of you.'

'I seem only to remember the poor devils who lost limbs and whose families will suffer because of that.'

'Yes, but at least their families aren't grieving because they died!'

'I wish I could be as positive as you are.'

'That's only because you're confused at the moment, eventually everything will fall into place.'

He let out a deep sigh. 'I do hope you're right. I'll be better when I get back to work. Being idle isn't my style.'

'Why don't you go away for a break somewhere? Then you'd have a change of scenery and things to do to fill your time.'

'Strange you should say that, Ann suggested it only the other day and I refused.'

'Then go home and change your mind.' She rose from her seat.

'You're leaving?' he asked with some surprise.

'Yes, Richard. I think it's for the best. You came to ask me a question and I've given you my answer. There's no point in prolonging our meeting. I'll always remember our time together, but now we have both to get on with our lives. I just hope eventually you'll be happy.'

He stood up and pulling her close to him he said, 'You too. I think you are in for a tough time with Havers but I wish you well, both of you.' He kissed her softly on the mouth.

Helen walked away, filled with mixed emotions. They had been so close for so long, she and Richard, and now when it was far too late – he wanted to marry her. What a mess! She walked around for some time to try and calm her inner turmoil. Richard was a brilliant surgeon with a great future, she only hoped that his wife would be there to share the accolades that were certain to come his way.

He had said she would have a tough time with James and she knew that he was probably right in his assumption, but she would manage somehow. Feeling somewhat better, she headed for the shops.

Chapter Fourteen

An hour later, Richard checked out of his hotel and caught a train to London. As he sat in his carriage, he went over his conversation with Helen. So she was set on giving up her career to marry James Havers. She was adamant that she loved him and he believed her, but he was fearful for their future. Helen seemed sure that James would recover and it was possible that the dreams would eventually fade, but during those times, would their marriage survive? The men suffering with this problem usually became deeply depressed and depression was debilitating and difficult to handle. Helen would need all her knowledge and patience to cope.

Now he'd seen her and realised she wouldn't be part of his life after all, he had to make some serious decisions himself. Helen had rightly said his wife must be suffering, knowing that their marriage was in crisis. I'm such a bastard, he thought, treating Ann so. He'd been so selfish, so immersed in his own needs, he'd given her little thought and now he felt guilty. I have two choices he decided. One, to move out and live alone, or two, to try and repair my marriage.

He tried to think back to before he was sent abroad. He and Ann had a decent marriage, they chugged along well enough. They'd never had children, it just hadn't happened and they had accepted that. Richard and she had a busy social life – yes, he thought, their marriage, although not exciting, had been solid. Poor Ann, she must be unhappy and totally confused by his actions. He made a decision. When I get home, I'll say I've changed my mind and we'll go away. Start again. It was the right thing to do.

Ann Carson was sitting reading the paper when she heard the key put in the door lock. She looked at her watch, it was almost five o'clock. She rose to her feet and walked to the hallway. She'd not expected Richard until tomorrow as he'd said he'd be away a couple of days. She saw him hanging up his coat in the hall.

'Hello, I wasn't expecting you today.'

Walking over to her he kissed her cheek. 'Well the meeting was over sooner than I expected. Any chance of a cup of tea, I'm parched?'

'Yes, of course.' She wandered into the kitchen. He seemed alright, she mused. Perhaps it was a genuine business meeting, after all, and not one with this woman, Helen. Maybe she was worrying about nothing . . . or was she?

As Ann prepared the tea, Richard called to her.

'You know you suggested a trip to the West Country before I left? Well, I've given it some thought and I think your idea is a good one. It'll be nice to have a break before I go back to work. What do you think?'

She was so surprised she didn't know what to think, but

she didn't hesitate with her answer. 'I think it would do us both good.'

What did she mean by that, Richard wondered? Was she making a point? He decided to let it be.

'I'll try and fix something up in the morning. Would you like to go out to dinner this evening? It'll save you cooking.'

Ann walked back into the room with the tray of tea and looked at him, wondering just what had changed his mind? The irritable man that she'd had to cope with since his return seemed to have mellowed. Well, thank God for that! She was sick to death with his attitude.

'Yes, that'd be lovely. I'll go and change after I've had my cup of tea.'

Later that evening they walked to a nearby restaurant where they were led to a table and ordered. Richard asked for the wine list and chose from it.

'My dear Ann, I feel I owe you an apology,' he said.

She looked at him in surprise. 'Really? Why is that?'

'Because I've been so difficult to live with since my return. I know I've been like a bear with a sore head and treated you badly and I'm sorry.'

Ann stared at him across the table. 'Yes, you have. You've been impossible to live with at times, however I made allowances for you. I realise that anyone returning from the war would find the change difficult. It hasn't been easy for me either!'

He felt guilty and the sharpness of her tone only showed how much he'd put her through. He knew he'd have to try and make it up to her if their marriage was to be stable once again.

'That's why I realise we have to go away. A fresh start, to get back to normality.'

'But we can't ever get back to normality, Richard.'

'What on earth do you mean?'

She was determined to hold her ground. After all, she too had had to make a life during the time he'd been away, never knowing if one day she'd receive the news that he'd been killed, living with that uncertainty. Now he was back, a different man, and she, a different woman.

'I've had to make a life for myself during your absence, as you know. I told you about the committee I'm on, well that's only one. I have other commitments too and I have new friends who kept me going whilst you were away. I'll still see them. Your being home doesn't change any of those things. They are as important to me as your work is to you.'

He was amazed. This wasn't the woman he'd left. The wife who was always at home. The wife who accompanied him to the many social events his life had required. He didn't know how to handle it. He tried to placate her.

'Of course I wouldn't expect you to give up your charity work. I think you're doing a great service to the men who fought for their country. I told you so.'

'Good. As long as you understand I won't always be available.'

He gazed at her with a certain admiration. He liked a woman with spirit, but was surprised to find it in his wife who, before, had always been so compliant.

The waiter came and served their first course.

As they ate, Richard asked her if there was anywhere in particular she'd like to go to down in the West Country.

'Not especially,' she said. 'I'll leave the choice to you.'

They chatted during the meal, Richard asking about mutual friends, finding out what had happened to them, until they walked back to the house where they had a nightcap before going to bed.

But when in bed and Richard reached out to her, Ann caught hold of his hand.

'I'm tired,' she said and turned her back to him, smiling to herself as she settled.

Rejection works both ways, Richard, she thought. Now it's your turn!

Chapter Fifteen

Back in the Cotswolds, James had told his parents about his engagement and they were delighted. Edward shook his hand warmly.

'Helen is a lovely woman,' Frances said as she gave him a hug. 'I can't think of anyone who would make a nicer daughter-in-law.'

'Well that's a relief, Mother,' he teased, 'because there isn't anyone else I'd want as my bride!'

But later when he was with his father in his study, he asked Edward's advice.

'Do you think I'm doing the right thing, marrying Helen?'

Edward looked concerned. 'Bit late to begin to have doubts, isn't it, James? You love her, don't you?'

'Of course I do, but you know my position health-wise, my nightmares haven't gone away. What if they never do? Am I being fair to Helen, asking her to live with this cursed thing?'

'Come now, haven't you discussed this with her?'

'Of course! But she says we'll work it out. She's under the impression that eventually they will cease. I'm not so sure.' He grinned broadly. 'She actually gave me a lecture about my attitude, about being a pessimist.'

'Quite right too. You are a lucky man, my son, to have such a woman by your side. What else has she had to say about your future?'

'She suggested when I leave the army, I start a riding school. I quite like the idea – what do you think?'

'I think it's splendid! You have Cleo and Miss Millie, they are both suitable for beginners, and if it's a success, you could expand.'

'It means using the stables, would you and Mother mind?'

'Absolutely not!'

'I intend to find us somewhere to live nearby, so we will have our own home.'

'And the wedding? When do you intend to have that?'

'We haven't yet discussed it, but Helen doesn't want to wait too long.' He frowned. 'I hope she only wants a quiet wedding. You know how I am with lots of people. I wouldn't want to have a panic attack and spoil her day.'

'Then you must tell her.'

Helen was having a similar conversation with her mother, sitting in the kitchen drinking coffee.

'It has to be a small wedding, Mum. James isn't good with a crowd and I don't want him fretting, not on our wedding day. Besides, a wedding should only be shared by those who are close to the bride and groom, who mean something.'

'I agree, Helen, and I understand, but I do hope you'll have the ceremony in our local church.'

Helen put an arm around her mother's shoulders.

'Of course, where else would I go? But before that, James has to resign his commission and we have to find somewhere to live.'

The following Saturday, James and Helen drove into Cheltenham to the jewellers to choose an engagement ring. She had a great time, trying them all on, but in the end she chose a half-hoop of emeralds and diamonds. Then they went into a hotel where they drank a glass of champagne as he put the ring on her finger.

James held up his glass. 'To us!'

She did the same. 'To us!'

He leant forward and said quietly. 'Now then, don't forget your promise to me.'

She looked puzzled. 'What promise was that?'

He held up his left hand and wiggled his fingers at her.

Helen was convulsed with laughter. 'You have no idea just how silly you look doing that.'

'Yes, maybe, but remember what you said. I'm keeping you to your word.'

She just grinned at him and sipped her champagne, but over the rim of her glass, her eyes twinkled, full of mischief.

To James's relief he discovered that he could write to his commander to resign his commission, without the dreaded trip to the metropolis. As he was doing so on medical grounds, he had to submit his doctor's report with his letter and then wait for a reply accepting his resignation. It was a relief to both him and Helen.

She was staying at Gately Manor to continue her riding lessons and to be on hand whilst they searched for a house.

They had decided to hold the wedding in June, three months hence. It was a busy time and James was coping really well. His room downstairs had now been moved to his old bedroom upstairs and Helen was ensconced next door.

When they went to bed on the first evening, James waited for Helen to open her door. She turned and saw him leaning against the wall, smiling.

'What?' she asked.

'I've come for my promise,' he said. 'You have the ring, so . . . ?'

Helen grinned at him and holding out her hand she said, 'Come into my parlour!'

During her stay, they behaved in a considerate manner, respecting the rules of morality to all outward signs, but slipping into each other's rooms on occasion to make love, returning to their own room after.

One night after having sex, James was holding Helen in his arms when he started to chuckle quietly.

'What's so funny?' asked Helen.

'Well you don't think we're fooling anyone, do you? I'm sure both my parents are aware of our arrangements, but are marvellously ignoring it.'

She was horrified. 'Do you think so, honestly?'

'Now don't go all shy on me, darling, or I may have to cancel the wedding!'

She playfully punched him. 'Don't even think about it.'

But at breakfast the following morning, she looked at Edward who was eating his toast and began to blush. James saw her cheeks redden and guessed why.

* * *

Unable to find a house they liked, he and Helen rented a small thatched-roof cottage nearby. It was nicely furnished, with a small garden which would suit their needs temporarily, when they married.

Both parents met with the happy couple to plan the wedding, the reception to be held at a hotel near to the church. They eventually arrived at a list of thirty guests, chose a menu, then sent out the invitations.

Helen and her mother decided to shop in London for her wedding dress.

'We'll go to Selfridges,' Margaret said, 'and I must find something to wear too. I'm sure we'll find something suitable there, then after we can go out to lunch.'

The assistant in the wedding department was most helpful. She eyed Helen's slim figure and questioned her about her preferences.

'To be honest, I've come with an open mind, apart from something classic and not fussy.'

The women sat as the girl brought out several wedding gowns to show them, then Helen tried on one after the other, until she was shown an ivory-coloured silk dress. It was beautifully cut, with a V-neck, long sleeves, a fitted waist with a wide, pleated waistband and handkerchief skirt, just below the calf.

'Helen, my dear, that's absolutely lovely,' declared Margaret.

Turning back and forth, Helen agreed.

'I love it and it fits perfectly, but what about a veil and headdress?'

'I have just the thing,' said the assistant and disappeared, only to emerge minutes later. 'As you are wearing your hair short, madam, this lace skullcap and veil would be perfect I think. Try it.'

The veil was gossamer thin, attached to the back of the delicate laced cloche-shaped cap. It was simple and classy. They all agreed that it couldn't be bettered and when the assistant sent for a pair of court shoes in matching satin, the outfit was complete.

'Now, young lady,' said Margaret, 'as the mother of the bride, I need something elegant. What do you suggest I wear?'

Eventually Margaret decided on a light, burgundy-coloured gown with a round neck and a draped bodice that finished with a bow on the hip. To go with it, a broad-brimmed matching straw hat decorated with a long feather across the brim and crown.

'If I may say, ladies, you both look very elegant,' said the assistant.

They thanked her for her time and trouble. As they waited for their purchases to be wrapped they were delighted to be served a glass of champagne.

'Mr Selfridge insists we serve champagne when anyone purchases from our bridal section,' said the girl. 'I wish you every happiness, madam,' she said to Helen.

As they left the store, Margaret turned to her daughter.

'Well, darling, after that there is but one place to go to lunch, and that's the Ritz!'

Whilst Helen and her mother were enjoying their trip to London, Richard and Ann were settling into their hotel in Torquay. Their room was at the front on the first floor, overlooking the sea. They unpacked and decided to go for a walk before eating. Ann had taken sandwiches for the journey to sustain them and so they were able to wander without feeling ravenous. They came across a local pub and decided to stop for a drink.

Once settled, Richard took a sip of his beer and looking out of the window, spoke.

'I wouldn't mind retiring down here, you know.'

Ann looked at him in surprise, then started laughing. 'You'd hate it! You like the bustle of the city, your club, socialising. Without that, you'd go crazy. Let's be honest, Richard, you enjoy your place in society; here you wouldn't know a soul. You'd be like a fish out of water.'

He pondered over her words. Ann was right. He did like his life in London. He did enjoy a social life surrounded by friends with like minds. He did hold a certain position and enjoyed his place in society. She was correct in every way, but he was surprised to hear her put it into words. He wasn't used to his wife having such strong opinions of her own. The woman he'd left behind had been a gentle soul, quiet. If he was honest . . . a little dull because of it. Now – it was like being with a different woman. It was intriguing, to say the least.

'You've changed, you know,' he said as he looked at her. 'It's like coming home to a new woman. You have become more decisive, with a mind of your own. How did that happen?'

'I had to fend for myself, Richard! Before, you made all the arrangements. Where we would go, who we would meet and sometimes even which gown I should wear. I was like a puppet! Now I'm not and, if we're being honest, I wasn't happy. I was just an appendage to you, I now realise.'

He was taken aback at her remarks. 'That's being somewhat harsh, my dear. I'm sure it wasn't like that at all.'

'You know very well that it was, but not any longer. I'm a woman with responsibilities to others now and I'm afraid that sometimes you'll have to fit in with me, as I won't always be available.'

He had to smile at the change in his wife. He rather liked it. He'd always liked spirited women, but just not in the one he married. His eyes twinkled as he looked at her.

'I have to say, Ann, this new you is quite fascinating.'

Her expression didn't change at his flattery. She met his gaze, her eyes glittering.

'More so than Helen?'

He froze. 'Helen?'

'Yes, Helen. Tell me about her.'

'I only know one woman by that name and that's my theatre sister, Helen Chalmers.'

'How long have you been working together?'

'This past year. We arrived at the front at the same time.'

'Is she good at her job?'

'Yes, she's the best theatre sister I've ever worked with, but why all these questions?'

'Oh, I think you did more than work with her, Richard, or why would you call her name in your sleep?'

He was shattered and at a loss for words. Furious, also, that he could have been so stupid to have called her name. Whatever was he to say?

'I must have been dreaming about an operation,' he said.

Ann studied his face. Was he lying? It could be the truth, but how far did she want to push it, she asked herself?

'Where is she now, do you know?'

'As a matter of fact I do. She's at home in the Cotswolds with her family, planning her wedding to an army captain that I operated on.'

Now it was Ann who was lost for words. Had she been wrong in her suspicions? Even if she was right and Richard had been having an affair, it was obviously over and if she wanted to remain married, she'd have to leave it there. She stared hard at her husband and thought of the years she'd stood beside him at some social event as his wife, therefore being also held in esteem. Well, now she'd achieved a life of her own, which she intended still to follow, being his wife would suit her very well. She had a beautiful home that she loved, and a position that she'd probably enjoy more now that she'd discovered who she was. Yes, she would leave the matter there. Richard had been shaken by her questioning and that would have made him realise she wasn't a fool. She smiled softly at him.

'Well, let's hope the couple will be very happy together.'

Richard felt his shoulders relax. He'd been very tense during Ann's questioning, wondering if his affair was about to be discovered. He lifted his glass.

'I'll drink to that,' he said.

Chapter Sixteen

It was the day of the wedding and the weather had been kind. The sun was shining and there was a gentle breeze. The wedding was to be at noon, which gave everybody time to prepare. Helen and her mother had an early appointment at the hairdressers for their Marcel Wave before they started dressing in their regalia.

The Havers had booked into the hotel the night before to save them having to drive over from Cheltenham for the ceremony.

As James had told her, 'It will be safer as Dad is driving and it would be terrible if the car broke down and I was late.'

'I should think so,' Helen said, 'after all, it's the bride's prerogative to be late, not the groom's!'

Henry was relieved that it wasn't raining as he'd arranged for the bride to be driven to the church in a horse-drawn buggy and it would have ruined the whole thing had it been wet.

Then it was time to leave. Margaret had gone ahead, giving Helen a kiss before she did so.

'You look absolutely beautiful, darling,' she said. 'I'll see you in church.'

Now Henry looked at the bride. 'Are you ready, my dear daughter?'

'Yes, I am.' She leant forward and kissed his cheek.

He led her outside where several of the neighbours stood waiting to catch a glimpse of the bride, calling out their best wishes and watching as Henry helped Helen into the buggy, holding her veil so she wouldn't crush it, then they were off.

James was standing by his seat in the aisle beside his best man, Alexander Hardcastle, a fellow officer and friend, both resplendent in the grey coat-tails, with Alexander trying to calm the groom.

'For goodness' sake, James, take a deep breath or something, it won't be long. Sit down for a moment, we'll know when she's here because the organ will play.'

James sat and tried to relax. It wasn't as if he was worried Helen wouldn't come, he knew that she would, but he couldn't shake off the fears of his mental illness and its consequences. The organ struck up and he rose to his feet.

To the strains of the 'Wedding March', Henry, smiling, proudly walked his daughter down the aisle and in the absence of a bridesmaid, took her bouquet as he handed her to James.

Helen took James's hand and squeezed it; seeing her groom's tense expression, she grinned at him and poked her tongue out just a little.

This immediately broke the tension and she heard him chuckle as he squeezed her hand in return.

* * *

155

An hour later, Mr and Mrs James Havers walked out of the church together, where they stood in the doorway to have their picture taken. James leant forward and kissed Helen.

'Hello, Mrs Havers, my wife. I do like the sound of that.'

'I quite like it myself,' she laughed. 'My husband . . . just practising.'

The rest of the guests filtered out and stood for the photographs and then showered the couple with confetti as they made their way to the buggy for their short ride to the hotel.

'Best not let Cleo know about this,' he teased, 'she'd never talk to me again.' He put his arm round Helen. 'You look absolutely beautiful, darling. I'm such a lucky man.'

'Indeed you are and don't you ever forget it. But you're not bad-looking yourself, so I don't think I've done too badly either.'

James started laughing. 'Oh, Helen, don't ever change. A sense of humour is as essential as life itself.'

The reception was laid out in small round tables where guests had been seated so they intermingled both families and friends to make it more friendly, without any demarcation, everyone introducing themselves to the others. A top table had been dispensed with, making it a less formal affair, although the married couple shared a table with their parents, best man and his girlfriend.

James was prepared as the champagne bottles were opened for the toast after the meal and allowed himself a sly smile as he remembered the scene at the manor when he'd been taken by surprise and hit the floor thinking the noise was gunfire.

Alexander, as best man, stood up, tapped the side of the glass for silence and gave his speech.

'Ladies and gentlemen, thank you for coming here today to see this fine young man wed this beautiful lady. Frankly I never thought I'd see the day. I was convinced that the only woman in his life would always be Cleo.'

There was laughter from those who knew of James's love of his favourite steed.

'Therefore I'm greatly relieved to see that he has come to his senses at last! Obviously being sent across the Channel has broadened his outlook on life.' He didn't speak for long, just exchanged a few stories of their friendship and how he was delighted to be the best man.

'Now, ladies and gentlemen, please be upstanding and drink to the health of Helen and James.'

'Helen and James,' they all said as they stood and raised their glasses, then sat down.

James rose from his chair. 'Thank you all for sharing what is the happiest day of my life. How I ever persuaded Helen to marry me, I'll never know. We met during the war and then when I was injured, she nursed me back to health. I think she invested so much time in doing so, she decided she'd better marry me to make sure I didn't undo all her hard work.' He looked down at her and smiled, then spoke directly to her. 'Whatever the reason, darling, I promise you'll never regret it.' He leant forward and kissed her, then sat down, amidst loud applause.

At the same time as James was giving his speech, Richard, sitting alone in his club in London, silently raised a glass of Scotch and toasted the couple. Their forthcoming wedding had been announced in *The Times* newspaper and he'd seen it, and although he knew it was taking place, he felt saddened. Today Helen became Mrs James Havers and was lost to him for ever. If he was honest, she had been back in France, when James had been brought into the operating theatre, so badly injured. He realised then he no longer had a place in her life, other than a memory.

During their holiday in the West Country, he and Ann had resumed marital relations. She seemed to have put her suspicions of Helen behind her. But he had been glad to be working again, back into a routine. He didn't enjoy having time on his hands, but now he had to consider his wife's busy schedule too, which had taken him some time to get used to. She wasn't always at hand to share his mealtimes, but she would leave something for him to warm in the oven – a covered dish, with written instructions as to how hot the oven had to be and how long to leave the dish inside to warm. It wasn't something he enjoyed but he had no choice, Ann had made that very clear. Sometimes, if he knew in advance she was to be out, he would dine at his club, which suited him better. He wasn't domesticated and, never having had to be so, wasn't comfortable with having to look after himself.

By contrast, Ann was enjoying her life. She had become more independent and confident during Richard's absence, making a new life for herself, and she thrived on it. Today she was being taken to lunch by Clive Bradshaw. They enjoyed working together at the forces charity and had become firm friends and for the past couple of months had met for lunch once a week, after the committee meeting.

'How's your husband settling now he's back at the hospital?' asked Clive.

'Oh, much happier. He likes routine and being busy.'

'If he likes routine, it must be a surprise to him that yours has changed so much.'

Chuckling she said, 'Oh, he doesn't like it at all. Richard was used to me being at his beck and call and finds it difficult to have to cope for himself when I'm not there. He's used to being waited on.'

Clive studied her for a moment. 'Are you still in love with him?'

Somewhat startled by his question she said, 'What a very strange thing to ask. He's my husband.'

'That's hardly an answer. Forgive me for being so blunt but when you speak of him, it's never with any note of affection. You told me when he first returned things were difficult – well that was to be expected – but now, there still isn't any warmth in your voice when you mention him.'

Ann was silent as she pondered over his remark and thought back to her first meeting with Richard.

'I suppose I was rather overwhelmed by him when first we met. He was headed for great things even then. He had a strong personality, and if I'm honest, I was in love with him then, or rather who he was and what he was and that he'd asked *me* out when he could have had anyone.' She paused for a moment. 'Now, I love Richard, but I'm no longer *in* love with him. Does that make sense?'

'Perfect sense. During his absence, you've blossomed, come out of your shell and what's more important, you have grown in confidence. I've watched it happen.'

She laughed with glee. 'Oh, Clive, you are so good for me.'

159

'I just think you're wasted on that man. He doesn't appreciate you and that's not only unfair but an absolute travesty. You deserve *so* much more.'

Ann gazed at her companion and saw the affection in his eyes as he spoke. It was only then she realised that he had feelings for her that were more than friendship and wondered why she'd not noticed it before. She didn't know what to say because deep down she liked what she was hearing. Richard had never looked at her like Clive was doing at this moment.

'I don't know what to say,' she murmured, feeling her cheeks flush.

'If you were mine, my dear Ann, you would be cosseted, cared for and loved as you deserve.'

'You have to stop this, Clive. I am married to Richard, for better or worse. Please don't complicate my life any further.'

'Very well, if that's what you wish.' He changed the subject. But as they parted after their meal, instead of his usual goodbye, he lifted her hand to his lips. Then walked away.

Having arrived home, Ann removed her hat and gloves and made her way to the living room and poured herself a stiff drink, sat down and sipped it. She was still reeling from the conversation over lunch. Then she smiled slowly. Having someone declare their love for you was very pleasing and when it was when you were married to another man, it seemed a bit naughty too, which made it even more pleasurable.

Leaning back against the sofa, she let her imagination

160

run. She was in a hotel room with Clive and he was kissing her, caressing her. She stretched languidly as she enjoyed the fantasy.

Then she sat up straight. How stupid! She was behaving like a lovesick girl. She took another sip of her drink and smiled softly. Nevertheless, it had been fun. But of course now, she realised, the meetings at the charity would continue but the relationship she and Clive had shared for a year as friends would have different connotations. Despite herself, Ann couldn't help being excited by this. How interesting life had suddenly become!

Chapter Seventeen

James and Helen had chosen the New Forest in Hampshire for their honeymoon. Somewhere reasonably quiet, without too many tourists, which James would have difficulty coping with. Their hotel was in Brockenhurst, in the middle of the forest, where they could walk, look at the New Forest ponies and enjoy the beautiful countryside.

It was an idyllic time for both of them. The weather remained kind, so they took the train to Lymington one day and ate in a small restaurant near the harbour, enjoying the change of scenery, and James was improving as each day passed. He was learning to cope with enclosed places as long as they weren't too crowded, and if he found it was too much, he'd quietly say so and they would leave. But his confidence was growing, which thrilled Helen.

They began making plans for him to start his riding school on their return, now that James was no longer in the army. He had the two horses, he'd use the stables, he had a practice ring, and all he needed were clients. They planned to advertise in the local paper.

'Won't you be lost without your nursing?'

'No, darling, I'll be looking after the cottage and I can take care of the bookings and appointments. I'll be your receptionist.'

'We'd better get a telephone installed in the cottage. I can't encroach on the manor too much, it wouldn't be fair.'

'Will you be teaching your female clients to ride side-saddle or astride, like me?'

'It will depend on the client, I suppose. How much experience they've had – if any – and whatever they choose. Mother sometimes rides side-saddle and there are a couple in the tack room. I don't want you to worry about finance, darling. I mean yes, I want to work and keep occupied but I do have money of my own that my grandfather left me.'

Her eyes twinkled. 'Are you telling me the man I married is wealthy?'

'I'm just saying you've nothing to worry about. But what I do know is you married me only for my good looks and not my fortune!' He beamed at her, then started laughing. 'Oh, Helen, if only you could see your face. Believe me, we'll have a good life, no matter what.'

They decided they'd return to the hotel, so calling the waiter over, James paid the bill and rose from his seat, holding Helen's chair for her. As they started to walk towards the door, a young waitress tripped and dropped the tray she was carrying, which was full of dishes and glasses. The noise was thunderous.

James grabbed Helen and threw her to the ground, covering her with his body, eyes closed, body tense. Around them lay spilt tables he'd knocked over as he dived for the floor.

For a few moments, Helen, winded, stunned and disorientated, lay still, then she realised where she was and what had happened.

'James,' she said quietly but firmly. 'You can get off me now. It's alright, it wasn't a bomb, a girl dropped a tray.'

He slowly got to his feet and saw the chaos around him, the upturned tables, the faces of the diners, the staff who just stood like statues, staring at him. Helping Helen up from the floor, he immediately began to apologise.

'Ladies and gentlemen, I'm dreadfully sorry for all this and I hope I didn't scare you too much. Frankly, it scared me to death. You see, ever since I came back from the war, loud noises make me dive for the trenches. I forget where I am for a moment.'

There was a murmuring of acceptance from those sitting down, and walking over to the manager, James apologised again. Giving him a business card, he told him he would settle for the damage he may have caused.

Helen walked over to him and took him by the arm. They left the restaurant together.

James walked a few yards, then sat on a low wall and with trembling hands lit a cigarette, took a deep drag of nicotine and looked at his bride.

'Christ! What a mess that was. Are you alright, darling? I do hope I didn't hurt you, throwing you down like that.' He looked at his feet, shaking his head.

Helen sat beside him and tucked her arm through his. 'You are my hero.'

'What?' James looked up at her. 'Hero? Bloody idiot, more like!'

'No, my darling, definitely hero. You thought you

164

were saving my life. You lay on top of me to protect me. Definitely my hero!'

'Oh, Helen, you are too kind, but it is what it is. Just another war wound, but not wrapped in a bandage. This one is deadly, because it's hidden and makes an appearance unexpectedly – like today. I scared those people in the restaurant half to death and I'm lucky that I didn't do you any physical harm.'

'Every word you say is true and I can't tell you this won't happen again, because it probably will, but in time, it'll happen less and less. You just have to be patient.'

'But imagine if I open a riding school, what if that happened when I was out with the horses and a client? I could spook the horses, they could take off. Can you imagine a learner rider and a runaway horse? I must have been mad to think I could start that kind of business.'

'Then we'll have to think of something else. Come along, darling, you can't give in that easily. It's just a setback, that's all.'

But it was far more than that. It was as if the wonderful light of happiness that had been in James's eyes had been turned down and he sank into despair. No matter what Helen did to try and get him out of his darkness, she couldn't reach him. Eventually they went home two days early, without telling anyone of their arrival in the hopes that being at home among their own things and background, James would be able to pull himself out of the pit of depression he was in.

The morning after their arrival as they sat having breakfast Helen made a decision.

'Don't be too long, James, because you and I are going

riding when you've finished. It's time to return to a routine. Sitting around isn't going to solve anything.' She was relieved to see a spark of interest in her husband.

'Poor Cleo, she'll think I've abandoned her, although Mother did say she'd see the horses were exercised.' He glanced at Helen. 'Are you ready to ride with me?'

'Of course. It'll do us both good.'

They walked to the stables along the country lane. When they arrived, they found Frances feeding the horses. She looked up in surprise as they entered.

'Good heavens, you're back already. I wasn't expecting you until the weekend.'

'We decided we'd had enough and wanted to come home,' Helen offered as an explanation.

James kissed his mother and walked over to Cleo's box and chatted to his horse, as was his habit.

Frances looked at Helen, her eyebrows raised in question. Helen met her gaze and just shook her head. 'We're going for a ride,' she said.

'Then I'll leave you to it. Pop in whenever you like.' She left them alone.

James saddled up the two horses and they walked them down the road to the field and cantered around it several times, James being considerate to Helen's capabilities, but she knew he needed to feel free and unencumbered. She rode up to him.

'I'll wait over by the trees, you take Cleo for a good gallop and jump if you want to.' His look of gratitude was her reward.

She watched him as he galloped Cleo round the field,

then jump the hedge. She waited for him, knowing that he needed to be alone, hoping this would renew his confidence and lift the black dog that was hanging over him like a dark cloud.

Eventually, he appeared, cleared the hedge and rode over to her, a broad grin on his face. She breathed a sigh of relief.

'God, I needed that,' he said as he brought the horse to a standstill and stroked its neck. 'You are a good girl,' he murmured as he did so. Looking at Helen he said, 'You rode really well this morning. I'm so proud of you.' He leant over and kissed her. 'Let's go back now.'

Once at the stables, they unsaddled the horses, wiped them down and gave them water.

'Better go and say hello to the parents,' James said and taking Helen's hand, they walked to the house.

She wondered what James would say about their early return and decided to follow his lead. She wasn't sure if he would give the real reason for them leaving the New Forest.

Edward, having been warned by his wife of their return, greeted them warmly.

'How lovely to see you both. Your mother said you'd been riding. I bet Cleo was pleased to see you, my boy. Would you like some coffee? Your mother made a new pot, in case you dropped in.'

They sat down and Edward poured the coffee and handed it to them.

'Thanks, Dad. We came back early because I had one of my turns in a cafe,' James said. 'The waitress dropped a tray and I hit the deck, taking Helen and several tables with me.'

'Oh dear.' Edward was at a loss for words.

'They were all very good about it, and of course I offered to pay for any damage.'

Edward glanced at Helen. 'That must have been difficult.'

'Not really. James soon recovered and when he explained why he'd reacted that way, everyone was understanding.'

'Of course, it means I'm not yet ready to open my riding school. Couldn't have that happening during a lesson, could I?'

Helen intervened. 'It doesn't mean you can't do so later, darling. These things take time. We just have to be patient, that's all.'

A spark of anger showed as his eyes brightened. 'So you say. All I can say is it's taking its time.'

'These things can't be solved in five minutes, James,' his father said. 'I'm sure it must be frustrating for you, but time is a great healer.'

James changed the subject and asked what had been going on during their absence. But Helen was pleased to note that at least he wasn't as depressed as he'd been. For the moment, that had been lifted. She would have to keep him busy and not give him time to think about his health. Richard had said she was going to have a difficult time and he'd been right, but she was determined to fight to get her husband back to health, one way or another.

Chapter Eighteen

In the mail the next morning, Helen received an invitation to go to a reunion in London for the medical teams that had worked together in Rouen. She was delighted. She'd made good friends during her time at the hospital and the thought of seeing them again thrilled her. It was to be held in a hotel where those who had to travel any distance could stay. She showed it to James.

'You should go, darling. You all went through so much together, it will be great to meet up again in peacetime.'

'You don't want to come with me? The invitation is for two.'

'Do you mind terribly if I don't? I'd only be on edge in case someone dropped a tray.' He managed a smile but she could see the concern mirrored in his eyes.

'No, of course I don't mind. But I will go, it would be a pity to miss it because I doubt we'll ever meet up again.'

Three weeks later, Helen was on an early train to London, with a small suitcase packed with her night attire and new gown to wear at the dinner that night.

On her arrival she bumped into Jenny Palmer, the nurse she'd worked with, and Harry Gibbs, the orderly. She was surprised to see them together.

'We got married!' Harry said, with a broad grin. 'Imagine that, she actually said yes when I asked her. You could have knocked me down with a feather.'

She hugged them both. 'Congratulations! Let's go to the bar and have a drink to celebrate.' They left their cases with the concierge at the reception desk.

Once settled at a table in the bar, they caught up with each other's news.

'We're both working,' Jenny told her. 'Saving to buy a flat. I see you're wearing a wedding ring. Did you marry Captain Havers?'

'Yes, in June. We've only been back from our honeymoon about a month.'

'How is he?' asked Jenny, who had nursed him.

'He's recovered from the surgery but I'm afraid he still has those nightmares and loud noises can throw him into a panic. But in time we hope he'll get over it.'

One or two others joined them and began reminiscing. Then it was time to get changed for the evening.

Richard and Ann, living in London, hadn't needed to book a room and dressed in the comfort of their own home. Ann was delighted to be invited as well as her husband and wondered if she would meet the mysterious Helen. She hoped so, then she could make up her mind about the woman who had worked with her husband for so long. She wondered if Helen's husband would also be in attendance.

Outside the dining room of the hotel was a list of the

tables and who would be sitting at each one. The organisers had kept the teams together, so when Helen found her name and table number, she saw that Mrs Ann Carson was listed with her husband, but fortunately not sitting next to Helen. She was shaken by this as she'd not considered the fact that Richard would bring his wife. She wasn't worried about meeting Richard again – after all, it had been a while since she'd met him in Cheltenham and since then she'd been married – but his wife . . . that was another matter. She was thankful that Harry and Jenny were next to her. Harry would be great company and hopefully she wouldn't have to speak much to Mrs Carson.

Ann had done much the same on her arrival and looked at the list, but she had searched for Helen's name in particular. This could be an interesting evening, she thought. If Richard had been having an affair, would he be able to talk to this woman without giving away the fact they had been lovers? She found the whole thing intriguing.

Everyone started to filter into the dining room and seating themselves at their designated places. When everyone was settled, Richard looked up at his team.

'Good evening, all of you. I can't tell you how happy I am to see you all, and for once in comfortable surroundings. This is Ann, my wife.' There were mutterings as they all acknowledged her.

'Aren't you going to introduce me to your colleagues, Richard?' Ann asked.

He looked startled. 'Yes, yes of course.' He started with the man next to him, then named each one. Nurse Jenny Palmer, Helen my theatre sister, Harry Gibbs our orderly . . .

Ann didn't hear the rest of the names, she was looking at

Helen. So this was the mysterious woman in her husband's life. Attractive, she thought, wearing her wedding ring, beautifully dressed in a lace-covered gown that was obviously expensive, but looking somewhat uncomfortable under my scrutiny. Ann smiled at her and nodded. Helen smiled back.

As Richard's wife stared hard at her, Helen's first thought was – she knows about us. Then she realised it could only be an assumption on the wife's part because no way would Richard have told her about their relationship, but Helen was convinced by her expression that Ann had her suspicions. She would have to be very careful this evening not to give any indication of their past relationship.

During the meal, stories were exchanged, incidents recalled. They all kept away from the serious side of their work, instead talking about the amusing things that had happened, but all the time, Helen was aware of Ann's interest in her. She busied herself talking to Jenny and laughing at Harry, who was a natural comedian.

At the end of the meal, they all made their way to the bar at Richard's invitation. He ordered champagne to thank them for their service to him. They all milled around, talking and drinking. Out of the corner of her eye, Helen saw Ann talking to one after another of the team and knew that soon she'd come over to her.

'So you are the theatre sister that my husband holds in such high regard.' Ann stood in front of Helen, a definite challenge in her voice.

'Your husband is a talented surgeon, Mrs Carson. It was a privilege to work with him. He saved many lives during the time I worked beside him. My own husband owes him his life.'

'So I believe, Richard did mention that. How is your husband? I see he's not with you.'

'No, crowded places unnerve him so he decided to stay at home. But I wanted to see my old friends; we went through so much together during the war and we probably will never see each other again. It was an opportunity not to be missed. I'm sure you are delighted and relieved to have your husband home with you, safe and sound?'

Ann stared hard at her. 'Indeed I am. Wars are such dangerous times. Apart from the obvious, life is tenuous and people live for the moment. Reality disappears.'

'All I remember is being absolutely worn out,' Helen said, smiling. 'But thankfully that's all behind us and now we can hope to return to normality, as much as is possible after being surrounded by death and destruction. Now if you'll excuse me I have one or two of my colleagues I've yet to talk to and I don't want to miss anyone. It's been nice to meet you.'

Ann watched her walk away, still unable to decide if this woman and her husband had been lovers. It still niggled at her but she must try and put it behind her. As Helen had said, the people in the room would probably never meet again.

Eventually the evening came to an end and everyone began to leave. Ann was standing with Richard as his team lined up to say goodbye to him and thank him for the bubbly. There was no way that Helen could escape this meeting, it would have looked very strange, so she waited her turn.

'Richard.' She held out her hand to shake his. 'So good to see everyone again. Thank you for the champagne.'

He went to introduce his wife but Helen stopped him. 'Mrs Carson and I have already met.'

'Oh, good. How is your husband, Helen?'

'Physically recovered, but still suffering with nightmares, loud noises and enclosed places, but I'm hoping in time all this will fade.'

'I do hope so. At least you're looking well. Take care and give my regards to James.'

'I will.' She nodded at Ann and walked away, letting out a sigh of relief as she did so.

A little later, Richard opened the door to their house and walking into the drawing room poured himself a brandy. 'Would you like a nightcap, Ann, my dear?'

She said she would and they sat together on the sofa.

'Well, I think the evening went really well, don't you?' he asked.

'Yes, it was splendid. It must have been interesting to see them all, away from the war. Your theatre sister, Helen, is an attractive woman.'

Richard was immediately watchful. 'Yes, I suppose she is. She's going to have many months of worry ahead of her looking after her husband, and to be honest, I've no way of knowing if he will ever recover. No one understands this condition well enough to know how to treat it properly.'

'But she's a nurse, surely that's a good thing?'

'Well, it helps. She's in the best place to watch over him and her nursing knowledge will be an advantage, certainly.' He changed the subject. 'I'm tired now, I'll think I'll go to bed. Are you coming?'

'In a while, I've a few things I want to do in preparation for tomorrow's committee meeting.'

He leant forward and kissed her cheek. 'I'll leave you to it, then.'

As he undressed, Richard went over the events of the evening in his mind. He wasn't a fool. He knew that Ann had made sure she'd met Helen. He knew also that his wife was still suspicious about his relationship with her but never would he admit to it. He smiled softly. Helen had looked so beautiful tonight in that gown. He'd wanted to take her in his arms and hold her. The only thing he'd held was her hand as she left. It had seemed strangely formal.

Downstairs, Ann stayed until she'd finished her brandy. Tonight was now over; it had been interesting, but tomorrow was the committee meeting and her lunch date with Clive. It was now her time to have a bit of fun! What if Richard *had* bedded the nursing sister? It was definitely over, Helen was married and had her own problems.

She stretched and smiled. She was going to dine with a man who had declared his love for her and that made her feel good – and excited. It was like an illicit affair, but it wasn't quite that . . . yet. How far would it develop? That would be up to her and she hadn't as yet made up her mind what she was going to do about it. Richard's affair, if it was one, was over, hers was about to begin. She rose to her feet, plumped up a cushion and danced her way out of the room.

Chapter Nineteen

Helen rose early and made her way to the dining room to have breakfast before she travelled home. She was pleased not to see any of last night's diners there, which allowed her some peace, and as soon as she'd finished she paid her bill, called a cab and was taken to the station.

When she arrived home, James was there to meet her in the car after she'd called him from the hotel giving him the time of her arrival. He met her on the platform, carried her case to the car and drove home.

Once settled in the cottage he made a cup of tea and plied her with questions.

'Who was there other than Richard?'

'Jenny Palmer and Harry, do you remember them?'

'Of course I do. They both nursed me. Harry always made me laugh no matter how rough I felt. Nice man, and Jenny, she was a great nurse.'

'They're now married!'

'No! Well that's a surprise, I would have never matched them as a pair.'

Laughing, Helen agreed. 'Harry said you could have knocked him down with a feather when she said yes.'

'That's typical of him. Well, good luck to them. And our great surgeon, how was he?'

'Much the same. He brought his wife with him.'

James looked at her. 'You didn't like her, I can tell. Why?'

'She made a point of speaking to everyone and was quite charming, but I felt she had an agenda. Making her mark as "the wife", so to speak.'

'She wouldn't have much time for you then, darling.'

Startled, Helen asked, 'Why do you say that?'

'Think about it. You and Richard worked closely together for a year. You were his right hand, he was lost without you by his side in the operating theatre. It was almost like a marriage, you were so in tune with each other.'

She didn't know what to say – it was too near to the truth to be comfortable.

'You could be right, I did feel her hostility when she spoke to me.'

'Perhaps she thought you were more to her husband than his theatre sister.'

This unexpected remark took Helen completely by surprise and she felt her cheeks redden. 'What nonsense!'

James stared at his wife and saw her discomfort. His eyes narrowed.

'I've hit the nail on the head, haven't I? Your relationship *did* go much deeper. I always wondered about that. When I turned up at the hospital that Christmas and took you outside, on our return I saw Richard's face. He was furious . . . and now I realise he was jealous.'

Helen, at a loss, didn't know what to say. She just looked at James.

'Were you in love with him?'

There was no point now in denying the relationship. 'At first I thought I was, but Richard made it quite clear that he wouldn't contemplate leaving his wife.'

'Did you ever ask him to?'

'Only once and when he didn't answer I knew where I stood.'

'But you continued to be lovers?'

'Until that Christmas, when you arrived out of the blue. Then I told him we were finished.'

There was a coldness in his voice when he asked, 'And why was that?'

'Because I liked you and wanted to know you better. There was no future for me with Richard and I knew I had to start living my life . . . without him.'

'And I happened to be the lucky man around at the time, is that what you're saying?'

Inside, Helen's heart was racing. She couldn't bear to see the hurt in her husband's eyes. He was already in a fragile state, and this would only make things worse if she couldn't persuade him of her deep love for him.

'No, that is not the case. How dare you even think I could be that shallow! I felt there was a chemistry between us and when you were brought in, near to death, I knew that I was in love with you. I'm still in love with you! I'll always be in love with you.'

He sighed. 'War is a swine, isn't it?'

She knelt beside him. 'James, you are my life. I don't want to be anywhere else but with you. Richard was of the moment. You know what war does to people, how when you're scared you cling to others for comfort in one way or another. That's all it was and it was over when you left me that Christmas.'

'It's alright, darling. After all, you were free, even if he wasn't.' He leant forward and kissed her forehead. 'You go and unpack and I'll rustle up some lunch.'

But as she took her case upstairs, she knew that James had been hurt and she prayed that eventually she could make him forget her indiscretion.

Downstairs, in the kitchen, James took some cold ham out of the larder and made a salad. He fried up some cooked potatoes that he found and kept busy, but he couldn't get out of his mind that his wife had once been Richard's lover. It wasn't that he hadn't understood her reasoning. War drew people together, he knew that. He'd seen it happen. Not to him, he was too busy trying to keep his company alive and when the opportunity had arisen from time to time, in some bar or other on a short leave, he'd passed up on the invitations from the prostitutes working there.

He'd seen his men taking refuge in the arms of such women and knew they needed the comfort they gave, but he didn't need it that badly and after he'd met Helen, he knew she was the woman for him. But now he understood why she'd kept from making any commitment to him in the beginning. It had been because of Richard.

It wasn't that he didn't believe that she loved him, he knew that she did, but somehow this sudden revelation had thrown him and he didn't know how to handle it.

* * *

Whilst James was trying to sort his dilemma, Ann Carson was enjoying her life. The committee meeting had finished and she and Clive were seated in their favourite restaurant.

She'd dressed with extra care that morning, wearing a cream silk blouse and dark-brown skirt, just above the ankles, with a neat pair of court shoes with a low heel. On her head a straw hat trimmed with a dark-brown ribbon matching her skirt and cream gloves.

After they'd ordered, Clive took her hand and smiled.

'You look most elegant, my dear. I'm proud to be your escort.'

She beamed at him. 'Thank you, Clive, and I'm delighted you are here.'

'Are you flirting with me, young lady?' he asked, his eyes twinkling.

'Would I do such a thing?' she asked, feigning indignation.

'I'm not sure, to be honest, you are full of devilment today. I've not seen this side of you before, but I must say I like it. How was the reunion, did it go well?'

'It was interesting meeting Richard's team. Especially his theatre sister.'

There was something in the tone of her voice that made him question her.

'Interesting in what way, may I ask?'

She hesitated. 'This Helen worked alongside my husband, closely, for a year. Medically her position was important and I hear she was more than efficient. They worked brilliantly together – or so I'm told.'

He immediately understood. 'You are wondering if she was more to him than that. Am I right?'

'Yes, you are, and to be honest I'm still not convinced that they were not having an affair.'

'If they were, how would you feel about it?'

'Oh, I'm not broken-hearted if that's what you mean. Just curious . . . and I suppose a bit peeved. After all, he wasn't a free man, he was married.'

'Do you believe he could be unfaithful to you?'

She thought about it for a moment. 'In this case, yes I do. She's an attractive woman, they have so much in common with their work. They'd have been together constantly. It would have been so easy to get involved. Especially under wartime conditions, not knowing if you were going to die from a bomb, or enemy fire. You'd grasp at straws for comfort.'

'So, what happens now?'

'Absolutely nothing! She's married, her husband is still suffering from his war. She and Richard are no longer involved. I'm still recognised as the wife of a brilliant surgeon and I have my own life to lead. Why should anything change?'

Clive shook his head. 'You are an amazing woman. If only we had met years ago instead of now. How different it all could have been.'

'But we have met, Clive, my dear friend, and I for one am delighted that we have.'

Frowning, he said, 'Only last week you asked me not to make your life any more complicated, so what are you telling me now?'

'To be honest, I'm not sure.'

He chuckled softly. 'I'm a patient man, Ann. When you've made up your mind, let me know. But be very sure of your decision, that's all I'm saying. I'm in love with you, you know that, but I won't be used as a pawn in your marriage just to pay back your husband.'

'I wouldn't do that to you,' she declared.

'Then we both understand each other.'

After eating they walked through a nearby park, chatting about the charity and the things to be done for the next meeting. There was a small summerhouse in the grounds. It was inviting and it was empty. Clive led her inside.

'Come here,' he said and took her into his arms.

Holding her close he kissed her tenderly and thoroughly, eventually releasing her.

'I would never be unfaithful to you if you were mine, darling Ann.'

Her head was spinning, her heart thumping. Never had Richard's kisses thrilled her as those she'd just shared. She placed her hands either side of his face and she kissed him.

Staring into his eyes, she said, 'Oh dear, what are we to do?'

'That will be entirely up to you, Ann. Choose wisely.'

Chapter Twenty

In the heart of the Cotswolds, Helen and James kept busy, working on the garden of the cottage, she tending to the shrubs and flower beds, he digging a vegetable patch. The rest of the time they spent at the stables or riding out, with Helen becoming even more proficient and enjoying it. James had set up some small jumps for her and was pleased with her growing confidence. To an outsider it would appear that they were a really happy couple, but she knew that although they still were close and in love, now there was this invisible wall between them, one she failed to penetrate, and since her return from London and his discovery of her affair, James had suffered with nightmares again.

Edward, concerned for his son, had called in Doctor Coombs for a chat and it was decided to send James to a psychiatrist in London for a consultation.

'It's the only thing I can suggest,' said the doctor. 'It may not help, but I think we have to give it a try. But first we have to get James to agree to it. Let's hope he does.'

James, summoned to the manor house, walked into the

drawing room and was surprised to see the doctor sitting with his father.

'Hello, you two, what's going on?'

The doctor stood and shook James by the hand. 'Sit down for a minute, old chap. We need to talk.' He waited for his patient to be seated, then continued. 'Your father has informed me that you've been having your nightmares more frequently and we would like you to visit a psychiatrist I know in Harley Street in the hope that he may be able to help you. Are you prepared to give it a try?'

'Why not? Do you think he'll be able to stop them?'

'I won't lie to you, my boy, I don't know, but there's only one way to find out. Would you like me to make an appointment?'

'Yes, please do. Perhaps he can help me to be a real man again.'

Edward rose to his feet. 'What are you saying? You are *still* a real man and will always be one. You diminish yourself and I won't have it! You are a casualty of war, as are many others, but *every* male who went over the top of those trenches will always be a real man, a hero, no matter how they are when they return home.'

James stared at his father in surprise. He was deeply touched by his words and tried to smile, fighting the emotions it had evoked. 'Alright, Dad, calm down. I'll certainly go and see this chap.'

'I'll go now and give him a call, shall I?' the doctor asked Edward.

'Yes, use the phone in my study.' When they were alone Edward said, 'I have to go to London to the Stock Exchange, so if you like I'll go up with you. We can stay in a nearby hotel for a couple of days, spend some time together. What do you think?'

'I think you are terrific, Dad. That would be great. We can leave the women together for a change.'

Doctor Coombs returned. 'He has booked you in for next week, but he said he'd like at least two sessions to begin with.'

'Good heavens,' James remarked, 'that's quick.'

The doctor grinned. 'He owes me a couple of favours so I called them in. Normally you have to wait much longer. I'll mail him your medical records today.'

'You'd better go and let Helen know what's happening, son. She'll need some warning, and I'll let your mother know too.'

Helen was delighted when James gave her the news. She blamed herself for the bad nights and thought they had been brought on by James's discovery about her and Richard and was at a loss as to which way to handle it, without again having to bring up the subject. Yet skirting around it wasn't solving anything.

'I think that's a splendid idea, darling, and to spend time with your father is an added bonus. He thinks the world of you, as I'm sure you know.'

'Oh, I'm well aware of that,' he said, thinking of his father's outburst.

The following week, the two men boarded the train and sat in the first-class compartment on their way to London. They sat in comfortable silence reading the morning papers, exchanging remarks on the news, enjoying the journey.

On their arrival, James went straight to Harley Street,

leaving his father to take their cases and book into the hotel, where they would meet later.

'Good luck, son,' said Edward as they parted.

It was with some trepidation that James entered the rooms of the psychiatrist and spoke to the receptionist. She checked his name and smiled, asking him to take a seat.

He did as he was asked and looked around the small but comfortable room. It was very calming with its white walls, soft chairs and a table with the latest magazines. Some aimed at the male patients, like *The Field* and *Punch*, and *The Queen* for the ladies.

The door beside the reception desk opened and a gentleman walked out, smiled at the receptionist and left.

'You may go in now, sir,' James was told.

Taking a deep breath, he rose from his seat and walked towards the door, knocked gently then walked in. A tall man stood up behind his desk and walked round it to greet his patient.

'Good morning!' He shook hands. 'I'm Hugo Beresford. Please take a seat.'

James studied the psychiatrist carefully. He put his age at about mid-to-late forties, dark hair, beginning to turn silver at the sides, generous mouth, and blue, penetrating eyes, well spoken, but with a softness to his voice that James felt was sympathetic. He liked him.

James looked about him and with a grin said, 'No couch?'

Hugo laughed. 'Over in the corner. You missed it.'

Glancing over his shoulder James saw that he had. 'So I did,' he said and chuckled softly.

'I've read your medical files,' said Hugo. 'My goodness, you caught quite a packet, didn't you? I must say the surgeon, Richard Carson, has done a fine job on you. His notes are very detailed and meticulous.'

'Oh yes, he's a meticulous man in many ways.'

The psychiatrist looked sharply at him and made a quick note on a pad in front of him. 'Do you suffer any pain from your operations?'

'I'm a bit sore sometimes, and I get the odd ache but nothing more. I've healed very well, considering.'

'You've recently married, I see. Congratulations!'

'Thank you. Helen, my wife, nursed me after my operation. She was Carson's theatre sister.'

'Oh, that's how you met?'

'No, we actually met when we were staying at the same hotel on leave somewhat earlier.'

'Oh, I see. Now, James, let's get down to business. Tell me about these nightmares – exactly what do you see?'

Taking a deep breath, he began. It wasn't easy for him, he wanted to give an honest account, but the images he was recalling were distressful and at one stage he couldn't continue.

'That's alright, take a break, continue when you feel able.' Hugo sat back and waited.

Eventually James was able to finish, perspiration beading his forehead, his breath laboured.

Hugo poured a glass of water for him and watched him drink it. 'Right, we'll leave it there until tomorrow.'

James looked disappointed.

Hugo immediately understood. 'It takes time, young man, your condition didn't happen in five minutes, it was over a long period and that's not going to be solved just like that. You have to learn to be patient.'

'Do you think you can help me?'

'At this moment, it's impossible to say. Patience!' He stood up. 'I'll see you at the same time tomorrow.'

Looking at his watch, James was surprised to see just how long he'd been talking.

He shook hands with the man and left, then decided to walk to Regent's Park, a short stroll away, where he found an empty bench and sat thinking about his meeting. It had been strange that the very man he and Helen hadn't mentioned since her return from London had been at the forefront of his discussion with Hugo Beresford. He'd been forced to do so and it hadn't been a pleasant experience. After all, he owed his life to his wife's ex-lover!

After walking round the park, he found a small restaurant and ate a light lunch, then made his way to the hotel, feeling suddenly weary. After checking in, he undressed to his underwear and lay on one of the single beds and fell asleep. This time his dreams were of a lighter vein. His mind took him back to when he and Helen rode on bicycles into the village in France when first they met and he had bought her a scarf. He remembered her delight.

It was Edward who disturbed his son when he entered the bedroom late that afternoon. As James stirred his father apologised for waking him.

Looking at his watch, James was surprised to see just how long he'd been asleep. He rose from the bed and dressed.

'Let's go and get a beer in the bar downstairs,' Edward suggested, 'and you can tell me about your day.'

Once settled, James began. 'Nice bloke, I liked him immediately. We chatted, then he asked me to tell him about the nightmares. It wasn't easy but I did so and then he said come back tomorrow. So far, so nothing!'

Edward looked amused. 'You youngsters have yet to learn to be patient.'

With a broad grin, James said, 'That's what Hugo said. How was your day?'

The two of them sat chatting, catching up, exchanging ideas, laughing over shared memories of past days before the war. It was therapeutic for both men. They decided to take a walk and get some fresh air, then find somewhere to eat, which they did.

As they entered their chosen restaurant, Edward noticed James looking round, taking in every detail of the room, the waiters, the diners, looking slightly anxious.

'Are you happy to stay here, my boy? We can go elsewhere if you like?'

'No. It's alright, Dad. I'm just getting familiar with my surroundings, just looking for anything that might make a sudden noise. I don't want to dive for cover again. I prepare for it all the time after my last experience. Don't take any notice.'

The waiter came over and took their order and James was able to relax.

The following day he sat again in the waiting room without any expectations, other than curiosity, and when summoned entered the consulting room and sat down, wondering what came next.

Hugo Beresford smiled at him. 'How are you?'

'Fine,' and with a wry grin added, 'trying to be patient!'

'Good! You're learning. I do have some news for you, but hear me out before you make a decision. I don't think I am the one to help you, but I do believe I know the person who can.'

This made James sit up in his seat. 'Really?'

'Yes. There's a man in Devon, Arthur Hurst, who has a hospital that deals only with such cases as yours, and he's been having great results. His approach to your condition is far from any other that's been tried, with a fair amount of success, but it means you having to go and stay there for maybe as long as a month, or longer if he thinks it's necessary. If anyone can help, in my opinion, he's your best bet. I took the liberty of giving him a call and he has room for you if you would like to go and give him a try.'

'Whatever does he do that's so different?'

'To be honest, I don't know, only that I've heard of his success. What do you think?'

'I think I need to try. I can't go on living as I do, it's not fair to my family and certainly not to my wife. But I need to go home first for a few days.'

'Of course. You have to put your house in order, I understand. Here is his number and the address. Give him a call and make a date to start.' He rose from his desk and held out his hand. 'Good luck, James. I hope it works out for you.'

As he walked back to his hotel, there was a lightness in his step. This was the first bit of good news he'd had about his condition. Before it had all been so negative and had filled him with despair. Now there was at least some hope. He packed his bag, left a message at the Stock Exchange for his father and caught the next train back to Cheltenham. As he sat in the carriage, he wondered how Helen would react to him having to leave her so soon after the wedding? The timing couldn't have been any worse. But their future was at stake and he hoped she would understand that he felt he had to go – and soon.

Chapter Twenty-One

When James arrived back at the cottage and gave Helen his news, she was delighted. For the first time in ages, her husband had reverted to the man she first met. He was full of excitement and amusing, teasing her about the new man she may meet if the treatment was a success.

'I know, darling, I've not been the easiest man to live with lately and I'm sorry.'

'Now stop talking like that, James. None of this is your fault and you know that, and of course you must go. I'll miss you, of course I will, but I wouldn't have it any other way. I suggest you call this man now and book in.'

James gave her a quick hug and walked into the house, appearing a while later to tell her he'd be off in three days' time. He needed a break to prepare himself mentally for whatever lay ahead and he wanted to spend some time with his bride before he left. He felt he owed her that much.

With at least some hope for the future, James was relaxed and the three days was like a honeymoon all over again. The wall between them seemed to have vanished and they spent their time together, riding, eating quiet meals in the garden and making love.

As he held her in his arms at night, he told Helen just how much he loved her and if, on his return, everything was alright, how great their lives were going to be.

Although she was thrilled by his enthusiasm, she was also fearful. If the treatment failed, James would be devastated and she wondered then how would it affect him, but she kept such thoughts to herself.

Three days later, James, packed and ready, caught a train to Newton Abbot in Devon. Now he was on his way, he was full of trepidation. What if the treatment didn't work? But he decided that negativity was a wasted emotion and he would put such thoughts behind him. After all, Hugo Beresford wouldn't have sent him to this place unless he felt there was some hope.

Eventually James arrived at Seale Hayne Hospital by pony and trap, which had been sent to meet him at the station. He enjoyed the short journey through the Devon countryside, listening to the chatter of the man with the reins, talking about his horse.

On his arrival, he was taken by a nurse to a single room, nicely furnished, if a little sparse. After all, this was a hospital and not a hotel, he told himself. There was a single bed, a small table and chair, a washbasin and wardrobe. He unpacked then made his way back to the reception, as instructed.

Apparently he had an interview with Arthur Hurst after lunch and he was shown where the dining room was and how to find the consulting room after.

'If you get lost just ask someone,' the nurse told him. 'We don't stand on ceremony here, James, we like to keep things informal.'

He smiled, thanked her and walked into the dining room.

'Hello, mate!' one of the men greeted him. 'You just arrived?'

'Yes, I have.'

'Then grab a tray and join the queue. I'm Tom, by the way.' He held out his hand.

'I'm James,' he said as he shook the proffered hand and walked behind him, picking up a tray. 'Bit like being back in the army,' he laughed.

'In a way,' Tom replied, 'but there's no bloody Boche here, mate.'

After collecting their food, a hearty stew with potatoes and vegetables, with an apple pie and custard for dessert, they sat together and chatted, but neither mentioned their medical problems or the war.

Later James said goodbye to his new friend and made his way to the consulting room where he was asked to wait. I've been here before, he thought to himself, but this time with a different man. He wondered what would happen now.

Arthur Hurst was very different from Hugo. He was an army major and had a quiet air of authority about him. He shook hands with James and asked him to sit.

'Have you settled in your room?' he asked.

'Yes, thanks. I'm all unpacked.'

'Good.' Hurst handed him a list. 'Here are the mealtimes. Make sure you have a good breakfast tomorrow because you'll be working at the farm. A truck will pick you and the others up outside the hospital at 08:00. The kitchen will give you a packed lunch, then at the end of the day, you can have a bath before dinner.'

James looked puzzled. 'Working on the farm? I don't understand. When do I start my treatment?'

Arthur Hurst grinned at him. 'This *is* part of the treatment. Trust me, James, go along with me. Just do as I ask for the moment. We have a way to go, this is the beginning. Now I suggest you take yourself off outside, get a book from the hospital library, find a quiet spot and relax. Save your strength for tomorrow!'

It was a very puzzled man who walked out of that room. Working on a farm? James couldn't make head nor tail of the situation, but then he was told this man had a very different way of handling his sort of case. He found the library, chose a book and wandered into the garden. There he found several men sitting, some together, others alone, but all seeming quite happy to be there. He chose a spot on the grass beneath a tree. Leaning against the trunk, he lit a cigarette and relaxed. It was like being on holiday, but tomorrow it was work. What kind, he wondered?

James was given a packed lunch with his breakfast. Tom, his new friend, saw it and spoke:

'Oh, you're one of the working party too, eh mate?'

'Yes, are you?'

Tom held up his package. 'Yes, me too. I love it, been doing it a while. There's nothing more therapeutic than digging. It clears the mind.'

They sat at a table together.

'What are we digging for?'

'Vegetables. The hospital grow their own. Well, mate,

they've got to feed the patients. We've got spuds, parsnips, onions, beans. It's bloody marvellous what they've done.'

There were about a dozen men who piled into the waiting truck. Tom quickly introduced James and they were soon on their way. On arrival, the men were given spades and forks and sent to a field of vegetables and told to dig, putting the chosen vegetables in boxes to be carted away and the next one filled.

It was a warm day and James found the sweat soaking his shirt, but somehow it was a great feeling once he'd started. It reminded him of his vegetable patch back at the cottage. The banter among the men was amusing and before long it was time for a lunch break. They all made for the shade of the trees where they were given water to drink and some to pour over their heads to cool them down.

An hour later they returned to the fields until four o'clock when the truck came to take them back to the hospital. James couldn't wait to sit in a bath and soak his aching bones. He was worn out, yet strangely peaceful. In his room, he washed out his shirt and hung it to dry over the washbasin, dressed in fresh clothes and walked out into the garden and sat on a wall. What a strange day, he thought, but what an enjoyable one. He was tired but at the same time content. After all, they'd all worked hard and achieved a great deal between them. It was very satisfying. He would write to Helen tonight and tell her of his first day. She would be surprised. How long would it continue and what happened next, he wondered?

It was a further two weeks of working on the farm before James was summoned for another meeting with Arthur

Hurst. By now he felt fitter, was tanned and had settled into the daily routine. The camaraderie of the men lifted everyone's spirits. He sat in front of Hurst's desk.

'My word you look fit, James. How do you feel?'

'Thank you, I feel great. Still somewhat puzzled by it all, but I'm fine.'

'No nightmares, I believe?'

'No, no nightmares.' James laughed. 'I'm far too tired for those!'

'Let's talk about the war for a moment. It's the officers who are the men who suffer the most, I've found,' Hurst said. 'Tell me, honestly, how did you feel as you blew your whistle and took your men over the top to face the enemy?'

'Bloody terrified, if you want the truth!'

'Exactly! But you had to set an example. No way could you show your fear to your men, right?'

'How could I expect them to follow me if I showed I was scared?'

'And because you and others like you had to smother those feelings, they manifested themselves in other ways. Like in your nightmares. There, nothing stopped the fear. It had to come out somewhere.'

'I never thought of it that way. But yes, I suppose that makes sense.'

'Now I believe you are ready for the next step.'

James was intrigued. 'And what, may I ask, is that?'

'We have reconstructed, in our own way, the battlefields of Flanders. Tomorrow you and several others will go and fight your war again. Relive your experiences. It won't be easy but I believe it's imperative to your recovery.'

James didn't know what to say. He'd hoped to have put

all that behind him and now he was going to have to face it all again. He felt sick to the pit of his stomach.

'If you say so, sir.'

Helen, unaware of this new scenario that faced her husband, was content to be a housewife, pottering round the cottage and helping Frances exercise the horses. James had written to her telling her about his working on the farm and how much he was enjoying doing so, although unable to understand the reasoning behind it, but Helen immediately saw the result as she read his letters. He was enjoying the task, enjoying the camaraderie of the men, being out in the open at one with nature. He was happy. She could well understand the thinking behind it.

Ann Carson however had no intention of playing the housewife! Yes, she cooked meals for Richard and sometimes she was there to share them with him. A woman came into clean and see to the laundry once a week, which released her time to spend attending various meetings for the charities she supported. In particular, the one where she worked with Clive Bradshaw. She actually saw very little of her husband, which suited her very well, and although Richard complained about the time she spent away from him, she ignored his protests.

Ever since Clive had kissed her in the summer house in the park, she was in a quandary about their relationship. He had made it clear that he wasn't to be used as a weapon against her husband and he hadn't kissed her again, to her great disappointment. She was playing the dutiful wife in the bedroom, but it was without enjoyment or meaning and she made excuses sometimes, keeping the physical side of the marriage at bay as much as she dare. It was Clive's arms she longed to feel about her, not those of her husband.

Things came to a head a few weeks later when an annual general meeting had been called for all the branches of the charity to meet in Birmingham for two days and to which the two people in charge of each charity had been invited. In their case it was Ann and Clive

'Will Richard allow you to come, Ann? If not, I'll take another member of the committee.'

She was incensed! 'Allow me? I don't have to ask permission, for goodness' sake. I'll tell him that I'm going, then he can dine at his club whilst I'm away.'

With a deep frown Clive stared at her. 'Be very careful, my dear. You are in a unique position for a lady of our times. Not many women have the freedom that you have. This may be a step too far for your husband. He might baulk at being told, whereas if you *asked* for his permission, that would be different. You wouldn't be undermining his authority.'

She thought about it for a moment and realised that Clive was right. Richard had always maintained he was the head of the house and her time spent away irritated him, she knew that. She also knew it was only after meeting Helen that she had been even more dismissive of her duties as a wife, almost as a punishment to both of them for what might have been between them.

'Yes,' she said, 'you're right, of course. I'll talk to Richard this evening.'

* * *

Later, Ann took the time to cook a delicious meal. She changed into one of her exquisite gowns, dressed her hair carefully, sprayed herself with perfume . . . and waited.

Richard was delighted to see her in attendance when he returned from the hospital. It had been a particularly difficult day and he was weary, but as he smelt the aromas coming from the kitchen he looked at his wife and smiled.

'You look lovely, have I forgotten something? Is this a special occasion?'

She laughed as she poured him a drink. 'No, not at all. I realise that I've neglected you somewhat as I've been so busy. This is my way of making it up to you. Sit down and rest before dinner.'

Over the meal, she asked Richard about his work, appearing for once to be interested, and then she took a deep breath and brought up the subject of the annual general meeting in Birmingham.

'As one of the heads of the committee, they will expect me to attend, Richard. I do hope you won't mind me going? I realise it is somewhat inconvenient for you, but as you know, the work we do is of the utmost importance and I really have to be there.'

He was not pleased. 'For goodness' sake Ann, I see little of you as it is! Surely they can do without you?'

'Oh, no doubt they could, but that would mean I would have to spend time catching up with all the changes that are on the agenda, which will mean I'll have to spend even more time away from the house and you wouldn't like that.' She held her breath.

He muttered to himself, then looking very disgruntled, he agreed.

'Oh, very well. I'll eat at my club when you've gone. How long will you be away?'

'Only a couple of days, you'll hardly notice I'm gone.'

He just glared at her and continued to eat his meal in silence.

Ann didn't say a word either in case he changed his mind, but she was filled with delight at the thought of being away from him and with Clive, staying at the same hotel. She would be the one to make the arrangements and would make sure they were in rooms next to each other.

Chapter Twenty-Two

Back in Newton Abbot, there was a subdued air among the men who were being sent out to the so-called battlefields. They had all been issued with uniforms and as they dressed, their minds automatically returned to their days in the army and the carnage they had seen and tried so hard to forget. Every man was nervous and afraid, and as they left the safety of their rooms at dawn and climbed into the waiting lorries, not one of them spoke.

The following twenty-four hours were horrendous. The men were forced to relive their daily battles, going over the top, to the sound of machine-gun fire, explosives that had been carefully placed so as not to injure anyone, returning to the waterlogged trenches time and time again. Hurst had brought men in who had been designated to be killed and were screaming in mock pain, using fake blood to cover them as they fell. It was so realistic, the patients were calling for the medics to take care of the wounded. It was like the opening of Pandora's box.

They returned to the hospital at dusk, exhausted and

emotionally drained. They piled out of the trucks and went to their rooms.

James closed the door behind him, kicked off his shoes, climbed onto his bed and sobbed until there were no tears left to shed. Then, still fully dressed, he fell asleep.

During the following days, the men were kept quiet and sent daily to a room where masseurs waited for them, giving every man a full body massage until eventually they were sent to a peaceful place in the Devon countryside where there was no work for them to do. Just a quiet place with books to read, walks to be taken, no regimentation at all apart from the opportunity to gather one's thoughts and to recover.

Four days later the men were returned to the hospital and James was told to report to Arthur Hurst's office. As he made his way there, he wondered what was going to happen next.

'Sit down, James,' said Hurst. He studied his patient for a moment. 'How do you feel?'

With a smile James said, 'Rested. After the massages and the time away from here, I feel, yes, rested is the best way to describe my feelings.'

'Excellent! I think it's time for you to go home.'

'Does that mean I'm cured?'

Hurst shook his head. 'I can't honestly say you are, but I have high hopes that your condition will certainly improve. I expect you may have the odd nightmare. The sound of a sudden noise I can't do anything about, nor your fear of confined places; that you'll have to try and overcome by yourself, if you can.'

'Going back to the battlefields was horrendous!' James declared.

'I know, but it was time to face your fears. I know it was a lot to ask, but I've found it's the only way.'

'I'd hoped to have put that time behind me.'

'You buried it! It was time to dig it up and face it and you did.' Hurst rose to his feet.

'Any problems, get in touch, but I hope not to see you again, young man.'

James went to his room and packed.

As he sat on the train, homeward bound, he thought about his time spent at the hospital. Working on the farm had been therapeutic, and completely satisfying. The camaraderie of the men, enjoyable. He didn't remember a time before when he'd laughed so much and had looked forward to the following day with such enthusiasm.

There was no one there to condemn those suffering with shell shock as cowards, as many had been during the war. They had been treated with humanity and dignity, which had alleviated the feeling of guilt. He had faced his fears and survived. It was like being renewed. Only time would tell if it had been any kind of cure, but for no apparent reason, he felt hopeful about the future. He smiled softly. Helen would be surprised when he walked in. He'd purposely not told her of his return, wanting to surprise her.

Helen was in the stables grooming Cleo. During the time her husband had been away she'd been schooled carefully by Frances on how to care for the horses and was now very able. She was brushing down Cleo with a curry comb, chatting away to the animal.

'We've got to keep you looking beautiful for when your master comes home,' she said, 'he'll expect to see you looking pristine.'

The horse gave an answering neigh.

Helen laughed with delight. 'James always said you understood every word, and to be honest, Cleo, I really didn't believe him, but I do now.'

'How could you possibly doubt a word I said?'

Helen spun round and let out a cry of surprise as she saw her husband leaning over the stable door. 'James!' She dropped the curry comb and ran to him, flinging her arms around him and kissing him soundly.

'Perhaps I should go away more often,' he teased.

'Oh no! Please tell me you're home for good and not just a few days.'

Holding her close he said, 'No, darling, they've kicked me out. Now I'm all yours . . . and of course Cleo's too.' He opened the stable door stepped inside and stroked the nose of his favourite horse. 'Hello, old girl. It's so good to see you again.'

Half an hour later the two of them entered the kitchen of the manor house, where James was greeted warmly by the cook, before they went into the drawing room to find his parents.

Edward put down his paper and, getting to his feet, greeted his son with a warm embrace.

'James! What a lovely surprise and, my God, you look well.'

Frances rushed over to kiss him 'How lovely to see you, darling. It's seemed such a long time ago. We wondered when you would ever return.' She poured them all a glass of sherry.

He told them about his time spent in Devon, about working on the farm, the massages and the time spent in the country, but he left out the war games, as he now thought of his day in the trenches. Those he didn't want to talk about.

After a while, the two of them left the manor and went to their cottage. James looked around and remarked on some of the changes Helen had made. The new cushions and curtains, furniture moved. Then he held her.

Nuzzling her neck he said, 'You have no idea how much I've missed you.'

'About as much as I've missed you I expect,' she answered. 'I hated every moment we were apart.'

He led her towards the stairs. 'We have a lot of catching up to do. I hope you haven't made any plans for the next few days.'

'If I had, I'd cancel them,' she laughed and walked ahead of him to the bedroom.

During the following days, they were hardly ever apart. They went riding together and James congratulated Helen on her progress in the saddle. They sorted out the vegetable patch, which had suffered during his absence.

'I'm sorry, darling, but I thought it best to leave it in case I did something wrong,' Helen told him.

'Not to worry, I've learnt so much working on the farm that we can start again. I spent some of the time when I was alone working out a plan for planting.'

Early one evening Edward found James alone at the stables. They sat together and chatted.

'How was it at the hospital, James? When you told us

about it, I had the feeling you were keeping something back. Don't tell me if you'd rather not.'

James told his father about the long day spent in the trenches that had been built, how there was the sound of gunfire and the explosions.

'It was so real, Dad. It was horrendous! It was as if the clock had been turned back. But it was to make us face our fears and relive those moments.'

Looking perturbed his father asked, 'Did it do any good, though?'

'Strangely enough it did, although it took several days for me to realise it. I can only describe it as a sort of cleansing.'

'Extraordinary!' Edward exclaimed. 'But, of course, the mind is a fragile thing.'

'Major Hurst hopes I'll now only have the odd nightmare. Loud noises and confined places I'll have to work out for myself. Not a bad bargain, if it works. Time will tell.'

'I thought I'd go out for a hack, fancy coming with me?' Edward asked.

With a wide grin, James agreed. 'I don't remember the last time we did that. I'd love to.'

The men saddled up their mounts and set off. It was a beautiful evening and they rode for a couple of hours before returning to the stables.

As they both attended to their horses, Edward said, 'That was great. We should do it more often.'

'Indeed, we should,' his son agreed and with a broad grin added, 'Good to see you're still able!'

'You cheeky blighter! I could still give you a run for your money.'

After the horses were settled they both made their way to their own homes having enjoyed each other's company.

Over the next few weeks, James and Helen worked on the renewed vegetable patch. She quietly observed him, pleased that he seemed so fit and relaxed. He'd not suffered any nightmares and when they'd shopped, she saw him steel himself to deal with the dreaded confined spaces, but said nothing.

James had decided to see the year out, pottering at the stables and garden before making a decision about the future.

'After all, I can't spend the rest of my life not working. That *would* be soul-destroying.'

'You'll know when you feel ready, darling,' Helen said. 'It just needs patience.'

'Now you sound like Hugo Beresford!' But he laughed as he chided her.

Whilst James was sorting out his life and his future, Ann Carson was only complicating hers. She'd booked adjoining rooms for Clive and her at the hotel in Birmingham and was now on the train with him, clutching a small suitcase packed with her prettiest lingerie, and a briefcase with the necessary papers for the annual general meeting. They were sitting in the dining car eating breakfast.

Looking across the table at Clive, she smiled.

'Isn't this exciting! I feel as if I'm on an adventure.'

He looked somewhat surprised. 'To be honest, not in my wildest dreams have I ever thought of an AGM as an adventure. It's usually very boring, sometimes annoying when people dither over decisions and I've always been glad when it was over and I could go home.'

'Ah, well, you've not had me with you before.'

His eyes narrowed as he scrutinised her face. 'You, my dear, look full of devilment. What are you up to, may I ask?'

'Absolutely nothing! It's just so lovely to get away from London, the house, Richard and everyday life. I know Birmingham isn't Paris, but I feel free for once.'

'You do realise this is a business trip? By the end of it, you'll be happy to return to the mundane, I can promise you.'

'Oh, Clive! Have you no sense of adventure?'

With a chuckle he said, 'Of course I have, but I fail to see how this trip is going to provide me with one.'

'Well who knows? You may be surprised.' She took a sip of her coffee and glanced out of the window at the passing scenery. I mustn't push too soon, she thought. This afternoon there is a meeting, then dinner tonight. A full day tomorrow, but in the evening there was to be a dance at the hotel and all the delegates were to attend. She could wait.

She glanced back at Clive and saw he was studying some papers in preparation for the forthcoming meeting. Men, she thought, they could be so obtuse!

Chapter Twenty-Three

When eventually Ann and Clive arrived in Birmingham, they took a cab to their hotel and booked in, signed the register and following the porter, took the lift to the first floor. The porter led Ann to her room, opened the door and took her suitcase inside, gave her the key and then asked Clive to follow him to the room next to hers.

Ann unpacked her things, hanging up her gowns and putting away her underwear, apart from an exquisite nightgown, which she held up against her and looked at her reflection in the long mirror of the wardrobe. She turned her body this way and the other with a satisfied smile. She'd purchased it especially for the occasion with the intention of seducing Clive. It was her only chance to lower the barrier of convention and failure was not on the agenda.

When she was ready, she left her room and knocked on his door.

'I hope your room is comfortable?' she said when he opened the door.

'Come and see for yourself,' he said and stepped back to let her enter.

It was furnished just like hers, with a single bed, wardrobe, chest of drawers and small washstand, and in the window a dressing table and mirror.

Turning to him she said, 'It's comfortable, just like mine.'

'Good.' He led her to the door, to her disappointment. 'Let's go down and see if any of the others have arrived, have a drink at the bar and then lunch.'

She had no option but to agree.

Some of the other delegates were hovering in the foyer, some at the reception desk, and Clive introduced her to one or two of them, saying he would see them in the bar.

There were ten delegates from five other branches of the charity and they sat together with Clive and Ann, chatting, then soon after made their way to the dining room. To Ann's dismay they all sat at one big table that had been prepared and she was drawn into conversation with those either side of her, Clive sitting opposite. This wasn't how she'd planned it at all. She'd hoped they would have a quiet lunch at a table for two, where she could begin to charm him.

After the meal, they gathered around a long table in the conference room. Only then did she realise what Clive had meant about the meeting being boring as they worked their way through the agenda. There were those who obviously thought their position was one of power and tried to push their ideas as being the only ones to consider for the changes to be made . . . then the arguments began.

'Ladies and gentlemen, please!' The chairman had had enough. As an ex-headmaster, he had a voice of authority and everyone stopped talking.

Glowering at those around him, he said, 'I began to

think I was sitting facing an unruly class of my students. You are adults, now please try and behave like one!'

He continued to run the meeting, controlling those with inflated egos and eventually getting them to vote for each item on the agenda, but it hadn't been easy and watching him, Ann was filled with admiration.

Three hours later the meeting came to an end and everyone breathed a sigh of relief. It had been exhausting. But tomorrow was a full day with meetings, followed by dinner and then the dance.

As they walked away, Ann tucked her arm through Clive's.

'Do we have to sit with any of the others over dinner? Only, after this meeting, I'd like to get away from everyone.'

He started laughing. 'What did I tell you? You didn't believe me, but frankly I don't want to see them again too soon either, so how about us finding a nearby restaurant and eating there? If we stay in the hotel—'

She didn't let him finish. 'Oh that would be wonderful! Please let's do that. I just need to get changed.'

'You go along, then, and I'll see you in the bar.'

It was late September and the evenings were beginning to herald a change in the seasons, so Ann wore a long velvet coat with a fur-trimmed collar to keep her warm as she and Clive strolled along the streets, looking in the shop windows, exploring until they found a suitable-looking restaurant and entered.

Clive took her coat and handed it to the waiter, then they ordered, Clive choosing the wine, which the waiter poured as they waited for their meal.

Clive raised his glass. 'To a good meeting,' he said.

'To our friendship?' she suggested.

'To our friendship,' he replied. They clicked glasses and drank.

'Was it difficult to persuade Richard to let you come here?'

'He wasn't best pleased but I talked him round.'

Her companion studied her closely. 'I would think if you really wanted something, it would be difficult for anyone to refuse.'

'Does that go for you too?'

He smiled softly as he replied, 'That would depend on what you wanted.'

'Then I'll have to think about it carefully, won't I?'

At that moment the waiter served their first course and they sat chatting about the delegates, especially the ones who had been difficult.

'They are the same every year. We all wait, knowing what will happen, irritated beyond reason, but the chairman, as you saw for yourself, is very capable of taking control.'

At the end of the meal, they walked slowly back to the hotel, managing to keep clear of any of the delegates, taking the lift to their rooms. Clive walked Ann to her door and waited for her to open it. She turned to him.

'There's a bottle of champagne on ice just waiting to be opened, would you like to have a nightcap with me?'

He started to chuckle. 'You are a devious woman!'

'Only when I have to be.' She opened the door, entered and stood looking at him. 'Well?'

Shaking his head, but smiling, he followed her inside.

Chapter Twenty-Four

James and Helen were off to Newmarket to a sale of horses. He had decided to buy at least one to break in, ready to sell on.

'It's what I'm good at,' he told Helen, 'and I enjoy doing it, as you know. Besides, I'll feel I'm doing a proper job!'

She was delighted by his enthusiasm and had encouraged him. It had been her first time at such a sale and she was surprised at the number of people standing round the show ring, waiting to bid. It had an air of excitement and expectancy and she found her heart beating a little faster as each horse was brought in and walked around the ring. The bidding was fast and fierce.

Almost an hour had passed without James making a bid. She'd not said anything as she didn't know just what he was looking for until a piebald pony was brought in. She felt James stiffen beside her as he watched the horse being walked round by its handler.

The bidding began. The auctioneer was in full flow and she had great difficulty keeping up with him. Beside her James was bidding, along with several others. She found she was holding her breath.

'Sold!' The auctioneer banged his gavel.

Startled Helen looked at James and saw he was beaming. 'Did you win?'

He gave her a hug. 'Yes, it's ours. Now let's see if there is another.'

By the end of the sale, James had bought another horse, a chestnut, which he had admired. He went to the office and paid for his purchases and arranged for them to be delivered the next day.

He joined Helen outside, waving his receipt. 'I'm in business!' He picked her up and swung her round, much to the onlookers' delight.

'James!' She was flushed with embarrassment, hanging on to her hat, but was delighted for her husband.

On the train home, he chatted enthusiastically about his plans, saying now was the time for him to really face the future.

'At one time, darling, I honestly wondered if I had one, other than that of some sort of invalid.'

'Oh, James, that's so sad, but do you realise that today you were in a big crowd and yet it didn't seem to bother you?'

'Oh my God! I hadn't realised. I was so concentrated on not missing buying the horse I wanted.' He beamed at her. 'It's been a great day and now I'm in business. You can help me sometimes, if you like. After all, now you are more than capable.'

'I'd love to, but you must show me what to do.'

Putting his arm round her he kissed her cheek. 'You'll see, we'll have great fun doing it.'

In a bedroom on the first floor of a hotel in Birmingham, Ann Carson was making her own fun. Having enticed Clive into her room, she let him open the bottle of champagne and they sat on the bed, drinking.

'There, didn't I tell you this trip would be an adventure?'

'You did, and I was proven wrong.' He stared at her over the rim of his glass as he drank. 'What else had you in mind?'

'Come along, Clive, you're not that naïve.'

He put his glass down on the bedside table and then took hers and did the same. Then he kissed her. Ann closed her eyes and wallowed in the pleasure of being held and kissed by a man who loved her. She had never felt that Richard had done so. He was fond of her and she was the perfect wife, or had been, but this was different.

'Ann, darling Ann, if only we'd met years ago,' he whispered as he kissed her eyes, her neck.

'But we've met now, Clive. Don't let us waste any more time. You know I can't divorce Richard, it would cause such a scandal. His reputation would be in question and I would be ostracised by society, but let's just enjoy each other.'

'You do realise that if we do and it was discovered, there would still be a scandal. Apart from Richard, we'd lose all credibility with the charity. They would ask us to leave. Our names would be whispered in corners and in living rooms, especially at the hospital where Richard works. A great deal is at stake here.'

'Are you prepared to take that chance?' she asked.

'I am, yes, but I really don't think you should, you have too much to lose.'

In her heart she knew that he was right. 'Can we not just enjoy the two nights we have here? After that, we will be respectable again. Please, Clive, that's all I ask.'

'As I said earlier, you would be hard to refuse and I haven't the strength to do so.'

They undressed and lay on the bed together, arms around each other. Ann closed her eyes as Clive kissed and caressed her. She returned his kisses with a fervour and without inhibition, enjoying every moment, listening to the words of love being murmured, feeling like a wanton woman and giving herself willingly until eventually, with a cry, she reached her orgasm. The first one for a very long time. She lay still, exhausted and thoroughly satisfied. Clive lay on top of her for a moment, then he moved beside her and took her into his arms and just held her close to him.

'Oh, Clive,' she said softly, caressing his face.

He just gazed at her for a moment. 'You are wonderful, my darling Ann, but when we return home, it's going to be so hard not to be able to hold you and make love to you.'

'I know, but we must enjoy our time together now, it's the only chance we have.'

He sat up, climbed out of bed and dressed. 'Tomorrow we have meetings in the morning, and in the afternoon we must be vigilant not to show any signs of affection, because if anyone even suspects, we are in deep trouble, remember that. Be very careful.'

He leant over her and kissed her softly, then walking to the door, opened it, glanced quickly to make sure the corridor was empty, then left.

Ann reached out and ran her hand over the place beside her where her lover had been and sighed. Whatever the risk, it had been worth it. Richard had never made her feel this good – lately she only slept with him out of duty – but he had never satisfied her as much as Clive had tonight. Tonight she'd been in a different frame of mind. She wanted Clive, had given way to the encompassing feeling of desire. She had surprised herself at her lack of inhibition, which made it all the more enjoyable, and the fact that their coupling was like playing with fire had only added to the enjoyment.

After taking a quick bath the next morning, Ann entered the dining room and saw that most of the delegates were seated. Clive was at a table with three others, which meant she had to sit elsewhere and chat to her companions. Remembering his warning, she didn't even glance across the dining room to where he was seated and continued in that vein all through the morning meeting, but at lunchtime she sat with two others who invited her and Clive to join them, mainly to ask questions about their branch. They were very businesslike in their discussion and Ann felt they had successfully covered their tracks. It was the same during the afternoon meeting and later at dinner, but as they entered the ballroom after, the band was playing a waltz and he held out his hand. Ann took hold of it and then walked onto the floor to dance.

'Don't look at me like that, darling,' he said, 'we are supposed to be business acquaintances, you'll give the game away.'

The dance seemed to go on for ever and Ann danced with several of the delegates, but Clive didn't come near her again until it was over and they both thankfully walked to the lift to take them to their rooms. As they arrived at their floor and walked along the corridor, not touching, Clive just smiled at her.

'I'll see you later,' he said quietly as, further down the corridor, two other delegates entered their rooms.

With mounting expectation and excitement, Ann donned her nightdress and waited. It seemed an age before there was a tap on her door. She ran to open it and let her lover enter, throwing her arms around him as soon as he'd closed the door.

Laughing, Clive picked her up and carried her to the bed.

'An eager woman is every man's dream,' he teased as he undressed and climbed into her bed.

After breakfast the following morning, they left the hotel for the station and the train home. Ann sat next to Clive and reached for his hand.

'Thank you for the best two days of my life,' she said.

He looked at her and laughing softly said, 'That's quite a compliment, thank you.'

She sighed. 'Now it's back to reality, and I can't say I'm looking forward to it.'

'Me neither, but we must return to our usual routines. Not to do so would be foolish. You know that.'

At that moment the train stopped at a station and two other passengers entered the carriage, which stopped any further private conversation, and when they arrived, they parted without touching each other.

Ann opened the door to her home without enthusiasm. It was pristine as the cleaning lady had been. She quickly looked in the larder to see what food was there and seeing it and the icebox empty, walked to the shops to replenish her stocks.

When she returned and sat quietly drinking a cup of tea,

she knew that this evening would be difficult when Richard came home. He was bound to be bad-tempered having to cope without her for two days and she also knew that she would find it hard to behave as normal, but she had no choice.

'You're back, then,' was Richard's greeting as he walked into the house.

'Yes, as you can see.' She stood waiting for his next remark, waiting for the complaints.

'It's no good, Ann, you just cannot go off on some jaunt again. It's most inconvenient.'

'Just as much as it was inconvenient for the soldiers my charity works for to be injured!' she snapped at him.

'Now that's an entirely different thing.'

'No it isn't,' she argued. 'You're put out because your routine has been upset, and I must say I'm surprised at your selfishness, considering you have been near the front during the war, having to deal with these men we are trying to look after.' She stomped away into the kitchen.

Richard sighed and poured himself a drink. He was tired and still aggrieved at having to dine at his club instead of the comfort of his home, especially after a trying day in the operating theatre. Why on earth Ann had to be involved with these charities he had no idea – it was commendable but it was time she stopped. He picked up the *Daily Telegraph* and sat reading it until Ann said that dinner was ready.

He tucked into his steak with relish. His wife was a good cook and it was so much more enjoyable to eat well at his own table.

'This is lovely, I can't tell you how I've missed you and

your cooking. It's no good, Ann, you'll have to give up all these charities, I hardly see you these days and it has to stop.'

Ann nearly choked on her food. This was *not* what she expected and if Richard insisted, what was she to do? She tried to remain calm.

'Yes, I know you're right and it is getting a bit hectic.'

He looked surprised. He'd expected an argument.

'I've been thinking of resigning from one or two, but not from the one I've represented in Birmingham. There are exciting plans for the future, which we discussed at the AGM, and I want to be part of it. I think I've earned that right.'

He heard the stubborn note in her voice and not wanting a night of discord, he agreed.

'Well, you have worked hard for this charity but if you resigned from the others, I'd see more of you and that would be fine. I'll allow you to do just that one.' He sipped his wine, feeling very self-satisfied.

Ann wanted to slap him. Pompous idiot, she thought. She did know that she was fortunate to have had the opportunity to live her own life during the time Richard had been away, not many women had that freedom, but she was not under any circumstances going to miss meeting Clive each week. Even if they had to behave in a decorous manner from now on.

Having made his point, Richard was most affable during the rest of the evening but in bed when he put his arm around his wife, she pushed it away.

'I'm tired, Richard, it's been a long day.' He can't have his way about everything, she thought as she pulled the sheet over her shoulders. My body, my choice!

Chapter Twenty-Five

There was much excitement at the stables at the manor house as the horses arrived the day after the sale. Edward was there to help James unload his purchases. Both animals were skittish and nervous after the journey but eventually were settled in their respective stalls and were munching away at the hay that was ready for them.

'You've chosen well,' Edward said to his son. 'They look in fine fettle. Once you've trained them there should be no problem selling them.'

James was delighted to hear this as his father was very knowledgeable when it came to horses. He entered the stall of the piebald filly, talking softly to it, feeding it a carrot, trying to gain the animal's trust. He stroked its neck as it ate, ran his hand down its legs, looking for any weakness, then left and did the same with the chestnut colt, but taking great care as the animal was still unsettled. It pawed the ground and then suddenly reared up on its hind legs. James moved out of the way very quickly.

'You, my beauty, are going to be a problem, but we'll get there in the end.'

At that moment Helen arrived just as James came out of the stall, closing the bottom half of the door behind him, leaning over it to see if the horse settled when it was alone. Helen joined him.

'I don't want you going into this stall,' James told her. 'This animal is still wild and unpredictable. It'll take some time to get him trained, but he's in great condition and eventually will be worth the money I paid. He's from good stock.'

Helen looked perplexed. 'I'm not sure about him, James, he's got a wicked gleam in his eyes, whereas the other one seems to have a sweeter nature.'

'Yes, the filly will make a good buy for a family, but you know, I have a feeling that this one could well be good for point-to-point or a hunter. He's spirited and built for speed. Time will tell.'

It was now mid December and in the three months that James had been training his new horses, he'd worked hard. Both were getting used to rider and saddle but the chestnut was still unpredictable.

He walked his wife over to the piebald's stall and holding out a carrot was delighted when she sauntered over and allowed him to feed her.

They had christened both the animals. The piebald was now known as Gentle Jane after one of Henry VIII's wives, because she was gentle, and the chestnut Genghis Khan, because he wasn't.

Stroking Gentle Jane's nose he said, 'She really is a joy, she'll be perfect for a youngster who has a little experience.'

Helen fed her another carrot and stroked her neck. 'Yes,

she's gentle, a child would be safe with her, but I still don't trust Genghis.'

With a frown, James agreed. 'It'll be a while before I can safely sell him on and then it will have to be to an experienced person who can handle such a spirited animal. But in my heart, I do believe he's something special.'

'How about us going into Cheltenham, James? I want to do some Christmas shopping.'

'Yes, if you like. I need to go home to wash and change first, though – I smell of horses!'

Whilst Helen waited for her husband, she thought how well he was doing, now that he was occupied. He'd only had one bad nightmare in the last three months, and the sudden sound of a gunshot one day when the farmer in the next field was shooting rabbits had only made him flinch and not dive for the ground. He was now more confident and no longer felt like an invalid. He was happy and content and so was she.

Christmas was to be spent with his parents at the manor, with an open house on Boxing Day. Frances and the staff had decorated the hall and downstairs rooms beautifully and everyone was beginning to get into the Christmas spirit.

Ann Carson had decorated their living room, dining room and hallway, but without a great deal of enthusiasm. Ever since her return from the meeting in Birmingham, she was a frustrated woman. She and Clive still lunched together after every meeting of the charity, sitting sedately, trying not to show any signs of intimacy, and it was driving her mad.

223

Today as she sat beside him at their usual table, she placed a hand on his knee.

'Ann! What are you doing? Stop it!' Her companion looked at her in surprise.

She took her hand away. 'I can't help it. I want to touch you, get close to you. I'm not sure, Clive, how much longer I can do this – we are just associates. I want more.'

He spoke quietly. 'You know that's not possible. You know what we said, we have to be careful. You asked for two nights and they were wonderful, but it can't continue, you know that.'

She appealed to him. 'Don't you find it hard or is it just me?'

'My darling girl, of course I find it difficult. How do you think I feel when we dine together and then you go home to your husband?'

'Tell me,' she urged, wanting at least to hear how he felt, even if that was all her lover could give her.

'I want to take hold of your hand and book into the nearest hotel. I want to hold you in my arms, feel the softness of your body and make love to you.'

'Oh, Clive darling, couldn't we do just that? Richard won't be home until the evening, we have the time.'

'Now you're being foolish. Of course we can't. What if someone saw us?'

She knew he spoke the truth.

Richard Carson removed his mask and let out a sigh of relief. That had been such a difficult operation, one that had used all his skills to save the patient. It had been touch and go, but the man had pulled through. As the patient was wheeled away he turned to his staff:

'Well done, everybody. Thank you, I couldn't have done it without you.' He walked out of the theatre, thankful that he'd finished for the day because he was physically and mentally drained. He made his way to his office and poured himself a stiff Scotch, added a splash of soda and sat drinking it slowly. It reminded him of working in the base hospital during the war, when he and Helen would sit and have a drink together in his tent after a heavy day.

He thought of her often when he was doing an operation and his theatre sister was not quick enough for him, comparing her mentally with Helen. No one had reached her standard in his eyes. She was the yardstick by which he judged his staff. He wondered how she was coping with her husband's shell shock, wondering if he still suffered badly and were they happy.

Sitting back in his chair he contemplated the state of his own marriage and found it wanting. Ann took care of the house, saw to his meals and now that she'd resigned from several charities, was at home more often. This should have pleased him, but most of the time when they were together, he felt her mind was elsewhere. She seemed distant. She answered any questions he put to her, but they didn't sit and chat as most couples did and she never showed him any affection. If they had sex it was as if she tolerated it, never seeming to enjoy it, certainly never instigating it – quite the opposite, often turning away saying she was tired. He'd have had more pleasure in a brothel!

Taking another sip of his drink, he couldn't help feeling bitter. He'd had his chance during the war when he and Helen were lovers. She'd asked him if he would leave his wife for her and he'd remained silent. What a bloody error that had been! She satisfied him in every way. Excellent at her job, a good companion and great in bed. He'd had it all and thrown it away. Then when he'd gone to Cheltenham to tell her he would leave his wife for her . . . it had been too late.

He rose from his chair, took his coat and hat off the stand and left the hospital. Outside it was cold, the sky was clear and no doubt there would be a heavy frost tonight. He wasn't looking forward to Christmas but had invited folk to drop in on Boxing Day for drinks and nibbles from noon until two o'clock. He'd better let Ann know, he'd forgotten to tell her.

When Richard informed his wife of his plans, she was furious.

'How thoughtless of you not to discuss this with me first of all. Now you spring it on me with two weeks' notice.'

'Oh for goodness' sake, Ann, all you have to do is go to Fortnum and Mason's and order what you need there and they'll prepare it for you. All it needs then is collecting the day before.'

'As if I don't have enough to do!' she complained.

'Come now, let's not exaggerate your position. You have a cleaner and someone who does the ironing. All you have to do is give your orders and do a bit of cooking. It's not as if you're overworked. I've never seen any sign of that and certainly not in the bedroom, but I suppose at a push you could pay for someone to do that for you too!'

She was speechless with rage for a moment and then she flew into a temper.

'How dare you speak to me like that? How dare you?'

He just looked disdainfully at her. 'Because it's the truth, that's why! You're not interested in me at all. You have little to say when we're together. It's almost as if you are not in the room, your mind is elsewhere, and as for sex . . . I may as well be mounting the ironing board, except you never touch that either!'

'No doubt your wonderful Helen would have treated you better,' she said spitefully.

'You're probably right. Perhaps I should have married her instead.'

Ann was so angry she threw caution to the wind.

'I'm sure she was a pleasure in bed!'

'Sadly, Ann, I was never in a position to find out – to my regret.' He got up from the table. 'I'm off to my club. At least there I know I'll have a decent conversation with somebody.'

She just sat at the table and watched him leave, then picking up a dinner plate, she hurled it at the door and burst into tears. Tears of anger and tears of frustration. He was right, her marriage was a sham, she was only playing at being his wife. She didn't love him any more . . . how on earth were they to continue to live together?

At his London club, Richard was asking himself the same question. He no longer looked forward to going home as a man should. He could manage without Ann, really. A cook would look after his meals and there was already the cleaner and a woman who could do the washing and the ironing. He could find Ann a small flat, give her an allowance and live the life of a bachelor without too much of a scandal. Then they would both be happier. He would wait until after Christmas, though. With guests arriving on Boxing Day it wouldn't be seemly to do it before, then who need know of the arrangements? Ann wouldn't want it known, he was sure of that. It would interfere with her charity work, and that to her was more important than he was. Yes, that was the answer. After Christmas it would all be sorted. Tonight he'd move into the spare room. It would be a start.

Chapter Twenty-Six

There was a snowfall in Cheltenham just before Christmas, which enhanced the enjoyment of the festivities. James and Helen had moved in to the manor house for two days, which made things easier. Helen was on hand to help her mother-in-law, which was much appreciated, especially as they prepared for the influx of guests on Boxing Day.

The extensive buffet had been laid out in the dining room and trays of glasses ready for the champagne and wine. It certainly looked very festive and the two ladies were wearing new gowns for the occasion. Helen in the latest fashion, a coffee-coloured dress with a dropped waist and handkerchief hemline. Frances, in a long black gown, trimmed with white lace. They both looked a picture of elegance.

The gathering was a merry affair with much laughter and conversation and when the champagne corks were pulled, one or two of the guests cast an anxious glance in James's direction, but he was fine. He'd anticipated the noise and had opened some bottles himself.

But their worried expressions hadn't escaped his notice.

He said nothing but just smiled to himself, delighted that these days he seemed more able to cope.

As the last guests left, Helen went up to her husband and kissed him.

'I was so proud of you today,' she said.

James started to laugh. 'One or two of our guests were worried for a moment when the champagne was opened, did you notice?'

She grinned broadly. 'Indeed I did, I found it very amusing, but you were fine, as I knew you would be. And you coped with so many people in the room. It *was* a bit crowded.'

'I had to prove to them that I was recovered. I'll never forget the last time, when I dived for the floor. I wasn't going to make that mistake again. Grab a coat and let's go and feed the horses, they need a treat too.'

They took a load of carrots and sugar lumps and walked to the stables where they were greeted with neighs and snorts of pleasure. James went over to Cleo and Helen to Miss Milly.

After, they both went over to Gentle Jane, who accepted their offerings willingly, then it was to Genghis, who looked at them with suspicion, pawing at the floor as James talked softly to him. Then the animal wandered over and took the offered carrots.

Helen stood back and watched. She didn't like this animal at all, didn't trust him and made sure she wasn't near him when James saddled him ready to ride. No way would she ever ride him. She felt the horse disliked her as much as she disliked him and she would be happy when he left the stables for a new home.

As they walked back to the house, Helen thought of other Christmases, during the war in the hospital, surrounded by her patients, and wondered how they had fared on their return. The boy with the burnt face, the sergeant who'd lost his leg. She prayed that they had learnt to cope as she had done.

Boxing Day at the Carsons' home had not been such a happy day for Ann. She'd been shocked when Richard had moved into the spare room after their confrontation, although relieved she no longer had to share a bed with him. But what was to happen next?

She wasn't left wondering for long as when all their guests had left Richard poured her a drink and asked her to sit down as he wanted to talk to her.

'First of all, thank you for today, Ann. The buffet was magnificent, but then Fortnum and Mason are always to be relied upon and as always, you were the perfect hostess. However . . .'

She held her breath, wondering what was coming next.

'However, it's perfectly obvious that our marriage no longer works, neither of us is enjoying being together, so I've decided to buy an apartment for you to live in.' Seeing the consternation on her face he added, 'Don't worry, Ann, you will be provided for financially. I will give you a generous monthly allowance and you can live your life and I can live mine.'

She was shocked at first, then she was angry.

'How dare you think you can treat me this way! I will *not* leave my home just because you're feeling put out.'

'It's rather more than that, Ann. I no longer want to share the same space with you, knowing that you're only filling it because we are married, not because it gives you pleasure when quite obviously it does not.'

'You can't do that to me! I'll lose my place in society. I'll be ostracised.'

'Nonsense, who's to know? I certainly will not be making this arrangement public and I'm sure you won't and when you are required to be at my side at some function or another, you will be there. I think it will work for us very well.'

'Do I have *nothing* to say about this arrangement?'

'No. I will start looking for a place as soon as the estate agents open after Christmas. Now, if you'll excuse me, I have some papers to see to in my study.'

She was stunned. This was not at all what she expected. She loved her home. It was elegant, full of beautiful furnishings, her life was organised. The staff did her bidding, the house was cleaned thoroughly and she had her job at the forces charity . . . and she had her position in society. That was the most important of all. But then Richard had said he wouldn't make their arrangement public and she would still be at his side when required, so it would seem to others that things were normal. She then decided to look for a positive side to his plan. He said he would provide for her generously, and she would be free to live her own life, as would he.

She poured another drink and sat contemplating this new life and she started smiling. If she lived alone, she could invite Clive to her apartment. Suddenly new vistas emerged. She'd insist that Richard didn't hold a key to her apartment. If he wanted her to move out, then he wasn't to be in any position to dictate to her. She'd refuse to move unless he agreed. Suddenly, things didn't seem quite so bad. She wouldn't have to see to Richard's needs, only her own. She could hire a cleaner but then, if she were to invite Clive over, it would be best that no one should know and a cleaner may well discover the fact she had a male visitor, and that wouldn't do at all. She'd think about that. A few domestic chores in exchange for a lover was a small price to pay.

Richard didn't waste any time. As soon as the estate agents opened he let several know of his requirements and began his search. At the end of January, he found a place in Chelsea. It was on the first floor, with two bedrooms, a living room, kitchen and bathroom.

'It hasn't a dining room,' he told Ann, 'but then you won't be having visitors to dine or they will discover we have separated and neither of us want that to be known. There's room in the living room for a small table and chairs for you to sit at. I've arranged a viewing tomorrow afternoon at three o'clock. Here's the address. Get a cab and I'll meet you there.'

She was pleased to see that it was a decent address and not in an unacceptable part of the city. After all, she still had her standards. She agreed to meet him.

To her surprise, Ann liked the apartment. It overlooked the Thames, the rooms were of a decent size and she felt she could be happy here. But she didn't show too much enthusiasm. Why should Richard have it easy?

'Yes, well it's not too bad, I suppose,' she said.

'Don't play games with me, Ann. This will be where you live. It's a nice size in a good position and will suit your needs. So let's have no argument about it!'

She saw the stubborn look in his eyes and knew that he wouldn't change his mind.

'There's just one thing that I do insist upon,' she said firmly.

'And what is that, may I ask?'

'If we are to live our separate lives, I want to be the only key holder.'

He thought about this for a moment. 'Very well, but that means you have to return the keys to the house. Then neither of us can encroach upon each other's lives. If I need you, I'll call. I've taken down the number of the telephone. I'll give you a budget to furnish it, but do not go over it! In other words, Harrods is out of the question.'

During the time that the contracts were drawn up, Ann had packed her clothes and personal belongings: one or two of her favourite figurines, some bed linen – there was more than enough for two households in her airing cupboard – a pair of matching bedside lamps and a standard lamp that Richard had never liked. She had taken the measurements of each room and had chosen her furniture, paid for by her husband, which would be delivered to her new abode when the contracts had been exchanged. She should be settled in March, she hoped.

She hadn't told Clive about the new arrangements, gleefully keeping her secret until she'd moved in. Then she intended to surprise him, hoping he'd be as delighted as she was and would be as anxious to take advantage of her new-found freedom. It had been difficult keeping it to herself when they had their weekly luncheon date, but she had planned to the last detail how she would tell him.

Eventually the day arrived for her to move. Richard was at the hospital as usual and a small van arrived in the morning to take her cases and boxes she'd packed; the furniture would be delivered in the afternoon.

Richard had paid extra for the carpets, curtains and the

cooker in the kitchen and so when Ann walked in, the place didn't seem too bare. She waited for the furniture and when it arrived gave her instructions as to where every piece was to be placed. By late afternoon it was done.

She made a cup of tea with the kettle she'd purchased, along with a new tea set and matching dinner plates, and sat in her living room on her new sofa and relaxed. Looking around, she was delighted. She had excellent taste, and although she'd avoided Harrods, she had managed to furnish the apartment to her standard.

Getting up, she walked to the window and enjoyed the view of the Thames and the various vessels sailing up and down, and the pedestrians walking along the pavements and embankment. Yes, this would suit her admirably. She then walked into the master bedroom with its double bed, bedside tables, a chest of drawers in the window with a triple mirror, and gave a satisfied smile.

After the next meeting of the forces charity, she and Clive left together, as usual, and to his surprise, Ann hailed a cab.

'What on earth are you doing?' he asked.

'I'm taking you out to lunch to a different place. I hope you like it as much as I do.'

He was intrigued so said nothing.

The cab stopped in front of the building and they alighted. Clive was even more intrigued as they took the lift to the first floor. He followed her and waited until she opened the door and invited him in.

She'd cleverly placed the small dining table in an alcove in the living room. It was laid out with dinner plates, glasses and pristine napkins.

'What on earth's going on? What is this place?' Clive was now mystified.

'This, my darling Clive, is my new apartment and we are going to dine here.'

'What do you mean, your new apartment?'

'Richard and I have separated, we now live apart, although that isn't public knowledge. I will appear with him as his wife at official functions, so no one will be aware of our arrangement. Look, sit down, and whilst we eat, I'll explain.'

She disappeared into the kitchen and took a beef stew out of the oven and mashed potatoes she'd left to keep warm. Then when they were seated, she told him what had transpired.

Clive listened intently as her tale unfolded. But to her chagrin, he didn't seem very pleased about the arrangement.

'I think that's appalling!' he exclaimed when she'd finished.

This was not the reaction she was expecting.

'What do you mean?'

'He's your husband. He can't toss you out of the house just like that. What sort of a man is he?'

She took exception to his terminology. 'I've hardly been *tossed out* as you put it, Clive! He's bought me this apartment, has given me a generous allowance and my freedom. We were no longer happy together, so what could be better than this? As far as people know, we are together, so there's no scandal. I won't lose my position in society. It couldn't be more perfect.' She leant across the table and pleaded with him. 'Don't you understand? We can be together now, whenever we want.'

'Have you lost your senses? Of course we can't! Just

imagine if we were caught. The fact that you're separated will become common knowledge and your reputation will be in tatters, mine too. Then you will be completely alone. No longer could you appear beside Richard at official functions, because that would make him look a fool and he wouldn't have that.'

To her horror, he rose from his chair. 'We will still be able to dine after the meeting as people are used to seeing us and they also see us leave and go our separate ways, but that's all, Ann. I'm surprised you thought I'd be a part of this. I'm disappointed in you.' He walked out of the room.

Hearing the front door close, she burst into tears. All her carefully laid plans were destroyed. She'd been so happy at the thought of her and Clive being lovers again, was convinced that he too would have been thrilled at the idea. Hadn't he told her how he longed to hold her and make love to her, and now all of a sudden, it would seem, she was no longer desirable. Only now did she realise how lonely her existence was to be. If she went out to tea with some of the ladies in her social circle, she would be unable to invite them back as was the habit among them. They took turns in playing hostess. Now that would be denied her as, having moved out of her house, she'd be unable to take her turn. That would certainly cause them to gossip. Oh, how she wished she'd played her part as Richard's wife more skilfully. But it was too late.

Chapter Twenty-Seven

James was reading *The Telegraph* and saw that eight hundred special constables, known as the Black and Tan, because of their uniforms, had been sent to Ireland and were to be paid ten shillings a day. They were mostly made up of men demobbed from the army. He wondered if any were men that had been in his unit and had survived the war. It appeared only to have heightened the tension in the country, which was already running high. He felt sorry for the men, who he was sure had only joined up out of desperation. He was thankful that he was no longer part of the service, especially now that he was to be a father. Helen had given him the happy news early in the New Year. He'd been delighted, as had both parents. Doctor Coombs had examined her and had confirmed the news.

She had teased James, who had suddenly decided she needed to rest and that riding was now out of the question.

'Darling, I'm not sick, I'm having a baby. I'm healthy and can live a normal life. I'm certainly able to ride for a while, anyway, even if it's a gentle trot.'

He wasn't convinced until he'd called the doctor for confirmation.

'My dear James, your wife's a nurse. She knows what she can and cannot do. Relax and please stop fussing.'

In time he did, but he watched her constantly until she'd had enough and became irritated.

'For goodness' sake, James, will you stop behaving like an old woman! You are making me edgy, watching every move I make, now stop it before I lose my temper.'

He was immediately contrite. 'Sorry, darling. But you must remember I haven't been a father before.'

'And you certainly won't be again if you continue this way.'

He started laughing. 'I do hope you're not threatening to have me gelded, like poor Genghis?' The vet had suggested this may be a way to quieten the animal.

She looked at him slowly as if considering the suggestion.

'I was only joking, darling!' he protested.

'Well bear this in mind,' she teased, 'if you don't stop smothering me, I might have to call the vet myself.'

Approaching fatherhood had given James something to focus on as did the fact that he felt it was time to sell on both his horses. He'd placed an advertisement in *The Horse and Hound* magazine, stipulating that Gentle Jane was a perfect first pony for a child and that Genghis Khan would be good for point-to-point or as a hunter. He was delighted to receive several answers. As one prospective buyer was calling at the weekend, James decided to take out Genghis and put him through his paces.

He first rode him into the practice ring and took him

over a few jumps, then out of the stables to the field and raced him over the adjoining land, jumping hedges, as if he were in a hunt. The horse responded well, and pulling him up, James patted him, pleased with the workout.

'Good boy! You'll do well,' he said, then he returned to the stables.

Helen was there grooming Miss Milly.

'How did he go?' she asked as James dismounted.

'He was superb. Whoever buys him shouldn't have any complaints. Nevertheless, it has to be someone who is competent, because he's so strong, he could be a handful for a novice.'

On the Saturday, James and Helen were at the stables preparing for their visitor. Eventually a tall young man, in his twenties, arrived with his father. James introduced himself and then led Genghis out of the stall. As the men examined the horse, feeling its fetlocks and looking for any weakness, James was relieved. They obviously understood horseflesh.

'He's strong and can be a handful,' James explained. 'I wouldn't sell him to anyone who wasn't an experienced rider.'

The father nodded. 'Quite right too, but have no fear. My son, Toby, has ridden since he was four and is accomplished. He wants a new mount for point-to-point, which he does regularly.'

'I'll saddle him up for you and I'll take my horse and we can ride out together,' said James. 'Then you'll get the feel of him.'

Cleo had already been saddled in preparation and

once Genghis was ready, the men left the stables together.

The father, Percy Grisham, walked with Helen around the other stalls, looking at Miss Milly and Gentle Jane. He loved the piebald and stroked her neck as she nuzzled into him.

'She's got a friendly nature,' he said. 'Do you mind if I go into the stall and take a closer look?'

'Not at all,' said Helen and let him in. She watched as he examined her thoroughly, patting her and talking softly as he worked his way around her. Then he came out and smiled at Helen.

'I don't suppose this beauty is for sale also? Only I have a daughter of twelve who would love her. She has got too big for her Shetland, as you can imagine. This piebald would be just right for her. She has a gentle nature and I can see she is in good shape.'

'As it happens, Mr Grisham, Gentle Jane is for sale and there have been a few enquiries about her. Have a word with my husband when he returns.'

James and his client were now in the practice ring and James watched the young man put Genghis through several jumps and was relieved to see the rider was more than competent to handle the horse, who was jumping well, and eventually they arrived back at the yard where James climbed down and put Cleo in the stall until he'd finished talking.

Young Toby Grisham was very enthusiastic about purchasing Genghis, whose reins he was holding, and then his father approached James about buying Gentle Jane too. A deal was struck and the men shook on it.

'I'll let you unsaddle him and wash him down, if you like,' James suggested.

Toby was delighted. He took the saddle off, and talking to the horse he picked up a bucket of water and poured it over its back. Genghis started prancing and just as Helen walked past, he kicked out with his back legs and sent her flying.

There was a moment of panic as she lay still.

'Put him in his stall,' James called to Toby as he and the father knelt down to see to Helen, who was a bit stunned but awake.

'Are you alright, darling?' James asked anxiously.

'I'm not at all sure,' she murmured.

'Just lie still and don't move,' he told her, then turning to Percy Grisham, said, 'I need to call the doctor, will you stay with my wife?'

'Go, my boy, I'll look after her.' Looking at Helen, he held her hand. 'Now you lie still, there's a good girl.' He took off his coat and covered her.

Doctor Coombs came immediately, leaving others to run the surgery. He gave Helen a cursory examination to judge if she could be moved, then suggested that James and Toby make a chair with their hands and carry her up to one of the bedrooms where he could examine her thoroughly. He sent James out of the room, telling him to wait outside until he'd finished.

Toby was full of apologies but James stopped him.

'It wasn't your fault. The horse was frisky after the exercise then the water. There was nothing you could have done.' But he was deeply concerned because of her pregnancy.

After his examination, the doctor was also concerned. Helen had been kicked in the side and he was sure she'd fractured or broken a couple of ribs, but he was concerned for the baby, as Helen was bruised on one side of her stomach.

'I'm calling an ambulance,' he told her. 'You need your ribs strapped and I want you under observation for the next few days.'

'My baby?' Helen looked worried.

'We'll have to wait and see.' He left the room, called for an ambulance and told James what he'd done.

Percy Grisham suggested that he and his son should leave and for him to let them know when it was convenient to collect their horses.

'There's no rush,' he assured James. 'You need to see to your wife. We are so sorry,' he added. Then they left.

James watched as Helen was taken into the ambulance on a stretcher.

'I'll follow you in the car,' he told her, trying not to show his concern.

At last Helen was put into a side ward and examined by the hospital doctor who sent her to the X-ray department before making any decisions.

'When we get the results, then we can decide what we need to do,' he said.

James accompanied her as she was wheeled there and waited outside until the X-rays had been taken, then returned to the ward where he sat holding her hand. Both were too worried to make conversation.

After what seemed an eternity, the doctor returned.

'You have two broken ribs, Mrs Havers, which we'll bind – so far your baby is fine, but we'll keep you under observation for a few days, to make sure. You just need to be quiet and rest.'

Helen smiled at him. 'I am a theatre sister, Doctor, so there's no need to walk on egg shells around me. I am aware of the dangers to my baby.'

'Well that's a relief,' he said. 'I'll leave you with your husband, then you can tell him what to bring in here for you. Left to themselves, men always get it wrong, I've found.' He chuckled and left them alone.

'Well, this is a strange situation,' James remarked, 'you in the hospital bed and me being the one beside you.'

'I'll be fine,' she said, trying to reassure him, but they both knew that wasn't quite true, not at this moment in time.

'You had better give me a list of what you need,' he said, taking a piece of paper and a pen from his pocket. 'I'll leave you to rest and come back this evening.'

When he arrived back at the cottage, James packed the things on his list then drove to the manor to tell his parents the latest news. They were most anxious as they had been in the house when the accident happened. James at last was able to air his worries in the open.

'God, Mother! It would be terrible if anything happened to the baby.'

'Now stop that, James! Don't for goodness' sake be so negative. Helen is a healthy woman and she's in the best place, so stop it, do you hear?'

He couldn't help but grin at his mother.

'You have just made me feel like a naughty boy.'

She came over to him and held him. 'I can understand

your concerns, darling, but fretting won't help Helen or you. It's a waiting game and we all know about that, no one more so than you. It's your turn to be strong for your wife as she was for you.'

'I know and I will be. How about a cup of tea and a sandwich? I realise in all the excitement I haven't eaten and suddenly I'm starving.'

It was Edward who laughed now. 'Well, that at least is a healthy sign,' he said.

Chapter Twenty-Eight

Ann Carson was not a happy woman. Her carefully laid plan for her apartment to become her love nest was in tatters and now, unable to mix with her lady friends and entertain them in her marital home, she had time on her hands and no company. She began to long for her previous existence: even if it hadn't been a deliriously happy one at least she'd had a life. Now there was nothing. Not even Clive.

At the next charity meeting he'd declined to have lunch with her, saying that under the circumstances he thought it best if they kept their relationship purely on a business footing.

She had been livid!

'How dare you treat me like this? I am not some hussy you can enjoy one moment and drop the next.'

'Precisely, Ann. You are the wife of an eminent man, now living apart, albeit without anyone's knowledge, which in itself is a tenuous situation. No way can you compromise yourself further – and certainly not with me. If you feel you can't manage to do that, I'll understand if you wish to resign from the committee.'

She felt the blood drain from her face. Leave the committee? It was the only thing she had left and now Clive was prepared to take that away too.

'No, there's no need to go that far. You've made your position perfectly clear and I accept it, although, Clive, I do think you have taken advantage of me, but I'll forget about it for the good of the charity.'

He knew her well enough to see how she'd been hurt by his suggestion and he was still very fond of her. She looked so lost and that was a pity.

'My dear Ann, I hate to see you this unhappy. You shouldn't live alone, you need to try and make it up with Richard. You should be there in your rightful place, you know that. You could make it work if you really wanted to.'

She could feel the emotion creeping up inside and her pride wouldn't let Clive see her cry. She walked towards the door.

'I'll see you next week,' she called over her shoulder, blinking back the tears brimming in her eyes.

Clive was right, of course. She should be with Richard. She couldn't live like this, it would drive her mad without a social life. She already felt like an outcast. Not her style at all.

She let herself into her apartment, called the hospital and left a message with Richard's secretary to ask him to call her at his first free moment. She poured herself a gin and tonic and walked to the window and watched the life that was London passing by the Thames.

* * *

It was late afternoon when her telephone rang. She took a deep breath before answering.

'Ann? It's me, I've been in the theatre all day and just received your message, are you alright?'

There was something strangely comforting at the anxious note to his voice.

'I need to see you, Richard. Could we meet for dinner this evening – please?'

'Yes, of course. How about Luigi's, seven-thirty?'

'That'll be fine, thank you, Richard, I'll see you there.' She replaced the receiver with a sigh of relief.

Richard was puzzled as he put down the phone, wondering what Ann wanted. She certainly hadn't sounded herself at all. Perhaps there was something wrong with the apartment? He hoped not, a surveyor had assured him that all was well with the building. Oh well, he'd find out this evening.

Ann was very nervous as she dressed that evening. She'd changed her gown several times before deciding what to wear. Eventually she slipped into a deep-maroon creation that she knew was one of Richard's favourites, over which she wore a long string of pearls he'd bought her some years before and in her hair a small comb edged with pearls to match. Around her shoulders she wore a fur stole to keep out the night air. Twisting to and fro in front of the mirror, she knew she looked elegant, which would also please her husband.

She took a taxi to the restaurant, arriving fifteen minutes late, not wanting to seem too anxious, and was shown to the table by the waiter.

Richard stood up and kissed her on the cheek. 'Ann,

you look lovely. What would you like to drink whilst we order – an aperitif?'

'Thank you, that would be fine.' She smiled at him. 'You're looking well.'

'Oh, I'm fine, keeping busy, you know how it is, and what about you, my dear?'

She tried to keep her voice light. 'Well, Richard, I'm not busy and that's not like me at all.'

He looked puzzled. 'I don't understand. When we were living together you were hardly at home, as I recall.'

'But that was then. To keep our separation a secret, I've been unable to meet my friends because I would be unable to invite them back to the house, as was usual. You know how we would take turns every month. It would seem strange to meet them and then not take my turn. You see what a problem that is? It's like being a leper without the disease.'

He hid a smile at her terminology. Ann without her social life would indeed be a problem for her. He did have some sympathy, he at least could go to his club for company without any strings attached.

'Oh dear, I can see how difficult this must be for you.'

'That's why I asked to see you. I can't go on like this, Richard, I just can't!'

'Then what do you suggest?'

She hesitated for just a second. 'That I move back in to the house and we resume our normal life once again.' She held her breath.

The waiter came and took their order and all the time Ann was mentally screaming, go away and take the bloody order later! But she remained calm and gave him her choice, then looked at Richard – and waited.

He was deep in thought. Although things hadn't been right with Ann over the last couple of months before she left, he had missed her. It was never nice to walk into an empty home, however comfortable it was, but things would have to change if it was to work for him and he said as much.

'I'm sorry you're not happy, Ann, that wasn't my intention when I bought the apartment, but if we are to live together again, things would have to change.'

'Like what, for instance?'

'You popping off for meetings for a few days.'

'Oh, that won't be happening again, I can assure you, and indeed I was thinking of resigning in the future.'

'I would like you to be at home at dinner time. A man needs company and comfort at home with his wife after a long day. He doesn't want to have to put a meal in the oven to warm up and then to eat alone.'

'Yes, I understand.'

Richard became watchful. What on earth had brought about this great change, he wondered? Ann was only too anxious to agree to his every suggestion.

'What about the apartment? I invested a lot of money in it for you to live in.'

'Well, Richard, that was entirely your idea, not mine!'

He had to smile. She hadn't lost all her spirit, thank heavens, and she did look very attractive this evening. He hadn't enjoyed being celibate much, either.

'I suppose I could rent it out or sell it on. But there's no rush. I can decide later.'

She tried not to look too eager. 'Does that mean you'll agree to my coming home?' she asked casually.

'We can but try, Ann, and see how it goes. After all, there is still the apartment if it doesn't work out.'

You bastard, she thought. You're holding that over my head as a threat, but she smiled.

'I'll move back in tomorrow if you give me the spare key.'

He took it off his key ring and handed it to her. 'Welcome home, my dear.'

Chapter Twenty-Nine

It was deemed safe for Helen to return home after four days in the hospital, to everyone's relief, but she'd been told not to pick up anything heavy or to ride, other than that to continue her life as normal, with her own GP keeping an eye on her.

During her time in hospital, Percy Grisham had collected the horses as James had wanted Genghis gone by the time Helen came home, knowing she'd be nervous if he was still in the stables and he didn't want anything to upset her. He also thanked the man, who had sent flowers to the hospital.

'It was the least I could do,' he said. 'Give my regards to your wife and take care of the baby when it arrives.'

Once Helen was back and settled at the cottage, James suggested they go for a drive and look at the blossom trail in the Vale of Evesham. It was mid May and the trees would be at their best.

'We could stop and have a lunch somewhere,' he said.

After being stuck in a hospital ward, Helen was delighted with the idea.

* * *

The trail was several miles of apple orchards with the trees full of blossom; it was a beautiful sight as they drove slowly through and eventually stopped at a local pub for lunch.

As they waited to be served, James looked at Helen and said, 'You have no idea how scared I was that day in the stables. I thought I was going to have a coronary when I saw you on the ground. Don't you ever do that to me again!'

Raising her eyebrows she said, 'Now you have some idea how I felt the day they wheeled you into the surgery in France.'

'Mmm. You have a point. Well, darling, I think now's the time to seriously look for a permanent home as we are to be a family. The cottage was fine for us, but I'd like to see us settled before the baby's born and I want to buy more horses, set up a proper business.'

She was delighted with the idea. James had found his niche. He was at ease with his animals, at home in the stables. He still suffered with claustrophobia, but most times he coped and when it was too much, he had the sense to say so and it had been some time since he'd had a nightmare. The future was looking bright and often she'd mentally thank Arthur Hurst and the treatment James had received in Devon.

The search for a home was over. There was an old farmhouse at the foot of Bredon Hill, which suited them very well. The interior was in good decorative order, which meant they could move in immediately. James planned to have stables built in what used to be the old cowsheds, so he wouldn't have to use those at the manor house. There was some land that went with the property that was ideal for setting out practice jumps. There was also a small orchard with apples, pears and plums growing. It was ideal.

By the time the contracts had been exchanged and they moved in, it was July and Helen was heavy with child, with another month to go before it was due. James was concerned that the move would be too much for her, but Helen assured him she was fine. They had people in to do any heavy moving and before long they were settled, with builders outside working on the stables, and the weather was getting warmer by the day.

Helen stood in the kitchen and, leaning over the sink, she ran the cold tap and cupped her hands to fill them with cold water, which she splashed on her face to try to cool down. She soaked a glass cloth and, sitting in a chair, put it round her neck, undoing the buttons of her blouse. Closing her eyes, she sat still, breathing steadily. She needed to lie down but couldn't face the stairs, so she heaved herself to her feet and went into the drawing room and lay on the large sofa, closed her eyes and fell asleep. It was here that James found her an hour later.

'Helen,' he called softly.

She stirred in her sleep and gradually opened her eyes.

'Helen, darling, are you alright?'

'I was so hot,' she said. 'I felt tired and couldn't do the stairs and came in here. Would you get me a glass of water please?'

He rushed off to do so and returned to help her sit up and drink.

'Shall I call Doctor Coombs?' he asked.

'No, no, I'm fine. It's just the heat, but if you help me upstairs, I'll get undressed and lie on the bed.'

Eventually, she looked more comfortable. James helped

her into a cool nightgown, opened the windows to let in a slight breeze and sat on the bed beside her. He bathed her face with a cold flannel until she felt better.

'Can I get you something to eat?' he asked.

'No, I just need to be quiet,' she assured him. 'You carry on with whatever you're doing, I'll be fine.'

Reluctantly he left her, but went straight to the telephone to call the doctor. He explained what had happened.

'It's probably the heat, James, but let me know if anything changes,' the doctor told him. 'Try not to worry, I'm sure she's fine – after all, she's almost due and that's tiring. Keep me informed.'

Still feeling concerned, James rang his mother-in-law and told her he was worried and she agreed to come over for a couple of days to look after Helen.

Helen, though surprised, was delighted to see her mother when she walked into the bedroom.

'James panicked,' she laughed. 'I was just overcome with the heat.'

'You must remember that this is his first child, this is all new to him. He'll get used to it. Nevertheless, I'm delighted to be here. It makes a nice change and I can see what work is being done.' She wandered over to the window and looked out over the fields.

'This really is a lovely place, Helen. You did well to buy it.' She walked back and sat on the bed. 'How is James these days?'

'Busy, happy and keeping fit. He has the odd hiccup, but on the whole, he's fine.'

'I'm so happy to hear that. To be honest, although I love my son-in-law, it did worry me that you might have taken on more than you could cope with at the time. He's come a long way and I couldn't be happier for you both.'

Helen soon recovered, to James's relief, and Margaret returned home but not before saying she would come again if needed.

Three weeks later, Helen felt the start of her labour pains as she lay beside her husband. Looking at the clock she saw it was five o'clock in the morning. Climbing out of bed quietly, she opened the curtains and watched the dawn break. There was no need to disturb James as yet. He'd been working so hard and was in need of his sleep, she thought. She would go down to the kitchen and make a cup of tea.

As she poured her first cup, she was struck by a vicious pain that caught her unawares and she dropped the teapot, which clattered to the tiles on the kitchen floor and smashed, spilling hot tea over her leg. She screamed with pain.

James came rushing down the stairs to find her doubled up. He saw the broken pot and the red mark on her leg. Realising what had happened he soaked a cloth in cold water and applied it to her leg, then rang for an ambulance.

Holding her close, he talked softly to calm her.

'I'm in labour,' she told him as another pain gripped her.

'Don't worry, darling. The ambulance will soon be here and we'll soon have you in good hands.'

It was a long labour and, as every hour passed, James became more concerned. Margaret, who had been summoned to the hospital, tried to comfort him.

'Babies cannot be rushed, my dear,' she told him, 'they come when they're ready and not before.'

But as time went on, the doctors became worried that the baby was suffering and they worked hard with Helen, helping her and urging her to push, although knowing she was exhausted, worried that delay was dangerous to both mother and child.

At long last she managed to give birth, but the cord was round the baby's neck, stopping it breathing. The doctor immediately unwound the cord, slapping the baby until to everyone's relief it breathed and let out a cry.

Outside in the corridor, James was beside himself with worry. He and Margaret walked up and down, sitting then standing, not knowing what to do. Each silently praying, neither speaking their innermost fears, lest they came to pass.

Eventually, the doctor came out to speak to them. 'Congratulations, Mr Havers, you have a daughter.'

'My wife?'

'It's been a bit of a struggle but we got there in the end.'

'What do you mean exactly? What's wrong?'

'Your wife is very weak after such a long labour. She will need time to recover. She also has a nasty burn, which is painful, but we'll take care of that. Now, I'll let you see her but only for a few minutes, she needs to rest.'

His face drained of colour, James went into the room and looked at his wife, laying back on her pillow. She had dark circles under her eyes and was even paler than he was. He had never been more scared in his life as he took her hand.

'Helen? Darling, I'm so sorry to put you through this.' His voice caught in his throat.

'Don't be silly. This wasn't your doing, the baby was in trouble, but darling, we have a daughter.'

A nurse came over and showed him a small bundle wrapped in a blanket.

James stared at the small face and tears welled in his eyes. He looked over at Helen.

'She's beautiful, just like her mother.'

Helen gave a wan smile. 'I feel far from beautiful at the moment, I'm so very tired.'

The doctor quietly told James it was time to leave and so he leant over and kissed his wife.

'I'll come back tomorrow, darling. I love you.'

Outside in the corridor, he wept.

Margaret held him and tried to comfort him.

'If I lost her, I don't know what I'd do,' he said.

'But she's going to be alright, James. She's just weak, but thankfully everything is fine and you have a daughter!'

He smiled amid his tears. 'She's so beautiful, Margaret. You wait until you see her, but I can't see us having another, I couldn't put Helen through that again.'

'Oh, James, many people have said that and have gone on to have more. Time will take care of that. Come on, let's go home. Tomorrow you'll feel better and so will Helen.'

Two weeks later mother and daughter were allowed home. James had filled the house with flowers and Margaret had been baking. James had finished the nursery, ready for his daughter, Rebecca. Everything was ready for their return.

James collected his family from the hospital and drove home carefully. Then with great pride, carried his baby into the house where Margaret was waiting, kettle boiling, cups and saucers laid out on a tray.

Helen kissed her mother. 'It's so lovely to be home, Mum.'

'Now, you sit down, darling, and have a cup of tea and make yourself comfortable. Then you can do what you like, but it will give you time to unwind. Leaving hospital is always unsettling, I found.'

Helen gazed at all the flowers and grinned at her husband.

'The flowers are lovely, James. A few more and it would be like a funeral parlour!'

He looked horrified. 'Oh my God! That's the last thing I wanted.'

'I'm only joking, darling, but I have to say the florist shop must be pretty empty.'

Still holding the baby, he came and sat beside her.

'I just wanted to show you how much you'd been missed.' Leaning forward he kissed her. 'Welcome home, darling.' Then looking down at the baby he said, 'And that goes for you too, young lady.'

Margaret disappeared into the kitchen to give them some privacy.

'Now, Helen, you need time to recover so I've a lady to come in to do the cleaning and Margaret is in the spare bedroom and will be here to give you some moral support. I've been told all new mothers want their own mothers nearby with a first baby. Is that alright, darling?'

Seeing his worried frown, Helen hastened to assure him.

'That sounds marvellous,' she said. 'You have been really thoughtful and I do appreciate it. Now, please relax and have some tea.'

The following weeks seemed to fly past. The baby, Rebecca, thrived, Helen was restored to health, apart from a nasty scar on her leg from the burn, and James was busy breaking in his latest horses. As September passed, the trees shed their leaves and the first frosts of winter made their appearance.

Helen hadn't been riding, she'd been too busy being a new mother, but she had taken Rebecca into the stables with her one day and she and James introduced her to Cleo, who didn't seem particularly interested.

'She's just jealous,' James declared. 'Now I have two women other than her and she's put out, aren't you, my beauty?' he said and made to rub her nose. To their great amusement, she flicked her head away.

'There! What did I tell you?'

'If she had two legs instead of four, I'd be really worried,' Helen teased, 'but I can hardly accuse you of being unfaithful with a horse!'

Putting an arm around her he said, 'I would never be unfaithful to you, my darling. Why on earth would I?' He looked across at Cleo. 'You might as well get used to the idea that you are no longer top of my list, girl!'

As they walked away, Cleo whinnied and snorted loudly, as if in protest. They left the stables laughing at her performance.

Chapter Thirty

This year, Christmas was spent at the farmhouse. Both sets of parents drove over on Christmas morning in time to go to church whilst the turkey was cooking. It was a bright if cold day and snow had been forecast for Boxing Day. Larders were stocked for the holiday and knowing how heavy the snow could fall in the area, everyone was prepared.

Rebecca was far too young to understand what Christmas was all about but the rest of the family rejoiced in opening gifts after lunch, drinking champagne and collapsing on the settees and chairs in time for the King's speech.

As they listened, James looked around the room at his nearest and dearest, silently thanking God for seeing him through the war, for meeting the amazing woman who was his wife and mother to his child. Thankful that apart from the odd moment he seemed now able to lead a relatively normal life. Thankful that Helen had stood by him and hadn't walked away and left him when he'd thought he couldn't ask her to share his life, carrying such baggage after the war. His business was slowly becoming established and he was a happy man, unlike many who had returned and were standing on street corners selling matches to make a living.

The following week, Helen was reading *The Telegraph* and saw that in the honours list Richard had been knighted for his services during the war and his contribution in the medical field. She was delighted for him, it was well deserved, but she couldn't help but think his wife would now be insufferable!

Ann Carson was beside herself with glee. Lady Carson! It did have a certain ring about it, she thought. She couldn't wait to go to Buckingham Palace with Richard and see him kneel before the King. She would buy a new fur coat and hat for the occasion, after all she had to live up to her title also. She couldn't wait until her first meeting with the other wives, when she would swan into the restaurant to meet them as Lady Carson. She would insist on buying champagne to celebrate, making sure they marked the occasion.

Richard was delighted to be recognised for his work but he knew without his team, especially Helen, working with him, he could never have achieved his aims and was more than a little irritated by his wife's high-and-mighty attitude.

'Don't let this go to your head, Ann,' he said over dinner when she was crowing about being a lady. 'It is me that is being knighted for my work, not you! If I find you using your title inappropriately, I will be more than displeased and I will not tolerate it. Do I make myself clear?'

She sat up straight in her chair and glared at him. 'I think I earned my title too, Richard – after all, I married you, looked after you during your early years. Surely I earned some recognition?'

'You seem to have forgotten that we parted for a while, Ann. That in fact our marriage was all but over. If you hadn't realised you couldn't survive in society without me, you wouldn't be here now, so less of the good wife. Just be thankful that I took you back into the home! If anyone deserves your title, it's all of my team who worked with me in the field and here in London.'

'Like the sainted Helen, I suppose!'

'Indeed, she of all people. She worked with me under gunfire when sometimes we had to run for our lives, and in the operating theatre she is worthy of her own medal, to my mind.'

Ann lifted her glass and said spitefully, 'Well sadly it's me that has the title, not her. What a great shame!' She took a sip of wine with a smug grin.

He gave her a withering look. 'What a bitch you really are! But be very careful, my dear. I still have the keys to the flat in Chelsea, so behave before you find yourself back there.' He rose from the table, donned his coat and walked out of the house.

Taking another sip of wine, Ann was unconcerned. It was an idle threat on her husband's part. About to be knighted, there was no way he could send her packing, it would cause too much of a scandal. No, she was safe for some time to come and no one, not even Richard, was going to spoil her elevated position.

The great day arrived. A chauffeur drove them to the palace in a Rolls Royce hired for the occasion. Richard, resplendent in top hat and tails, Ann in a mink coat and hat, driving down the Mall looking out of the window of the car. It was all she could do to stop herself giving the royal wave to the pedestrians.

She sat and watched her husband kneel to receive the sword on his shoulders and his knighthood, pass a few words with King George V, step back and walk away.

Outside, the photographers took their picture with Richard holding his medal as she beamed at them, smiled lovingly up at her husband and kept saying in her mind . . . Lady Carson . . . Lady Carson.

They were then driven to the Savoy for a celebration lunch, with some of Richard's associates from the hospital. It was a happy occasion made perfect for her the first time she was addressed as Lady Carson. The only thing that spoilt her day was when they returned home and Richard received a telegram, which read *Congratulations on your very well-deserved knighthood. Helen and James.* But she wisely didn't comment.

Three days later, Ann walked out of a shop in Knightsbridge and stopped to gaze into the window when behind her she heard a familiar voice.

'Good afternoon, Ann, or should I say Lady Carson?'

Her heart seemed to miss a beat as she turned to face Clive Bradshaw. All her pomposity melted away as she gazed at the man who in the past had been her lover for two wonderful nights.

'Clive!'

'How are you, my dear? I was delighted to see your husband knighted in the honours list. That must have made you very proud.'

'Thank you, Clive. It did. It was richly deserved. How

264

are you keeping and how is the charity going – well?'

'Thank you, I'm fine. As for the charity, we do miss you. For me it hasn't been the same without you. I was sorry that you felt you had to leave.'

'At the time, Clive, you gave me little choice, as I recall!'

'And I have lived to regret it, I have to say.'

'Really?' Her voice softened.

'Yes, really. Look, can't we go and have some tea somewhere and catch up with each other's news?'

'I'd like that,' she said, 'it's been ages since we've seen one another.'

They settled in a nearby cafe, ordering tea and cakes. Clive brought her up to date with the charity business, then he asked, 'How is life with you these days? Are you happy?'

She thought for a moment. 'I suppose so. Richard and I chug along. As long as he has all the comforts of home, meals on the table, etcetera, all is well in his world. He's busy at the hospital, of course. Nothing much has really changed.'

'Oh, come now, Ann. Being a lady must have some kudos for you?'

She couldn't help but preen for a moment.

'Well, yes of course. I am given a table in restaurants very quickly, when I ring to book theatre tickets, I get great service.' She gave a chuckle of delight. 'I love it!'

Knowing her as well as he did, Clive added, 'Your social standing with the other wives too, no doubt, has elevated you?'

She looked at him with twinkling eyes. 'Some of them are really jealous. They try not to show it but I know they are. It's very satisfying. Isn't that naughty of me?'

Clive started laughing. 'Oh, my dear, you haven't

changed at all. It was that streak of wickedness that I loved about you.'

She gazed across the table at him and softly said, 'I've really missed you, Clive. Apart from our wonderful time in Birmingham, I missed those weekly luncheon dates we used to enjoy.'

'So have I, Ann. So have I.'

'Is there any real reason stopping us from meeting weekly again, just to sit and chat? I can't see the harm, can you? I know you were shocked when I was living apart from Richard when I hoped we could have been closer, but having lunch isn't doing anyone any harm, is it?'

He saw the vulnerability in her eyes and recognised the fact that beneath her bluster, she really wasn't truly happy and he felt sorry for her. He also still had strong feelings for this woman, even knowing her faults – and he was lonely.

'No, I can't see any harm in our meeting at all. It will do us both good.'

They made an appointment for the following week and as they left, he kissed her on the cheek.

'I'm so pleased we met today, Ann, and I look forward to our lunch date.'

Ann watched him walk away, filled with excitement and delight at the outcome. She wouldn't mention this to Richard, he'd only grumble at her having any tenuous link that might lead her back to working for a charity again. Besides, this was her secret, which made it feel somewhat naughty, and she liked that.

Chapter Thirty-One

The spring arrived all too soon it seemed to Helen. Almost before she realised it, Christmas and New Year had flown by and here was April! What happened to the months in between? She sat drinking a cup of tea in her kitchen after she settled Rebecca outside in her pram for a nap. Her baby was now nine months old and gorgeous, James was busy and at the moment keeping well, breaking in new horses, and he now had Mick, a young man helping him, but Helen was restless. It wasn't that she didn't have enough to fill her day, what with the baby, the house and helping James with his bookings when necessary, which wasn't that often; once he'd started training his horses, it took time before they were ready to sell on and it was this fallow time that Helen hated. Despite the fact that when she married James she'd been happy to give up her nursing, now she found she was missing it. She realised she had needed a break after her war years to recuperate mentally from the stresses and strains she'd encountered, but now she desperately needed more. She didn't tell James of her restlessness, she knew he wouldn't have understood, but Margaret, her mother, sensed the inner turmoil of her daughter, and that afternoon she called in to see Helen.

Walking into the kitchen carrying some home-made cake, she poured herself a cup of tea and sat down.

'How are you, darling? Rebecca is asleep, by the way. I peeped into the pram on my way in. Are you alright?'

'I'm fine . . . well actually I'm not, to be honest. It's odd, Mum, but I really miss nursing, something I never thought I'd say.'

'Why are you surprised? It has been your adult life and you were good at it. You're bound to miss it, especially now you are settled. So what are you going to do about it?'

'What can I do? I have a baby and a husband to look after.'

'That doesn't mean you can't find a way to satisfy your frustration. Why not apply for part-time work in the local hospital?'

'How on earth can I do that?'

'I could come and look after Rebecca a few days a week. I'd love it, and you could work so you'd feel happier. Have a word with Doctor Coombs, he would know if there was an opening, he goes to the hospital often.'

Helen looked thoughtful. 'I'm not at all sure if James would be happy about that.'

'Then ask him, for goodness' sake, instead of mooning about!'

Helen started laughing. 'Oh dear, was it that obvious?'

'Only to me. You know men, they haven't any idea how a woman's brain works.'

Helen hugged her mother. 'What would I do without you?'

'One day your daughter will say the same to you,

darling. It goes with the territory. Think about it.'

When she was alone, Helen couldn't get the idea of working out of her mind. With Margaret looking after Rebecca, she'd have no concerns leaving her for a few hours and it would make her feel useful again. She rang Doctor Coombs first to see what he thought.

'My dear Helen, I think it's an excellent idea. I do know a couple of the surgeons at the hospital, would you like me to sound them out for you?'

She took a deep breath before answering. 'Yes I would, but don't do more than that. If there is an opening I'd have to run it past James first.'

'Understood. I'll get back to you in a couple of days.'

A few days later, Helen received a call from the doctor with some good news.

'I've spoken to my surgeon friends at the hospital and they were very interested in your working a few days a week. They always need someone of your calibre to join their staff. Here is a number to call if you decide to go ahead. It'll be good for you, Helen. You shouldn't waste your skills when it could help others, that's why we enter the medical field, after all.'

She took down the number and thanked him. Now she'd have to tell James and she wasn't sure how he'd react. She would wait until they sat down to dinner tonight after the baby was in bed and they wouldn't be disturbed.

As usual, James had a bath before eating, then sat at the table telling Helen about his day, full of enthusiasm about the animals he was training. She listened, waiting for an opportunity to tell him of her news. Eventually he asked her how her day had been.

'I've had a really interesting day, as it happens,' she began. 'I have an opportunity to work part-time at Cheltenham's main hospital.'

'What?' James looked at her, a deep frown creasing his forehead. 'What are you talking about? You have a young baby to take care of.'

'Yes, James, of course I am aware of that, but Mum said she'd come and look after Rebecca when I would be at work, so there isn't a problem.'

'Oh, I do believe there is indeed a problem. The house, the baby and me, we're not enough for you? I thought you were content with your life.'

She knew this was going to be difficult. 'Darling, don't misunderstand my motives. I love all of that, but I need more, James. I need to work, to use my skills and not let them go to waste. I need that mental stimulation. What we have is wonderful, but it isn't enough. I feel stagnant.'

'Are you telling me getting married was a mistake, is that it?'

'Don't be ridiculous! Just try and remember back when you didn't know how you were going to work, because of your illness. How frustrating that was until you discovered you were happy breaking horses – and the thrill that gave you. I love you and the baby, our life together, but can't you understand? I need more to feel fulfilled.'

'Then I've failed you. I thought I made you happy.'

'Oh, for heaven's sake, no you haven't failed me in any way. You do make me happy – I *am* happy – I just need to work a few days to make my life complete. That isn't too much to ask, is it?'

'No, I suppose not, if that is what it takes. You don't need me to tell you how good you are at your old job: after all, where would I be today without your care? So why should I deny others from benefitting too? If it's that important to you, go ahead.'

Helen could see that her husband wasn't happy and that he had no understanding of her needs, but she'd made up her mind now and nothing was going to change it.

'I'll call the hospital in the morning, then,' she said. But the air was full of tension during the rest of the evening.

The next morning, she rang the hospital and made an appointment to talk to one of the surgeons later in the week. She then called her mother who would come over to be with the baby. Helen could hardly contain her excitement, but when she told James, she was very matter of fact, knowing he wasn't best pleased with her plan.

'On Thursday I have an appointment at the hospital, James. Just a chat to see if they can come up with an offer of work that would suit.'

He was very non-committal. 'Fine, if that's what you really want,' was all he said.

Paul Henderson, one of the hospital surgeons, sat behind the desk in his office talking to Helen. He asked her about her time spent in the field during the war and was impressed when he heard she had worked with Richard Carson.

'Sir Richard is one of our best surgeons,' he said, 'that must have been an experience.'

She agreed. 'He taught me a great deal during the year we were together, and now I want to return to medicine. I do miss that side of my life. Of course, it would have to be part time as I am married and have a baby.' She explained that her mother would be looking after Rebecca, which would allow her the time to work.

'That all sounds satisfactory,' he said. 'Can you manage three days? Wednesday through to Friday? You would be working with whichever surgeon is on duty on those days.'

Helen was delighted. 'Yes, that would be just fine, and thank you for the opportunity. It will be great to be back at work again.'

But on the way home, pleased as she was at the outcome, she wondered how James would react to her news.

James, still unable to understand why his wife wasn't content with her life, was out riding Cleo, trying to come to terms with her decision, which had shaken the confidence he had about the state of his marriage. He thought they had everything they needed as a family now they had a child. For him, his life was ideal. He was working with horses and doing well. They had a lovely home, a baby, why wasn't that enough for his wife? Was he lacking as a husband, was that it? Did he disappoint her? If so, how, he wondered? It was beyond his comprehension. He rode back to the stables, completely mystified.

When Helen returned home, she immediately told her mother the news and they arranged the time for Margaret to arrive the following week. She couldn't keep the delight she felt to herself.

'I'll have to get my uniforms unpacked and washed, ready for Wednesday. It'll feel a bit strange for a while, but Mum, I am so excited!'

'It'll do you good, Helen. Men have no idea how mundane a housewife's life can feel if you have been out in the world as you have. Let's face it, darling, how many women have had the chance to get away and lead such a life? Not many. Of course you want more. I understand, but does James?'

'No, he can't. He thinks he's failed as a husband and that's not the case at all.'

'Just give it time, he'll get used to the idea when he sees you are happier working.'

But when Helen told him she would be starting work the next week, he was taken aback.

'So soon? I thought you meant sometime in the future.'

'I didn't know when, darling, but it seems they would like me to start next week and I can't see any reason not to.' She gazed at him, willing him to understand.

'Be happy for me, James. It's what I need. I love my life with you and Rebecca. You have your work which fulfils *your* needs and this will do the same for me. It doesn't mean that I'm not happy being a wife and a mother. I just need to be *me* as well. I am a person in my own right, after all.'

A glimmer of understanding began to show in his face. 'Of course you are. I'm sorry if I seemed pig-headed. I forgot the woman I first met. The dedicated nurse, the horrors you had to live through, the war and how you gave up nursing to be my wife and now a mother. I just took it all for granted, I suppose. With me being as happy as Larry with my world, I totally forgot our past lives.' He took her into his arms. 'If that's what it takes to make my wife happy, then of course you must go.'

She kissed him soundly. 'Thank you, darling. You see, you won't regret it, we'll both feel fulfilled and what could be more perfect?'

'Just make sure those surgeons know you're married and spoken for, that's all,' he teased. 'Those eyes behind a mask can be damned attractive, as I recall!'

Helen breathed a sigh of relief. She'd managed to make him understand, at last. She couldn't have him in doubt about their marriage, which could have brought on a bout of depression and that definitely would have put an end to any hopes she might have had of working.

Chapter Thirty-Two

Helen soon settled into her routine at the hospital and was happy. She enjoyed the camaraderie, it took her back to earlier days in the theatre. Here the surgeons were appreciative of her skills and she was popular with the rest of the nurses. It lifted her spirits, which was now obvious to her husband.

James could see the difference in Helen after the first couple of weeks. She was excited about her work, of being useful, and once at home, she was happier around the house. He found her singing in the kitchen one morning, and walking up behind her, slipped his arms around her waist and kissed the nape of her neck.

'You sound happy,' he said. 'How about a quick cup of tea for a working man?'

'Only if you take off those dirty shoes, James. You're walking mud all over the kitchen.'

'Oops, sorry.'

They sat at the kitchen table together and she began telling him about her work. He saw how animated she was and was pleased for her. Helen was happy, which made him happy.

Margaret was a blessing and so good with Rebecca, it seemed as if the household had settled. He realised at last that his only fault had been to take his wife's happiness for granted, but now, all was well with them, which was a great relief.

Ann Carson was not a happy woman. Her week seemed to be all about her luncheon with Clive Bradshaw; the days between seemed to get longer and longer and she was frustrated. Her frustration stemmed from Clive himself. Being the gentleman that he was, he made sure that they remained just on friendly terms and Ann longed for more. She wanted to be held in his arms once again, to enjoy the intimate moments they had shared at the hotel in Birmingham. He had told her that he was in love with her in the past but now she wondered if those feelings had died during the time they had been apart. If they had, then nothing would change and she couldn't go on as they were, but . . . if he still felt the same, how different it could be. She had to find out today when she met him, she decided. After all, it was her birthday and he was taking her to the Savoy for lunch to mark the occasion.

It was with both excitement and some trepidation that Ann made her way to the hotel and she was relieved as she stepped out of the taxi to see Clive waiting for her. He stepped forward and paid the driver, then ushered her into the dining room where the waiter led them to a table by the window.

They had an aperitif and ordered from the menu. Just then a pageboy came over to the table carrying a bouquet of flowers and a small package. He handed them to Ann with a smile and walked away.

'Happy birthday, my dear Ann,' said Clive.

She was delighted. 'Oh, Clive, how very romantic. Thank you so much. May I open the package?'

'Of course, I can see you can hardly contain your curiosity,' he said with a chuckle. 'You're like a small child.'

Inside the gift wrapping was a bottle of L'Heure Bleue perfume by Guerlain. She was thrilled.

'This is one of my favourite perfumes.'

'I remember,' he said. 'You wore it when we went to Birmingham for the AGM. I saw the bottle on your dressing table.'

She gazed up at him, eyes shining. He *did* remember. Her spirits soared, but she didn't say a word. She had to be careful not to rush things. She could play the waiting game if the end result was to be what she desired . . . but a little word couldn't do too much harm.

'Those days were very special to me, Clive.'

He just smiled but said nothing more and they sat through three delicious courses, drinking champagne. Ann hadn't felt this happy in a very long time.

At the end of the meal, they decided to go for a walk in nearby Green Park. Despite drinking coffee at the end of the meal, Ann was feeling a little tipsy after the champagne and she held on to Clive's arm as they walked until, eventually, they sat on a bench beneath a wild cherry tree that was now in blossom.

'Oh, Clive, this is the best birthday ever!' she exclaimed and leaning forward, she kissed him on the mouth.

Taken by surprise, he kissed her back, then realising what he was doing, he stopped. 'I'm so sorry, Ann, I shouldn't have done that.'

She took hold of the front of his jacket and pulled him closer.

'But I'm so very pleased that you did,' she kissed him again and this time he didn't pull away.

'Do you still love me, Clive?' she asked softly when he eventually let her go.

He hesitated, but she saw the look of affection he couldn't disguise.

'We shouldn't be having this conversation, Ann. You know that.'

'How can we not? When two people feel as we do, why on earth shouldn't we talk about it? That's not normal.'

'But you know nothing can come of it,' he said. 'You're married.'

'To a man who's married to his career; I certainly don't feel he's married to me!'

'That is so sad to hear. You are a vibrant woman, crying out to be loved. It makes me so angry to see such a wasted relationship.'

'How can you say that? When I had my flat in Chelsea, you were appalled when I suggested we could become close again?'

'I'm sorry, my dear, but somehow the arrangement seemed so sordid and cheap. It didn't feel right under those circumstances, somehow.'

'But you make me happy, dear Clive. With *you* I feel loved. Why on earth must we waste such feelings when together, for however brief a time, we could be deliriously happy?'

'What you are suggesting is dangerous, you know that.'

She was now beyond being careful. She held his hands tightly.

'I'm in love with you, Clive, and if I'm honest, I have been for a very long time. I'm sorry if this isn't what you want to hear, but it's the truth and I can't hide it any longer.'

'Oh, Ann – what a predicament. What are we to do?'

She threw caution to the winds. 'Let's have an affair!'

To her surprise, he burst out laughing. 'You are outrageous!'

Now she too was laughing. 'But just think how much fun we could have. I'm so lonely . . . aren't you lonely, Clive?'

'Yes, yes I am.' He stared hard at her for a moment, then he said, 'Are you really willing to risk everything to be with me?'

She threw her arms above her head. 'Everything!'

'Are you certain it isn't the champagne talking?'

'Absolutely certain. At the risk of sounding like a loose woman, I want you so much, you can't imagine how I feel.'

'You make it very hard for me to refuse.' He hesitated, then he said, 'Very well, but we will have to take the greatest care not to be discovered.'

These were the nicest words anyone had said to her and she beamed at him.

'Oh, darling, I can be very devious when necessary!'

Chapter Thirty-Three

James Havers was a worried man. His beloved Cleo wasn't well. Instead of being her normal playful self, she seemed distracted and vaguely uncomfortable and when James checked and found a reduced amount of faeces in the stall, he was concerned that Cleo was suffering with colic and immediately called the vet, who told James to walk her round until he arrived. As he did so, his heart was beating that little bit faster and he fought to stop the feeling of panic building inside.

'Come on, Cleo,' he murmured as he led her round the stable yard. 'Don't do this to me. You cannot be sick, I won't allow it!' But deep down he was scared. Colic could be dangerous.

It wasn't long before Brian Dickinson, the vet, drove into the yard. Cleo was returned to her stall where the vet examined her. He checked her heart rate, her temperature and then felt the muscles on her rump and frowned when he felt how tight they were, and he was worried that the animal might have excessive fluid in her stomach.

James found he could hardly breathe as he waited.

'We need to get her to my place,' said Brian. 'I need to take an X-ray before I make a decision, so let's get her into the horsebox now.'

In Cheltenham, Helen had finished her work for the week, unaware of the dire situation that James was having to face. She changed out of her uniform and saying goodbye, made her way home, looking forward to the coming weekend as her mother had taken Rebecca to her house to give them time together.

Walking into the house, Helen called for James but he wasn't in there, so she made her way to the stables, calling out to her husband.

'James, I'm home! Where are you, darling?'

But no one answered. She called again, but there was silence, so she walked into the stable block, expecting to see James there, and when she saw Cleo's stall empty, immediately thought he'd taken her out for a ride, until Mick, the young man working with James, entered and told her what had happened.

Returning to the house, Helen was really worried. If anything happened to Cleo, James would be devastated. His relationship with his beloved horse was something very special. She remembered the touching scene she'd observed when James had returned from the war. How he'd cried when he first entered her stall after so long. She immediately rang the vet's number. The receptionist put James on the line and he told her what had transpired.

'Brian is about to operate on her. Her intestines are twisted, so of course we couldn't wait.'

'Oh, that's awful. Poor Cleo. Are you alright, darling?'

'No, I'm not, Helen. If anything should happen to Cleo, I don't know what I'd do. It would be just too much. You know what she means to me. To live a life and die of old age is one thing, that's acceptable, but this . . .'

Feeling helpless, Helen didn't know how to comfort him. He promised to call if he had any news and put the phone down.

It was a long night. James insisted on staying beside Cleo after her operation and had called Helen to tell her. She wasn't surprised, she'd have done the same in his place, but she hardly managed an hour's sleep that night.

It was early afternoon when she heard her husband's car in the drive and she held her breath wondering if he brought good news, but when he walked into the kitchen and she saw his drawn expression, her heart sank.

He sat on a kitchen stool. 'She's gone, Helen. I've lost her,' he said.

Rushing over to him, she put her arms round him. 'Oh darling, I'm so very sorry.'

'The vet did the best that he could, but she didn't make it.' He got to his feet. 'I'm just going to the stables,' he said.

She let him go. He needed to be alone with his grief she realised. There was nothing she could say that was helpful at this stage, but she had tears in her eyes as she made a cup of tea.

That night James had a nightmare. The first for several months.

* * *

It was now July, but during the past two months James had become even more depressed. He still worked training his horses, but it gave him little satisfaction. It was just something he did every day because he had to. He rarely held a conversation, just replied to anything anyone said. Much as she tried, Helen couldn't get behind the bleak exterior of the man she loved who was in this deep pit of despair, and she didn't know what to do.

Margaret also tried when she came to look after Rebecca, but without success.

'You just have to let him work through it,' she told her daughter. 'You can't do it for him.'

Edward came over to see his son but he couldn't get through to James either. He tried to chat about everyday events as he helped to groom the horses, but in the end James turned to him.

'Look, Dad, I know what you're trying to do and I do thank you, but I need to be left alone. I can't help the way I feel, I have just to find my own way. I know I'm a worry to everyone at the moment but in time I'm sure this will pass, though not if people keep trying to chivvy me out of it. It only makes matters worse.'

Helen was so concerned she even contemplated giving up her work, but Margaret advised against such a move.

'By doing that, you'll put even more pressure on him,' she said, 'and that's the last thing the boy needs. Just be patient, that's all you can do.'

Life for Ann Carson couldn't be better. Every Wednesday, she and Clive would go out for lunch, then they retired to his flat for the afternoon, undressed and climbed into bed together. Having made the decision to have an affair, they were like two young lovers, sating their desire, laughing, tumbling about the bed as they found ways to enjoy each other. She felt young again, surprised by her own lack of inhibition – delighting in it.

Clive too was happy. He'd been a widower for some years and now it was like a rebirth of his youth, despite the fact that this was an illicit arrangement. Now he just lost himself to the enjoyment of this insatiable woman's demands.

Ann lay back against the bed sheet, hot and breathless, stretching her arms languidly.

'Oh, darling, that was *so* good.' She curled her naked body round him, her arms enclosing his broad chest, kissing his cheek.

He held her close, enjoying the feel of her bare flesh against his, wishing that they could stay together for the night, instead of having to part, knowing that his lover would be returning to her husband, cooking his meal and eventually climbing into *his* bed. He resented the fact that Richard Carson had that right, especially as he had no understanding of the woman he had married. It was such a waste. But deep down he couldn't hide the feeling of superiority, of understanding the woman beside him, knowing that he could satisfy her needs as she satisfied his.

Richard was not unaware of the change in his wife of late. She seemed to have a spring in her step, to be more cheerful, less pompous; she'd finally stopped boasting about being a lady, which had irritated him so much. He began to wonder what had brought about such a change and at dinner that evening he asked her.

He placed his knife and fork down on his plate. 'That was lovely, Ann, thank you.'

She smiled happily. 'I'm pleased you liked it.'

He poured them both another glass of wine. 'You seem very chipper lately, I have to say. It's like having a different woman about the house. What's changed?'

She stiffened slightly. 'I have no idea what you're talking about.'

'It's as if you've taken on a new lease of life; it's so noticeable I just wondered what has brought on such a change, that's all. There must be some good reason for it.'

She silently cursed; she should have been more careful when she was with him. She had changed because now she was happy, but that was because of Clive, and Richard must never discover the true reason or she was in deep trouble.

Shrugging she said, 'It's because the summer's here. I so hate the winter months, they are so depressing. It's just so nice to be out and about in the sun. It lifts one's spirits.'

He wasn't convinced. In all the years of his marriage, summer had never had this effect on his wife, but why would she lie? He stared at her and saw a moment of discomfort, and was that perhaps an expression of guilt? Something was going on, but what?

Two weeks later, Richard was in a taxi on his way back to the hospital when the car slowed because of the traffic. Glancing out of the window of the vehicle, Richard was surprised to see Ann and Clive Bradshaw in deep conversation, sitting in the window of a small restaurant. Ann looked somewhat concerned, he thought, then to his further surprise, he watched as Clive reached across the table and took her hand as if to placate her. The cab moved on and they were out of his sight.

He tried to sort what he'd just seen. Ann had resigned from the charity she ran with Clive when she moved back into the house with him, so what on earth were they doing together? As far as he knew, all ties had been cut with all of his wife's charity work.

His eyes narrowed as he mulled over these thoughts. Was this man behind the change in Ann?

When he arrived home that evening, he hung up his coat and hat, poured a Scotch and soda and went into the kitchen where Ann was preparing the dinner.

'So what did you do with yourself today?' he asked.

'I met Henrietta and we went out to lunch together,' she answered immediately.

'And after?'

'We did some shopping, then I came home. Dinner won't be long. Go and read the paper whilst I finish off here.'

Richard sat in his usual chair, picked up the paper but didn't open it. Was Clive Bradshaw the reason for the change in his wife, he wondered? Well he certainly wasn't going to put up with that. But he would have to be certain and there was only one way to find out.

Chapter Thirty-Four

Brian telephoned Helen over the weekend to see if James was any better. He'd seen for himself the devastating effect that losing Cleo had on his friend, and like his family, was very concerned.

'No, Brian, he's much the same. He does talk to Rebecca sometimes when he feeds her for me, but other than that, there doesn't seem to be any improvement and I'm so worried. I really don't know what to do.'

'Try not to worry, Helen. It just takes time, that's all.' But as he put down the receiver, he had an idea.

The following morning, James was surprised to see Brian arrive in his yard driving a horsebox. He went out to greet him.

'Brian! How are you and what are you doing here?'

'Looking for an enormous favour, James. Come with me.' He led him to the back of the horsebox and opened the door.

Inside was a horse, but he was a sorry sight to behold. His coat was a mess, his bones could be seen and he was decidedly nervous. Brian spoke softly to the animal as they walked inside the box.

James was shocked when he saw the state of the animal. 'What the hell has happened to him?'

'You might ask. I found him tied up in a field and left. No one has come forward to claim him and if I could find who did this I'd bloody well horsewhip them for being so cruel.'

James walked up to the horse, talking quietly, and was appalled when it seemed to cringe away from him. He quietly stroked its nose and, putting a hand in his pocket, gave it a lump of sugar, talking softly as he did so.

'I don't have the time to take care of him, James, and I wondered if you would take him, otherwise I'm going to have to put him down.'

'No! Don't do that, please.' He stroked the horse's neck. 'You poor bugger, no one deserves to be treated like this. Now, you and I are going to work together and make you well, but you have to trust me, alright?' He turned to his friend. 'How could people be this cold-hearted. They should be shot!'

'If you keep him, my friend, I'll supply any medication needed, but the rest is up to you. Are you game?'

'Of course. I'll certainly do my best. It used to break my heart during the war to see the bloated carcasses of horses that had been injured then shot and left by the roadside. If I can save this one, it will in some small way make up for that. Does it have a name?'

With a rueful smile Brian said, 'It doesn't have anything. Feel free.'

James looked into the sad eyes that looked back at him. 'Well, we'll wait and see before we give you a name. Now come along, my beauty – and I use the term lightly – I've got a nice warm stall waiting for you.'

Brian watched as James slowly coaxed the new arrival out of the box and across the yard into the stable block. He smiled to himself. Two poor, sad creatures together. Maybe each would be the other's salvation. He certainly hoped so.

During the following three hours, James spent time with his new stablemate, brushing its coat gently, talking softly as he did so and trying to calm the fear that someone had instilled in this poor animal. His heart bled for the poor creature. Eventually he gave it a feed. Not too much too soon. This would have to be a very gradual care in every way. Then he stroked the horse.

'I've got to go to the house now, my lovely, but I'll be back. Now you rest up. Nothing bad will happen to you whilst you're in my care, understand?'

There was no response from the animal, but it had seemed to have settled a little and had stopped trembling when James was near him.

James burst into the kitchen and when he saw Helen he gave vent to his anger.

'Brian has just brought a horse in and asked me to look after it. You wouldn't believe the state it's in, Helen. He's been left in a field to starve! You can see the poor thing's bones, would you believe, and it's terrified of humans. It makes my blood boil to see the neglect!'

She was startled. This was the most that James had said in one breath for weeks. But she was thrilled to see him so animated.

'Can you help him, do you think?'

'I'm certainly going to try. No animal should be treated

like that, it's inhumane. I've just come in for a quick cup of tea and a sandwich, then I'll go back.'

As he sat and ate his sandwich, he began making a plan for the animal's treatment.

'Firstly I need to feed him to give him some strength, and secondly I have to teach him to trust me and not be scared, then we can really make strides, but it's going to take time.'

'And patience,' she added. 'But you have such a way with horses, darling. You'll manage in the end.'

'Mick can help me with the training of the others in the stable, but I alone need to look after this one until it feels more secure and safe.'

He drank his tea and rose from his seat. 'I have to get back. I'll be in in time for dinner.' He kissed her and left.

When she was alone, Helen went to the telephone and called the vet.

'Thank you, Brian, for bringing in that poor stray. You wouldn't believe the difference in James. He now has a mission and, believe me, he intends to carry it out. I do believe you've found the key to unlock that dark place where James was buried.'

'I do hope so. It was just an idea, but if it works, then I'm really happy. James has been through so much and, like you, I want to see him recover.'

Whilst James was sorting out his problem with the sick animal, Richard Carson was faced with a problem of his own. That morning on his way out of the house he'd picked up his mail and was now reading one of the letters in his office. It was a report from a private detective he'd hired.

There were also some photographs for him to look at.

First he read the letter then he looked at the photos, one after the other. It showed his wife and Clive Bradshaw in different places. In a restaurant, holding hands, walking through a park and a few of Ann leaving Clive's flat and kissing him goodbye. Richard was livid! How dare she do this to him? But now he had the evidence. This was why she was so cheerful these days. She was having an affair! This could not be allowed to continue. But how was he to handle the situation – that was the problem. He placed the report and photographs into a drawer in his desk and locked it. He needed time to think.

Completely unaware that her secret had been discovered, Ann was on her way to meet Clive. They chose different restaurants in which to dine, not wanting to become familiar figures in one and maybe recognised.

She had never been so happy. Clive loved her, spoilt her, buying small gifts she'd hidden in the drawers in her bedroom: a small brooch, a pair of earrings, a silk scarf. He was an ardent lover who satisfied her every need. What more could a woman want?

Entering the restaurant, she saw Clive waiting. He rose from his seat as she took hers.

'Hello, my dear, how are you today? You look lovely, as usual.'

She beamed at him. She was wearing a new outfit, bought especially for the occasion, knowing that he always remarked on her appearance, whereas Richard hardly ever noticed.

'I'm fine now I've seen you,' she said softly.

'Be careful, darling,' he warned. 'You mustn't look at me like that, you'll give the game away.'

She chuckled with delight. 'It's not as easy as that,' she replied. 'I want to kiss you hello, but I know I can't. But I'll make up for it later.'

'Behave yourself, Ann.' He handed her the menu. 'What would you like?' Seeing the mischievous expression on her face he added '. . . from the menu, I mean.'

'Oh, you're no fun at all!' she teased.

They ate a leisurely lunch, then walked to his flat . . . and eventually climbed into bed.

That evening when Richard arrived home, he could hear Ann singing in the kitchen, which enraged him even more, but after hanging up his coat and hat, he went into the kitchen, kissed her on the cheek as usual, then in the living room he poured himself a large Scotch and soda. Walking into the dining room, he lay out the photographs on the table where his wife sat – and waited.

Ann came into the room and placed his meal in front of him, then walked around to her own seat. She suddenly saw the photographs and, with a cry, dropped the plate of food, which shattered on the floor, her face suddenly devoid of colour as she looked at the evidence before her.

'Sit down, Ann,' Richard said in a voice tinged with steel. 'We need to talk.'

Chapter Thirty-Five

Ann collapsed into her chair as her legs had ceased to hold her, the photos still in front of her. She wanted to sweep them away, hide them. But it was far too late for that. She looked up at her husband. His face was like granite. His eyes cold. She felt sick.

'It would seem that it wasn't the summer making you so happy, after all.'

Still in shock, she didn't know what to say, so remained silent.

'I can't believe that you were so stupid as to embark on a sordid affair – and with a man like Clive Bradshaw. Really! How could you?'

At the sound of disgust in her husband's voice over her choice of lover, Ann recovered her composure through anger.

'How easy it is for you to denigrate Clive,' she retorted. 'If you were half the man he is I probably wouldn't have felt the need to have an affair, which believe me is *far* from sordid. He loves me and makes me feel like a woman, something you *never* did, I might add.'

Richard kept his temper under control as he spoke.

'What could he give you, compared with the life you have, married to me? You have money, a beautiful home, a position in society and now a title, which you delight in using at every opportunity. Could he do the same?'

'You know that he couldn't but he cares about me. I feel cherished with him, not an appendage as I do with you. He's interested in me as a woman, a friend . . . a *lover*!'

Richard, now furious, rose suddenly, sending his chair crashing to the ground.

'I'm happy for you, my dear, because from now on, he'll be able to care for you completely. Twenty-four hours a day. That should make you *very* happy!'

'What on earth do you mean?' Now she was worried.

'I mean that I can no longer consider you my wife. You have made your choice. If your *lover* cares as much for you as you say he does, he'll be delighted for you to move in with him – permanently!'

'I can't do that, think of the scandal!' She was white with shock. 'Think of your position.'

'Oh, I have, Ann, believe me. People will be shocked that the wife of such an eminent man could be so foolish. No blame will be laid at my door, it will all be yours. You earned it – now enjoy it!'

He walked into the living room and poured himself a drink, Ann following quickly behind him.

'You can't do this to me!'

'My dear Ann, I haven't done anything, remember? It's you that has broken your marriage vows, not me. It's you that society will shun. I hope you think it was worth it.'

He put on his coat. 'I'm off to my club. I suggest you

call Clive Bradshaw and ask when you can move in. Sooner rather than later would be acceptable, meantime move your things into the spare room whilst I'm gone!'

Ann was shattered by the turn of events. She'd thought she and Clive had been so very discreet, so how on earth had Richard become so suspicious? Then she recalled an earlier conversation when he'd asked her why she seemed so cheerful. It was her own fault, after all. She'd let her happiness show, that was her big mistake. What on earth would Clive say now? Would he desert her? She felt the tears begin to flow. If he did then she would really be alone. Her friends would ignore her under the circumstances, not wanting to be tarred with any hint of scandal. She walked to the telephone.

Clive was sitting, reading over the report he'd written for the treasurer of the charity, when the telephone rang.

'Hello, Bradshaw speaking.' He listened for a moment. 'Ann, slow down, I can't understand a word you're saying.' He listened and then said, 'Of course I'll meet you but whatever is wrong?' After a moment he replaced the receiver, grabbed his jacket and left his flat.

He frowned as he walked. Whatever had happened? Ann was in such a state and said she'd explain when they met. He hurried on.

Twenty minutes later he arrived at the park where Ann had asked to meet him, and he could see her just inside, sitting on a bench, looking more than a little perturbed. He hurried over and sat beside her.

'Whatever is the matter?' he asked.

She burst into tears.

He held her hands and waited until she managed to pull herself together.

'Richard has found out about us! He even has photographs showing us meeting!'

Clive was shocked. 'How on earth could that have happened, we have been so careful?'

She related the sorry story to him as he listened intently.

'He's told me I have to leave and move in with you. He said he could no longer consider me as his wife, that now I was to leave and as I had chosen you as my lover, you could take care of me. What *are* we going to do?'

'Well, you can't move in with me, that's not possible – you must know that?'

She was in despair. 'You're not going to desert me, are you, Clive? I couldn't bear it if you did.'

He looked at the woman he loved and his heart ached for her. They had played a dangerous game and now it was out in the open.

'No, of course not! But we have to be careful what we do now. You do realise whatever that is it will cause a great deal of gossip, don't you?'

'I don't care about that any more as long as we can still be together. I love you, Clive, these past months have been the happiest of my life.' She was silent for a moment. 'But what about you, darling? How will this affect you? Because it will be common knowledge eventually.'

Placing an arm round her shoulder he spoke softly. 'You make me happy, Ann. I have no family ties, no one to point the finger, unlike you. You have a husband, a place in society that will be denied to you now. You have so much more to lose.'

'Do you really think I care about that any more? Yes, once upon a time it was everything. Now it means nothing.'

He patted her on the back as you would to comfort a child.

'We could always move out of London. Go somewhere where we aren't known, set up a home of our own, together.'

She looked at him in astonishment. 'You would do that for me?'

'No, I'd do it for us!'

'But what about the charity – your work?'

'I can always work elsewhere.' He smiled at her. 'Why shouldn't we be happy together? It would be very different from the lifestyle you're used to. Do you think you could lower your standards just a little? There would be no fine house. No afternoon teas with the ladies. No Lady Carson. Just a simple life, the two of us.'

She started to laugh. 'Oh, Clive, it would be such an adventure, but we wouldn't be married!'

'Who would know? If Mr and Mrs Bradshaw moved into a new town or village, who would even question it?'

She leant forward and kissed him. 'I told Richard if he was half the man you were I wouldn't have had an affair, and I was right. You are my hero!'

'You flatter me, Ann. But we have to make plans. I suggest we find a small hotel for you to move into tonight, until we decide where to go, and then find a place to live. During that time, I suggest you keep out of the limelight. I doubt that Richard will tell anyone about the situation for now, which will give us time.'

'I'll have to go home and pack a couple of bags with my clothes and toiletries.'

'You do that and I'll find a hotel for you to stay. The

sooner you move out, the better. You can always return for the rest of your things when we find a place to move to. I'll call you when I've found a hotel, then you can get a cab to take you there.'

Ann let herself into her house and, taking off her coat, went to her bedroom and packed two large suitcases with her clothes and another with toiletries and some of her jewellery. She then went into the living room, poured herself a gin and tonic and sat on the sofa. She looked around at the elegantly furnished room, knowing that she was leaving for good. Did she really mind, she wondered?

When she'd left before she had minded, but not now. She'd not been really happy here with Richard. Not in the same way she was happy with Clive. With Richard it had all been about position, a place in society, being a member of the upper class – through her husband. But she now accepted that it was all rather shallow. What had been important to her then had no depth, no real value – not like Clive's love for her. He was prepared to start a new life in a new place so that they could stay together. That had true value. That was pure gold.

Whilst she waited she penned a short note to leave for Richard.

Richard,
I've packed a few of my clothes and I'll inform you
when I will return for the rest of my things.
Ann.

She smiled with some satisfaction. He would be surprised when he came home to find the place empty. But what did she care now?

The telephone rang. It was Clive with the address of a hotel.

'You're booked in as Mrs Clarkson. I'll come over and meet you in the bar,' he said. 'We'll have our own small celebration.'

She was delighted and rang for a cab. When it arrived she walked out of her house with a definite spring in her step. She was leaving Lady Carson behind with the furniture!

During this time, Richard was sitting alone in his club, having a quiet drink, collecting his thoughts, trying to calm down. His anger, still boiling inside, was like a volcano waiting to erupt.

He was still unable to come to terms with the fact that his wife, who for years had so enjoyed her elevated position, could have thrown it all away for sex. She said it was for love, he didn't believe it! And . . . for such an insignificant person as Clive Bradshaw, whom he'd met once when Ann had joined the charity.

He sipped his drink. Well he had shaken her little world this evening. He wondered what she would say to him when he returned to the house. Would she beg to be forgiven?

Well, she could try. He was so incensed at the moment, he certainly was not in a forgiving mood. Let her go to this little man who had nothing to offer. Let her find out just how different life would be. She'd hate every moment! This gave him a great feeling of satisfaction. Yes, he'd let the matter run its course before she came running back to him. He ordered another drink. Make her wait, he thought, as he picked up a newspaper.

*　*　*

It was ten o'clock when he arrived home. He opened the front door and walked into the living room where he fully expected to see his wife waiting. The room was empty. He walked into the kitchen, she wasn't there. On his return to the living room, about to go upstairs, he spied a piece of writing paper on the coffee table, picked it up and read it. Then he read it again before cursing loudly as he screwed it up and threw it across the room.

Chapter Thirty-Six

It was now early October and around the Cotswolds the leaves on the trees were turning colour. Children were collecting conkers from beneath the horse chestnut trees and there was a hint of winter in the air.

Helen dressed Rebecca warmly, then tucked her up with blankets in her pram and made her way to the practice ring where she knew that James was working with Valiant, the name they had chosen for the horse.

Ever since he'd taken him into his care, he and Brian had worked hard to make him fit and well and James had taught the animal to trust humans again. It had taken time, patience and energy, but eventually they were rewarded. Today Valiant had a beautiful coat covering a strong frame and at last the animal seemed to have lost fear of those he was familiar with. If a stranger stopped by his stall he was watchful, but no longer trembled at the sound of a voice.

Not only had the horse taken on a new life, but James was no longer suffering with depression and was back to his old self, much to everyone's great relief.

Helen watched as James rode around the arena, then took the horse over small jumps, encouraging it as he did so. Seeing Helen, he rode over and stopped, patting the horse's neck.

Beaming at his wife he said, 'Can you believe this is the same animal? Remember how he looked that day when Brian brought him over?'

She leant forward and stroked the animal.

'He looks wonderful,' she said, 'but then think how long you've worked to get him to this stage.'

'It was worth every minute. He's a brave soul, his name suits him and we'll keep him with us. Who knows, when Rebecca is old enough she'll be able to ride him. I'll take him back to his stall, we've done enough for today, he's earned a feed and a rest.'

Helen watched him ride away. She would never be able to repay Brian for what he had done for the horse, but even more for finding the answer to her husband's depression.

As James unsaddled the animal, he chatted away as he used to do with Cleo. He was also aware that he had been saved by caring for this animal. At first he'd been so incensed about the cruelty it had endured, he'd just wanted to repair the damage, but as the days passed into weeks, he realised just what was happening to him and was more than grateful to his friend. He had been in the depths of despair, unable to get out of it. Knowing how worried his family were about him had only made his situation worse. Now, he felt like a different man.

His business was thriving. Mick, the young man working with him, was an asset and had a way with horses too.

They worked well together and James trusted him enough to leave him in charge if he had to go off to any horse sales or on business.

Helen was still working part-time at the hospital, which fulfilled her need to be useful and continue with her love of medicine, and she had been invited to attend a two-day conference in London the following week, with two of the surgeons she worked with. Margaret and James had insisted she go. Margaret would move in until her return.

There were to be several speakers, discussing new methods and the latest update on operation procedures. She was looking forward to it. It was imperative for them all to keep up to date.

Helen travelled up to London with her colleagues and booked into the hotel where the conference was to be held. In their rooms was a programme of the event and she was surprised to see that Richard was one of the speakers. She wondered how he was these days. It had been a long time since they had seen one another.

At the end of the first day, Helen gathered her notes and walked out of the conference room. It had been a full day and she was weary. She wanted to go to her room and sit in a hot bath before dinner, but as she walked across the foyer she heard a familiar voice call to her.

'Helen! Is that really you?'

She turned to see Richard approaching.

'Richard! How lovely to see you.'

'And you, my dear.' He kissed her on the cheek. 'Fancy a drink?'

She could hardly refuse and followed him to the bar, where they sat at a small table and gave their order to a waiter.

'You look well,' he said. 'How's life in the Cotswolds?'

'Great. We live in an old farmhouse and James has built stables there to train horses, which he then sells on, and we have a daughter, Rebecca.'

'Congratulations! How is your husband?'

'Fine. He's busy doing what he loves and is good at it. He's keeping really well.' She wasn't going to tell Richard of the bad times because they were behind them now, there was no point.

'I'm delighted to hear that. There was a time when I wondered if he would ever recover from his ordeal.'

'Well, Richard, you had a great deal to do with that. By the way, congratulations on your knighthood.'

'Thank you, and for your telegram. That was kind of you and James.'

'Not at all, we were so happy for you. It was well deserved. How is Lady Carson?'

His expression changed. 'We are separated, I'm afraid, and have been for a while now.'

This was so unexpected that for a moment Helen was lost for words. 'I am sorry to hear that.'

'It isn't common knowledge at the moment,' he added. 'You know how people gossip. I'm trying to keep the situation quiet but eventually it will get out. Until then . . .'

'I understand. Anyway it's not anyone's business. They certainly won't hear it from me, but how are you, under the circumstances?'

'Fine. These things happen, although if I'm honest it

was totally unexpected. I thought Ann was content, but she found her contentment in another man's arms. That *was* a surprise.'

'Oh, Richard, I am so sorry.' What else could she say? She was surprised after meeting Ann Carson. She thought the woman would have gloried in being a lady.

He picked up his glass and sipped his drink. Then with a wry smile said, 'Imagine, Helen, this was the woman I put first before you. That was probably the biggest mistake of my life.'

Remembering how Richard had arrived in Cheltenham to ask her to marry him if he divorced his wife, she decided to stop the conversation from heading down the wrong path.

'That was then, Richard. It was in another life. I'm lucky, my marriage is solid, I'm just sorry that you are not as happy in yours.'

He shrugged. 'I have my work, and as you well know, that's what drives me, and if I'm honest, Ann and I got along, but it wasn't really a love match. It was more habit than anything else.'

'That's the saddest thing I've ever heard you say!' she exclaimed.

'It's not something I'm proud of, but it is the truth.' He downed the rest of his drink. 'I have to gather my notes for tomorrow. I'm giving a talk in the morning, then I'll be leaving. I can't tell you how good it is to see you and to know that you are happy.'

They both rose to their feet. He put his arms round her and kissed her on the cheek.

'I'll never forget you, Helen. We went through dreadful

times together in the base hospital and beyond, but you made me happy and made my life bearable and I'll always be in your debt for that. Take care.'

She watched him walk away. How sad that this man who had given so much of himself in his life was now alone – and lonely, she felt. Then she made her way to her room and the bath she'd been looking forward to.

The next morning, Helen and the other delegates sat and listened to Sir Richard Carson deliver an amazing speech on the latest surgical procedures and she felt proud of the man who had been her mentor as well as her lover. Everyone sat enthralled with what he had to say, and at the end of it they all gave him a standing ovation. He looked both surprised and delighted. He smiled and gave a short bow.

'Thank you all, how very kind of you. I don't get such accolades from my patients, of course, they're usually unconscious!' The audience laughed. 'Now, I'm ready for your questions.'

There were many from those eager to learn about new procedures from such a man. Richard was patient and fulsome in his explanations, it was really like a class with the master.

Helen sat listening with a feeling of pride to have been part of this man's life and again was sad that his home life wasn't a happy one. Richard needed someone to talk over his day with, as she well knew. Mind you, Ann wouldn't have been able to cope with the medical side as she had, but she could have been there to make his life comfortable. Thank goodness he had his work, but a man needs more than that. Perhaps in time he'd meet another woman to share his life. She certainly hoped so.

Eventually the questions had all been answered and Richard bid his audience goodbye. He walked towards the door, smiling at Helen as he passed her, but as the door was opened for him he let out a cry, clutched his chest and fell forward.

Several surgeons rushed to him, followed by Helen. But there was nothing anyone could do. Richard had suffered a severe heart attack that had taken his life. The surgeon kneeling beside Richard looked at Helen and shook his head.

'Oh, Richard!' Helen's anguished cry was the only sound in the room as someone removed their jacket and covered the body.

An ambulance was called and the body removed. Helen was overcome with grief and was comforted by those who understood how close she was to the great man. She was handed a glass of water and a handkerchief to wipe away her tears.

Eventually her sobs subsided and she sat, absolutely stunned by what had just happened, unable to believe that, in a second, one so vibrant could have been taken. There was a silent buzz among those who had been so enthralled by Richard's presence and were equally as shocked at his demise. They slowly began to filter out of the room.

One of the surgeons stayed with Helen until she recovered.

'Is there anything I can do for you, my dear?' he asked.

She shook her head. 'Thank you, but no. I just have to call my husband and then I'll go to the station and get a train to take me home, but thank you for your kindness.'

He patted her hand and walked away, leaving Helen to call James and tell him what had happened, then she packed her bag and made her way to the station.

Helen sat on the train gazing out at the passing scenery, but seeing nothing. She was still stunned by Richard's sudden demise. One moment he'd been responding to applause then minutes later he was gone. She thought over their earlier conversation, remembering his words and felt at least some comfort from the fact that she'd brought him a modicum of happiness during their time together. He had taught her so much in the operating theatre and he would always be an important part of her life. But how sad that his final days had not been happy. She wondered what his wife would feel when she heard the news.

In a small village in Essex, Mr and Mrs Bradshaw were sitting listening to the one o'clock news when an unexpected announcement was made by the newsreader.

Sir Richard Carson, the eminent surgeon, suffered a severe heart attack today after giving a talk at a seminar in London. He was taken by ambulance to a nearby hospital where he was pronounced dead on arrival.

'Oh my God!' Ann let out a cry as she heard the news. Clive sitting beside her was shocked into silence.

'I must go back to London,' said Ann, getting to her feet.

'Whatever for? You left the house and him, why do you have to return?'

'No one knows we've parted,' she said. 'As far as anyone is concerned we're still together. Now is not the time for any gossip. Besides, by law, I'm still Lady Carson, his wife.'

'But if you return, people here will know who you really are!'

'I can't worry about that. This is a small village, it'll be a seven-day wonder. But there will have to be a funeral. I have to be there as his wife, surely you can see that?'

'No, Ann, I'm sorry he's gone but I thought we had started a new life – that all the other was behind us.'

'We'll have to talk about this later. I have a funeral to arrange. I'll take a few clothes and catch a train this afternoon. They must wonder where I am. I have to go and now.'

As Ann arrived at the house in London, letting herself in with a spare key that she'd kept, she could hear the telephone ringing. She ran to pick up the receiver before the caller hung up. It was a colleague of Richard's on the line.

'Ann! Where the hell have you been? I've been calling you all day.'

'I'm sorry, I was visiting friends when I heard the news, I've just walked in the door.'

He told her what had happened. 'There will have to be a post-mortem, but it's pretty straightforward. Richard suffered a severe heart attack. I can't tell you how sorry I am, he was a great man. If you like, I'll come over tomorrow and help you with all the arrangements, that's if you want me to.'

She gladly accepted. There would be so much to do. Alone it would be just too much. She replaced the receiver, poured a large gin and tonic and, kicking off her shoes, sank onto the sofa. She looked around at the familiar room, happy to see everything was as it used to be, that it was clean and tidy as was usual. The last time she sat here was just before she left to live with Clive, thinking she would only return to collect the rest of her things, which she had done one day when Richard was working – and here she was back again. It was only then that Richard's death really began to sink in. In her rush she'd had no time to think, but now the enormity of his death became a reality. Never again would he walk through the door of the house. Then she slowly began to think of the many things she'd have to do.

She'd have to clear his clothes, go through his desk – well his colleague could do that tomorrow, he'd know what to do with all the papers and files. There would be the death certificate after the autopsy. The funeral to be booked, hymns chosen. Her head was reeling.

Then she thought, I suppose this house is mine now, and immediately felt more cheerful. As his wife, of course, she'd inherit everything. She knew that was in Richard's will as they had made their wills together. She'd be a wealthy woman. She tried not to feel too pleased about that – after all, the poor man was hardly cold. It didn't seem right . . . nevertheless!

Two weeks later the funeral of Sir Richard Carson took place. Ann, dressed in black and widow's weeds, followed the hearse in a black car to the church. There was a large crowd outside who were silent and respectful as she walked to the door and entered. As she made her way to the family pew, she was amazed to see that the church was packed, with people having to stand at the back. She straightened up as she walked, knowing that all eyes were upon her.

Helen, standing with James and some of her colleagues in a pew near the front, watched Ann with interest, knowing that she and Richard had parted, although as far as she could tell it wasn't common knowledge, and the way Lady Carson was walking, with a definite air, it would seem that was still the case.

It was a full service and at the end the vicar announced that a reception would be held at a nearby hotel and all would be welcome. It took some time to filter out of the church. Ann Carson was standing thanking those who stopped to talk. Helen would have liked to walk past her but it would have looked rude so she stood waiting her turn. But as Ann recognised her and looked at her with such an imperious air, Helen couldn't help herself. As she said how sorry she was she lowered her voice:

'I had a drink with Richard the night before he died,' she said. 'How nice of you to turn up today.' Then she walked away.

She and James went to a restaurant after the service. Helen couldn't face going on to the hotel and listening to everyone exchanging stories about their time with Richard, she felt too sad about his passing for that. She wanted just to be with her husband and enjoy a meal before returning to the Cotswolds, their home and Rebecca.

Lady Carson, however, was in a strange way enjoying her husband's wake. It was obvious that not a soul knew that they had parted and for that she was more than grateful. After all, she owed much to him and his position and she was happy that his name wasn't being besmirched in any way at his funeral. She was again enjoying the slightly deferential treatment she was getting. It made her feel good. Richard's solicitor was also there and he asked if she could go to his office the next morning as he wanted to read the will and set the wheels in motion.

'I always think it's best to get things over with as soon as possible, don't you, Lady Carson?'

'Yes I do,' she said. 'Eleven o'clock be alright?'

'Perfect. I'll see you then. My condolences, of course.'

That night, Ann returned to the house, but she slept in the spare room. She had looked at the bed that she and Richard used to share, but couldn't bring herself to use it.

The next morning, Ann made her way to the solicitor's office, wondering just what was the value of Richard's estate? There was the house and the flat in Chelsea too. In monetary terms . . . she had no idea, but it would be some considerable sum, she was certain.

On her arrival, she was ushered into the man's office and offered a cup of coffee, which she accepted.

Then the solicitor began, '"I, Richard Ellis—"'

Ann interrupted. 'Can we skip all the frippery bits and just get to the content, please?'

'Yes of course,' he said and then continued. 'There are one or two bequests first of all. "I leave three thousand pounds to The Royal British Legion that has just been formed, to help servicemen in dire need. These men served their country well and I wish to help them."'

Ann nodded her agreement, although she was surprised at the amount of money donated.

'"Fifty pounds each to my cook and cleaner, who have looked after me well" – I have their names and addresses. "My house in Knightsbridge,"' Ann sat up straighter and smiled in anticipation, '"and the contents are to be sold, the money to be added to my estate."'

'But he can't do that,' she protested, 'that's my house!'

The solicitor ignored her outburst and carried on. '"To Ann Carson, who left our marital home to live with Mr Clive Bradshaw and therefore removed herself from our marriage, I leave one hundred pounds each month, just to ensure that whatever happens to her in the future, she won't be without funds."'

Enraged, Ann glared at the solicitor. 'And that's it? Is that all that he left me?'

'There are other bequests but as far as you are concerned, that's it. Sir Richard made a new will a few weeks ago. He said his situation had changed and therefore so had his will. I'm sorry, Lady Carson, but I must ask you to hand over your keys to the house.'

Ann's eyes narrowed. 'What about the flat in Chelsea?'

The solicitor read from the will. '"My Chelsea apartment is left to my colleague Dr Ronald Gibbs, who has worked faithfully beside me for many years."'

'So who inherits his estate?'

The solicitor read on. '"The rest of my estate I leave to Helen Havers of Cherry Tree Farm, Beckford, Near Cheltenham, Gloucester. She worked beside me as my theatre sister during horrendous times throughout the war and it's my way of thanking her."'

'What!' Ann was livid. 'That bloody woman, she keeps cropping up in my marriage.'

'Forgive me for saying so, Lady Carson, but your marriage is over and I believe has been for a little while.'

She glared at him. 'I will contest this will. I'll go to court. After all, I am Lady Carson, his wife. I am entitled to more than he's left me.'

'You can do so, of course.' He took some papers out of his drawer. 'But if you do, I'd have to inform the court that Sir Richard had started divorce proceedings.'

'He what?' Ann went cold.

He held the papers aloft. 'Yes, I'm afraid so. But at least you've been spared that. The newspapers would have had a heyday when they got to hear about it, with Richard being so well known. No lady wants to be tagged a scarlet woman, do they?'

She glared at him. 'I beg your pardon?'

'At the moment your good character is unblemished as far as the public are aware, Lady Carson. After probate has been settled and a decent time has passed, you are a free woman to wed whom you wish without any whiff of scandal. But if you insist on contesting the will, that would be very different. Everything would be out in the open – in detail.'

She was beaten, she knew that, but it was a bitter pill to swallow. She had planned for Clive to move into the house in Knightsbridge with her and for them eventually to marry. After all, she would be a wealthy woman, she had thought, but Richard had made sure she had paid the price for her infidelity. She rose from her chair.

'Thank you, Mr Long. When will the first payment be paid into my account?'

'At the end of the first month after the probate has been settled.'

As she left the office, Ann was devastated. She had thought she was to be told she had inherited Richard's considerable wealth as well as his property. She had envisaged she and Clive, living the good life, back in her beautiful house, dining out as she'd done as Richard's wife in all the best restaurants, going to the theatre, enjoying the luxuries money could buy. But no. Richard had taken his pound of flesh and she would have to accept it.

But as Ann sat on the train back to her far more simple life in Essex, she couldn't help but think of what might have been, and now she'd have to face Clive's displeasure at her flying off to London to preside over her husband's funeral.

Chapter Thirty-Seven

Helen was surprised when, a week after the funeral, she received a phone call from Peter Long, Richard's solicitor, asking if he could come and see her as she'd been a beneficiary in Richard's will. They arranged a day the following week when she'd be at home.

When she told James about it, he was pleased for her.

'That's really nice of him to remember you, darling. After all, you worked together for some considerable time. It's his way of thanking you.'

Helen was pleased that James refrained from mentioning her close relationship with Richard. He'd eventually managed to put that behind him. But she was flattered to be remembered by Richard. That was kind of him, she thought.

Peter Long arrived just after lunch, and at Helen's invitation, joined them for a cup of coffee, before James took Rebecca with him to the stables, leaving Helen with the solicitor in the living room.

'Sir Richard made me the executor of his will,' Peter

explained, 'and of course it will be some time before probate will be granted as there is a property to be sold, but Sir Richard made you his main beneficiary and as there is a considerable amount of money involved, I thought I should come and see you.'

Helen was stunned. 'His *main* beneficiary?'

Peter nodded. 'Yes.' He read from the will to help convince her.

'What about his wife?'

'It wasn't known, but she was now living with another man. Richard has left her a small amount to be paid monthly, but there was no longer a marriage. In fact, he'd started divorce proceedings.'

'Yes, I did know she'd left, he told me. I was at the lecture when he died. We'd had a drink together the previous evening.'

'I didn't know that. It must have been a dreadful experience for you.'

'For everyone – it was so sudden. One minute he'd been talking, the next he collapsed and died.'

'Now, I'd better tell you what is involved here, Mrs Havers.'

'Helen, please.'

'Well, Helen, his house in Knightsbridge is to be sold. The proceeds, after any outstanding bills, to be added to the estate. It should be a considerable sum. All together, we estimate somewhere around this figure.' He handed her a printed paper.

Helen gasped when she looked at the bottom line. 'But this is a small fortune!'

Peter beamed at her. 'Indeed it is. Congratulations!'

'Oh my goodness, I don't know what to say.'

Getting to his feet, Peter said, 'I suggest you share the news with your husband as I have another appointment and must leave. It was lovely to meet you, Helen. I'll be in touch.'

After she'd shown him out, she went rushing off to the stables and found James on the ground, playing with Rebecca. She ran over to him and held out the piece of paper Peter had handed her.

James looked at it and frowned. 'What's this?'

'That's an estimate of what my inheritance from Richard will be.'

He looked at the paper again. 'Bloody hell! Are you certain?'

'Apparently there is Richard's house in Knightsbridge to sell first, apart from anything else. This is what they think will be the total amount.'

'What about his wife?'

'She'd left him for another man and he was about to divorce her. He left her a small monthly payment, that's all. I was his main beneficiary. I can't quite believe it. In the will it said it was to thank me for working with him during the war in horrendous times.'

'Well you did and it was. This is your reward, Helen. He was given a knighthood – this is your decoration for working beside him during the war!'

'But it's a small fortune!'

'You will be a wealthy woman in your own right.' He grinned at her. 'You won't leave me will you, now you're a woman of means?'

She put her arms around him. 'As if I would ever leave you, you idiot!'

'What will you do with the money?'

'I have no idea. I'll have to give it some considerable thought. It would be nice to put it to some good use. Come on, let's open a bottle of champagne and celebrate.'

James picked up Rebecca. 'Your mother is an heiress, how about that?'

The child chuckled, clapped her hands and chatted away in her own baby language.

'There! Rebecca's thrilled for you.'

But when Ann Carson returned to the village in Essex and Clive, she was far from being thrilled with the news she was about to impart. She was also uncertain of the reception she'd receive from Clive, who had not been pleased with her sudden departure to oversee Richard's funeral.

She opened the front door and walked into the living room where she saw Clive reading the newspaper. He looked up at her, folded his paper and waited for her to speak.

'Hello,' she said uncertainly. 'I'm back.'

'So I see. I wondered if you would decide to stay in London and reconvene your life as the recently widowed Lady Carson!'

She tried to ignore the sarcasm in his tone. 'As you can see, I didn't.'

'I have to confess, I'm surprised after your dash to maintain your position as Richard's wife.'

'But don't you see, I had no choice. No one as yet knows we had parted. I couldn't let his funeral be marred by any scandal. That wouldn't have been right. That much I owed him!'

'How very noble of you! But, of course, under those circumstances, you would inherit his money, let's not forget that. I'm sure you didn't!'

'That didn't enter my head for a moment. What a dreadful thing to say!'

'Come now, Ann, I'm sure it did at some time or another. Please don't lie to me.'

'Well, when I was sitting in the house, before the funeral, I did wonder.'

'I read about the funeral in the papers. It was well attended.'

She looked horrified. 'It was in the papers?'

'Oh yes, with lots of pictures. All the local inhabitants now know who you really are. I've had some strange looks when I've been to the local shops. Not that anyone has said anything, well not to me, but I expect it's been the topic of conversation ever since. Never mind, Richard's money will allow you to move to something bigger, elsewhere.'

This was even worse than she'd imagined. Now they could no longer stay in the village, they'd have to move. She looked at Clive, took a deep breath and spoke:

'Richard left me a hundred pounds a month, that's all. He left his estate, apart from a few bequests, to Helen Havers. So you see, I am not the wealthy widow. He's paid me back for leaving him.'

Clive looked at the sad figure sitting opposite him. He was still angry with the way she'd left him to return to London, but he was pleased that Richard's funeral went well and without any scandal. After all he *was* the injured party in this mess. Knowing Ann as he did, he knew she'd be devastated that Helen was the beneficiary of the will, but he could understand Richard doing this. After all, she'd worked with him during the war and that must have been dreadful. Why would he reward his wife who'd left him for another man?

'So what now, Ann?'

She was uncertain. Clive's anger was still obvious. Would he still want her? She really didn't know at this moment and it scared her. If he didn't, she was alone with a small annuity to keep her.

'Do you want me to leave?' Her voice was barely a whisper.

'And go where? Don't be silly, woman. I am the cause of Richard writing you out of his will, therefore I'm responsible for you.'

She felt weak with relief. 'Honestly?'

He came and sat beside her. 'Honestly. We'll have to move from here and start again, but at least you are no longer a married woman. You are free to do as you wish. In time we could get married, if that's what you want, but as you know, we'll be living a different kind of life. I'll get a job and we'll just be an ordinary married couple.'

She couldn't hold back the tears any longer. When at last she'd recovered, she put her hand to Clive's cheek.

'I do love you, you know. We were happy together until Richard died. I didn't mind living a different life, if it was with you.'

He smiled at her with affection. 'We'll give our notice to the landlord and move out. I'll look in the papers for a job, then we'll decide where to go. Now, let's get something to eat, I'm really hungry.'

Ann watched him walk into the kitchen knowing how

lucky she was to know such a man and vowing never to disappoint him for standing by her. She would marry him in time and this time she would have a happy marriage, of that she was certain. It would be a very different life from what she'd been used to with Richard, but now she didn't care any more about position. She'd experienced living alone and had hated it. But Clive loved her, despite everything, and that was worth a fortune to her. He'd always look after her – and care for her as she would for him.

Chapter Thirty-Eight

During the time she waited for the probate to be settled, Helen had given much thought to the considerable amount of money that would be hers and had decided to put it to good use. She'd been looking around the area on the days she wasn't working at the hospital and had found an old house that once had been a boarding school. It had been on the market a while and the owners had dropped the price. As she walked around it with the estate agent, she became more and more excited. This building, with some reconstruction, would be ideal for what she had in mind. She then arranged for a builder to look around and give her an estimate for the work involved. Then she went to the office of the estate agent and made an offer before she went home to tell James of her plan.

'You what?' James looked at her with surprise.

'I've put an offer in for an old boarding school, just outside of Evesham.'

He frowned. 'But I don't understand, why would you do that?'

'I want to put my inheritance to good use and I've decided to open a home for the treatment of the troops who came back from the war and are still having the same problems as you. I've an estimate from a builder for what needs to be changed and the decoration. The dormitories will be used as bedrooms for the patients. I thought I could have them dig up the back garden and grow vegetables as you did in Devon, with the appropriate staff, of course.'

'It's a wonderful idea, darling, but how long before you run out of money?'

'I've thought of that. I'll make it a charitable home so public funds will allow me to continue. I thought I'd get in touch with your man in Devon. What was his name?'

'Dr Arthur Hurst.'

'Yes, him. I thought he could advise me on the best way to run it. What do you think, James?'

He shook his head but he slowly smiled. 'I think you are wonderful. Richard would be so proud of you, I know I am. It's a great idea, if you can manage it.'

'Will you come with me tomorrow and look at the place? I could do with your input. After all, who better to tell me if it is viable?'

'Indeed I will. It'll be an outing for Rebecca too.'

The following day the three of them drove to the school to be met by the estate agent and were allowed to wander around unhindered, Rebecca toddling with them on her reins. James could immediately see why his wife had chosen this spot. In his mind it was ideal and he became as excited as she was. They were even more thrilled when the estate agent informed them her offer had been accepted.

'I thought I'd wait to give you the news after you had looked around to make sure you still wanted to buy,' he said.

'Oh, we certainly do,' Helen told him. 'Let's go to your office now and I'll sign any necessary papers.'

It was nearing Christmas so they decided to wait until after the holiday before starting any renovations. In the meantime, Helen, who had now given in her notice at the hospital, spoke with Arthur Hurst and told him of her plan and he kindly agreed to come up to Evesham and meet them, look over the site and help in any way he could with advice.

'I'll be delighted, Mrs Havers,' he said, 'and to see your husband again and have a chat with him.'

So it was arranged.

Meantime, Helen and James told Edward of the plan. He was thrilled with the concept and said he would like to make a contribution to the fund also, which was unexpected but would be a help towards the initial outlay, allowing Helen even more breathing space, financially. By mid December, she was the proud owner of Richard Carson House. She had long decided to call it after her benefactor; after all, without him, none of this would have been possible.

Shortly after, Arthur Hurst arrived and went with Helen and James to look over the school. He agreed that it was ideal, so they returned to the farmhouse for lunch and a chat.

As they sat at the table, Helen turned to Arthur. 'Obviously I can't do what you do, but I would like your advice as to what I *can* do to help these men, so any ideas would be so very welcome.'

After much discussion it was eventually decided that the home should be more of a refuge for the men who were still struggling to survive, due to the mental stresses they were enduring. Here they would do manual work in the garden, as James had done. The vegetables grown would be a help towards the food bills. Hens and pigs could be kept and cared for and they also would help towards the food chain as well as give the men jobs looking after them, keeping them clean. They would have dartboards, board games, books to read and writing facilities to fill the patients' leisure time.

'Don't get involved with surgical cases, Helen, although it's your field. Take only those who need nominal nursing. Yes, wounds to be dressed, if necessary, otherwise your money will soon run out. The men need to be occupied and worked during the day, and rested after. They need a place where they can find peace and unwind whilst they cope with their traumas. But I would suggest a psychiatrist is essential to let the men talk about their experiences. If you do all that, my dear, you'll be doing so much good to these poor devils. But I have to ask you one question, Helen. How are you going to finance this, other than with your inheritance?'

'I'm going to register it as a charity, but to do so, I have to find three trustees first.'

'No, my dear, you only need find two. It would be my pleasure to be the first one.'

'I can't thank you enough, Arthur. That's wonderful, and today you've already been a great help.'

'It is my pleasure and you can call me anytime if you have a problem.'

'I'll leave you two alone whilst I look after Rebecca,' she said and left the room.

'You're looking remarkably fit, James,' Arthur said. 'How *are* things with you after all this time?'

'Good, mainly thanks to you who started me on the road to recovery. I rarely have a nightmare these days, what with work and young Rebecca. Truth to tell I'm too damned tired when it's bedtime.'

Laughing Arthur said, 'There speaks a contented man.'

'I'm still edgy in confined spaces but I've learnt to cope with it most of the time and I no longer hit the floor if I hear a loud noise, as I used to do, to my great embarrassment.'

'You've come a long way and I'm delighted to see it. Helen must have been a great help to you, with her nursing experience. She would understand your illness more than most women.'

'My wife is an extraordinary woman, as you've seen for yourself. I am a lucky man.'

'You are indeed. But when she opens this home, you could be a help to her patients by talking to them about your own experiences. After all, you would understand exactly what they're going through.'

'To be honest, it's all happened so quickly I've not thought of that, but of course I'd gladly step in, if needed. What about riding? If I was to take my horse over and walked it on a lead rein, the patients could ride. Is that a good idea?'

'Indeed it is. It would give them an added interest and add to their confidence.'

James beamed at his mentor. 'Great. I'll tell Helen what you said.'

* * *

Christmas was a happy family affair at the farmhouse. Both sets of parents came over to stay and helped to entertain Rebecca now that she was a little bit older. She was in her element unwrapping her presents and, to everyone's great amusement, then ignored all the toys to climb into an empty cardboard box where she stayed for most of the afternoon.

'How typical,' Edward remarked. 'The simple things are the best.'

On Boxing Day, Helen laid out a cold buffet for everyone to help themselves and afterwards they all visited the stables to see to the horses. Christmas decorations hung over the stalls. As James said, 'They have earned the right to celebrate too,' as they were all given sugar lumps to hand out.

He picked up Rebecca to allow her to give hers to Valiant. Having been used to horses all her short life, she wasn't afraid and held out her small hand for the horse to take the offering, giggling as he did so.

In January, the builders moved into the Richard Carson House and started the renovations: new wiring was installed; new floors laid in some of the rooms; windows replaced; new doors fitted; walls plastered; the interior painted in cream; Helen had curtains made for the windows; beds were ordered, as well as new bedding; chimneys were swept; old fireplaces replaced with new, where required. Slowly it began to take shape.

Arthur Hurst had passed the word around among his colleagues, letting them know about the house, knowing there would be patients forthcoming in the near future.

Helen had advertised in various medical journals and

among her associates in the medical field and to her great delight, Edward had offered to be her second trustee. Not only that, but he said that a wealthy friend of his, Gerald Roberts, a retired businessman, was interested in the project and would like to be a third. She was thrilled – and relieved. They all had the knowledge to be of enormous help in the running of the business side of things. Then she started looking for her staff.

Chapter Thirty-Nine

It was now April and Richard Carson House was to be opened. Everything was ready, the staff in place: a doctor, psychiatrist, two nurses and two male nurses, plus a gardener to direct the men working in the garden. The local papers were there and the national press, interested because the house was named after the late but eminent surgeon who had also left part of his estate to the British Legion. The military background was the major point to it all, especially as Helen had been in the war with Sir Richard and had worked with him. It was a great human interest story and the publicity a boost to the charitable side of it.

All three trustees were there and Arthur Hurst cut the ribbon, then gave a heartfelt speech, talking about the men who had returned from the war but who still were suffering the traumas of their time under fire and how the house would play a major part in their recovery. He also made the point that it was to be run as a charity and any donations would be more than welcome. He also mentioned that Helen had financed the buying of the premises and the renovations, but now needed the public to help her continue this vital work.

'These men were the survivors of a terrible war and we owe them a future,' he said. 'They faced the enemy on our behalf and are still suffering. We have a duty to help them. I am honoured to be a trustee of this endeavour and will do my very best along with the other trustees to see it flourish and succeed. Tomorrow, our first patients arrive, may they be the first of many that we can enable their recovery.'

There was enthusiastic applause from the invited guests: bank managers, businessmen, those from the medical world, all summoned by Hurst and Helen. Men who were in a position of power who could help keep the coffers flowing. They were all given a tour of the house, during which it was explained what plans they had to treat the men who were in dire need of their help.

At the end of the day Helen was thrilled at the offers of financial help that had been promised.

When eventually all had left, apart from the family and the trustees who sat down to dinner back at the farmhouse, they were all exhausted, but filled with hope. A bottle of champagne was opened in celebration.

James stood up.

'I would like to propose a toast to my wife Helen, an amazing woman whose idea has today come to fruition.' He held up his glass. 'To Helen!'

They all got to their feet. 'To Helen!' Then they resumed their seats.

She blushed with embarrassment, then she too rose from her chair.

'Thank you, everybody, but don't forget, if Richard hadn't left me the money none of this could have happened and neither could I have done it without my three wonderful trustees. I thank you gentlemen from the bottom of my heart . . . and James who encouraged me instead of telling me I was mad to even consider such a move.'

Arthur Hurst had decided to stay on for three days to help monitor the first patients and advise the staff on their treatment. After that he would be returning to Devon but would come up at regular intervals to advise. Helen was giving him a bed at the farmhouse during his stay and was delighted with his help, which would be invaluable.

And so it began. Helen walked into the house the following morning dressed in her nurse's uniform, with Arthur, as the first patients arrived and were taken to their rooms. Here they had a bed, a locker for their clothes and a chest of drawers. The dormitories were not unlike army barracks but with a more homely touch. Then they were shown the public rooms and the facilities.

'Blimey!' said one, 'I might stay here for ever! This is a might better than my place.'

He was even more enthusiastic after eating a hearty lunch.

'Can I book in indefinitely?' he asked Helen.

She laughed as she answered, 'I'm delighted you like us, but we hope to send you home a fitter man.'

'Oh, Nurse, that may take some time.' But he grinned broadly as he spoke.

One or two were much quieter and withdrawn, but Helen understood this and let them get settled in their own time.

Arthur had a chat to each patient that day and met with the medical staff and in particular the psychiatrist, later going over each man's file with them. They had ten men in all, with more arriving in the morning. Tomorrow the first arrivals were to be sent to dig the vegetable garden.

'Oh, I remember that day well,' James remarked over dinner that night. 'I couldn't imagine it was part of the treatment, well not for a while, anyway.'

Arthur chuckled at the memory. 'I remember too. But my goodness it made you and the others fit.'

'Slave labour, that's all it was!' James teased, then turning to Helen he asked, 'Well, darling, how did today feel to you?'

'Exciting! I loved every moment. I remember just what a difference it made to you and there are a few today who I can already see really need us and that's why we are here.'

'I've already suggested to James that he could be a great help chatting to these men. He understands just how they feel and what they went through. His intervention could be most helpful.'

'I've already thought of that,' Helen said. 'I'll wait and see who can benefit from this the most to begin with. But I can see he'll be called to assist a few times. Nothing helps more than someone who has seen what they have and suffered the same. When they realise how well he's come through it all, it will give them some hope.'

The following morning, the first arrivals were sent to the garden and under instruction from the gardener, started digging, clearing the ground of weeds and raking it over, ready for planting the seeds. At first, some of them struggled, not being used to manual labour for some time, but cheered on by the others, started to work with more enthusiasm.

Whilst they were doing so, five more patients arrived and were shown their room and then were interviewed by Arthur

Hurst before being sent to the dining room for lunch.

Arthur and Helen went over the complete list together, he pointing out the men who would need particular care to begin with and suggesting ways of treating them. Each man had his own problem, which Arthur, with his experience, was able to recognise to a degree. Some, like James, still had nightmares, others had lost all confidence and had become morose. One or two covered their fears by being comedians, but beneath their veneer were still suffering with nerves.

'These men are used to regimentation and rules, they are more comfortable with them,' he suggested. 'Like children, parameters give them a feeling of safety. I suggest you have a strict timetable, then they'll know what is expected of them. They don't have to worry about when and where. Mealtimes, anyway, will have to be at set times for the cook, or he'll go crazy and we don't want that!'

Between them they wrote out a timetable, which was to be typed and put on the back of each bedroom door for the patients to read. It worked for the staff as well as the patients. And so, with fifteen men in all, the house began its work.

During the first week, Helen asked James to come over and talk to the men. She felt that he could help to settle a few who were finding things difficult, being away from their families and familiar surroundings.

He made his way to the garden first, now that all the men were working there. With his natural charm, he chatted to them, man to man, telling them of his experiences during the war, how it had left him afterwards and how working in the garden in Devon had been the first step to his recovery. He made them laugh at his embarrassing moments with loud noises, which was more than helpful to those suffering from the same things. In the evening, he played darts with them, helped them choose books from the library and encouraged some to write home, letting their families know they were alright.

The men, recognising a kindred spirit, would talk to him about their fears, which was good for them, and James was able to relay this information to the staff, which went a long way in helping the men concerned.

Some of them were still suffering from the effect of their war wounds and were on medication, distributed by the nurses. At night, those who still suffered with nightmares were cared for by the male nurses on duty. Those who had withdrawn within themselves began to talk after a day or two working hard in the garden, even if it was only to moan about their aches and pains.

To begin with, Helen's mother Margaret had moved in to look after Rebecca, but after a few weeks, when Helen felt the house could do without her, she only worked part-time, which enabled her to be with her child. Rebecca was growing so quickly and Helen missed being with her each day, watching her develop. Sometimes she would drive over to the house and take Rebecca with her, which cheered up the men who had children and were missing them. They loved to play with her, which in its own way was therapeutic for them. She would take her toy tea set with her sometimes and the men would sit on the floor, drinking from tiny cups and chatting. It was a delight to watch.

At the end of each day when the men returned to the house after doing their daily jobs, which now included looking after the chickens, pigs and a couple of goats, they would have a bath and gather before dinner. Then they would be handed their mail from home, an important moment for all of them. It wasn't always good news, which could set the patient back in his development. If it was a death or someone was seriously ill, then of course they were given leave to visit and return later. But mostly the families wrote cheerful letters, pleased that their men were settled and feeling better, hoping that when they returned home they could face the future so much more positively.

On this particular day, a month later, Jack Simmons sat down to read his letter in the room where the men relaxed. As he read the two pages he became enraged and started swearing loudly.

'What's up, mate?' asked one of the others.

'My fucking wife, that's what! She's only gone and bloody left me. She's gone off with that pillock who lives a few doors away.' He got to his feet. 'I'll bloody kill him!'

One of the male nurses overheard his remarks and as Jack made for the door, the nurse stopped him.

'Where do you think you're going, Jack?'

'I'm going home to sort that bastard out!'

The nurse took a firm hold of his arm. 'Now that wouldn't help. Come with me, let's talk about it.'

Jack tried to shake off his hold, but the nurse led him firmly away into another room.

'Bloody hell!' said one. 'I wouldn't like to be the man who's run off with his missus if he gets to him.'

Jack was persuaded to have a chat with the psychiatrist who managed to calm him down and persuade him that returning home wouldn't be a good idea, but he warned the staff to keep a wary eye on him.

'I'm not convinced that he's ready to accept what's happened and I'm not at all certain how he's going to react in these next few days.'

At first, Jack returned to his chores: working in the garden, cleaning the pigsty, feeding the chickens, but all that time he hardly spoke to anyone. The other men tried to chivvy him along, but in the end they left him alone. One morning they discovered his bed was empty.

The psychiatrist rang the police station nearest to Jack's home address to tell them what had happened in the hope that they could intervene in what was obviously going to be an altercation, which could get out of hand due to Jack's anger and mental state.

It transpired that by so doing, they had saved him from being in serious trouble. He'd returned home, gone to the neighbour's house to confront him and was about to set about him when the police arrived to warn the man involved.

Jack was hauled off to spend a night in the cells to cool down.

When Helen was informed about his situation, it was decided to offer Jack another chance if he returned to the house and continued his treatment. Both the psychiatrist and Helen had discussed it between them and had decided they could still be the ones to help him, but only if he was willing to abide by the rules. The police agreed to let him go with just a warning – and so he was returned.

It was to Helen that he was referred on his return, to his surprise.

She sat in her office and spoke to him.

'I can understand your anger, Jack. You feel you have been

betrayed, but your wife has made her choice and you have to be a man and accept it. She obviously wasn't happy so now you must move on. I know what you've been through on the battlefield during the war, I was there and had to try and mend the broken bodies that were brought into the hospital.' Her tone softened. 'My own husband has been through it too, and has suffered mental traumas as you have, but as you've seen, he has overcome them and now lives a mostly normal and happy life. If you stay the course with us, hopefully you can do so too and start afresh. But I have to tell you, Jack, there are other cases who would willingly take your place and I'm not about to waste my time on someone who isn't going to work with us. The choice is yours!'

He sat quietly for a moment. 'That night in the cells gave me some thinking time, Sister. Yes, I was bloody angry, but you're right, I need to pull myself together, and get fit so I'm in a position to start to live again.' He grimaced. 'If I'm honest, I wasn't easy to live with, it's no wonder that Gracie, my wife, left me. So my answer is yes. I will stay and do as I'm told and thank you for taking me back.'

Helen smiled at his reply. 'Good, now go and get yourself a cup of tea and see your mates.'

At the door he turned and looked at her. 'You're even tougher than my old sergeant, Sister Havers!'

She burst out laughing. 'On your way, Jack, and behave!'

Chapter Forty

It was now July. The house had been open for three months. The vegetable garden was flourishing, keeping the cook supplied with fresh vegetables. There were eggs from the hens and milk from the goats, although milking them wasn't easy for some of the men who had sustained a few kicks now and then, to everyone's amusement.

James had started giving riding lessons to those who were interested, but some of the men politely refused when actually faced with the saddled horse. Jack, however, was enthusiastic. He had a natural aptitude and, at James's suggestion, he worked at the stables two days a week, helping out.

'How much longer will Jack be with you?' asked James one evening when he and Helen were having dinner.

'He's settled really well since he came back. He's more stable now and hopefully we can send him home before too long, if he continues to improve.'

'But he'll be living alone, won't he?'

'I imagine so. He's not mentioned any family. He did have a wife but she left, as you know. Why?'

'He's good with horses. I could use him permanently, if he wants a job.'

'Really? Oh, James, that would be great, that's unless he has any plans. Ask him tomorrow when you come over to give your riding lessons. But where would he live?'

James gave this some thought for a moment. 'There must be somewhere in the village that would rent him a room and feed him. I'll ask around first before I say anything to him.'

James found such a place and then he had a word with Jack when he was working in the stables a few days later, grooming the horses together.

'What are your plans when you leave the house?'

'To be honest I haven't made any. I don't want to go back home and be near the now ex-wife. That wouldn't do at all. I'll look for a job elsewhere, I suppose.'

'How would you like to work here with me, looking after the horses? I could do with another pair of hands. Mick and I have enough to do as it is.'

'You serious, gov?'

Laughing, James said, 'Yes, why wouldn't I be?'

'Knowing what I've been through and everything?'

'You forget I've been in the same boat and suffered as you have. My wife said you would soon be ready to go home. There is a room for rent in the village, full board, so you would have somewhere to stay. What do you say? I'll pay you a working wage.'

Jack grinned broadly and put out his hand. 'Thanks, you have a new man and I do believe I am a new man!'

* * *

When Jack returned to the house at the end of the day and joined the others in the dining room, he gave them the good news. Everyone was happy for him, knowing about his broken marriage.

'You'll be able to chat up the women in the village,' teased one.

'Nah! I've sworn off women, thanks. I'll stick to horses.'

This brought forth lots of ribald joshing, but it made for a happy atmosphere among the men.

Although most of the patients were recovering in their own way from their stay, one or two were not making the progress the staff had hoped for and this was told to Arthur Hurst on his next visit. He had a talk with the men involved and suggested they should be sent to his place in Devon, where he could offer a more in-depth treatment. And so it was arranged and new patients were admitted from a waiting list to take their place.

During his visit he held a meeting with the other trustees who were running the business side of the venture. So far, the donations that had been promised at the opening were in place and in some cases the businessmen involved had promised regular payments, which was a great relief, but it was decided that in the near future they would have to make plans to feature the house and its aims, in the hope of raising even more money. They decided to hold a summer fete at the end of August. They could have stalls selling the home-grown vegetables. Some of the men were good at woodwork and it was decided they could produce useful items and perhaps some children's toys, and the cook could set up a stall selling home-made cakes.

When Helen made the announcement after dinner that

night, it caused much discussion among the men, giving them an added interest, and when Helen asked them for volunteers, several put up their hands and offered up ideas about what they were prepared to do. It made for a lively discussion.

To everyone's surprise, Tommy, one of the men, offered to sketch portraits of the visitors.

'I didn't know you could draw,' said Helen.

He flushed with embarrassment. 'It's something I've always done, Sister. I've got a sketchbook full of drawings I've done since I've been here.'

He was sent off to his room to fetch his book and when he returned and showed his work, it was obvious to all that he had a real talent. There were drawings of many of the patients and the staff. There were pictures showing the men at work in the garden, all drawn in either pencil or pen. The admiration shown by everyone boosted his morale, which delighted Helen as Tommy had been one of the patients who had been very withdrawn to begin with, and although he integrated well eventually, he remained a quiet man.

So it was decided. The necessary wood would be supplied for those who needed it. The gardener would oversee the vegetables to be sold and any other goods needed in the cause would also be supplied. The two female nurses offered to make rag dolls together, which was an added bonus, and the cook was pleased to bake cakes for the day.

When Helen went home that evening, she was thrilled with the outcome and told James what had transpired.

'You should have seen the men, James. It gave them something new to work towards and you should see

Tommy's sketchbook, he has a real talent for drawing. He's going to draw portraits for a small fee.'

Seeing how animated his wife was, James was delighted for her.

'If you like, I could bring three of my horses over and give rides to children. I'll let Rebecca ride on Valiant first to show that it's safe.'

'That would be marvellous and Rebecca would love the fete. I'll take her round the stalls. It was suggested by one of the men to have a coconut shy. He said he'd build the cups to put them in if we supply the nuts and the balls to throw. I said yes, of course. I thought we could put up notices in the local shops asking for items to be sold on a white elephant stall. Women love knick-knacks.'

Edward offered to supply items for a raffle, which was a brilliant idea, and Margaret said she had items for the white elephant stall and would be willing to run the stall for them.

During the coming weeks, there was an air of excitement in the house among the patients as they started work on their items. Those who were not so competent at making things helped in other ways, working extra hard in the garden, filling in for the men who were doing other things for the fete.

As Helen walked around with the psychiatrist watching those at work she was thrilled when he said how being so involved was great therapy for the men.

'Just watch their expressions, Helen. They are so engrossed, they're in another world, one that doesn't hold any fears for them. Most of them have overcome the worst of their mental problems being here. They are beginning to realise that they can cope with life in the real world, after all. Working in the garden, being allowed to live at a slower pace without any pressure, sharing their fears with me and the others who have suffered the same has been exactly what was needed to get them back on their feet. I'm so proud to be a part of it and so should you be. Sir Richard certainly would be.'

She was very touched by his words. Having been part of the war and seeing how the troops had suffered, she knew that now she had the means, thanks to Richard, to be in a position to help these poor souls. She remembered how helpless she'd felt when she'd been behind the lines working in the hospital, knowing these men would be returning home, unfit, still suffering mentally from what they'd seen, and how it would have affected their marriages. Hopefully, through their treatment here, marriages and home life could be saved as hers had been. But for Arthur Hurst and his care for James, it could well have been a different story.

The day of the fete arrived. Breakfast was served early, allowing time for all the stalls to be set up and filled with the goods on offer. The vegetable stall looked very colourful, the vegetables arranged so carefully by the gardener.

The white elephant stall was full to overflowing with many small items donated by the villagers and others. Margaret had arranged things really well and with a female touch that made it look so inviting to the ladies, and next to that a stall displaying delightful rag dolls, made by the nurses.

There was a vast display of handmade wooden items:

troughs for the garden, lidded boxes for storage and many small toys, plus a wooden fort, which any small boy would love.

The coconut stall was set up, with a couple of the men ready to run it when the fete opened at two o'clock that afternoon. They were practising knocking the nuts out of the holder, making sure everything worked, anxious to start.

Tommy had a chair for his clients to sit on whilst he drew their portraits, plus plenty of spare paper and pens. He decided to use pens for his drawings as they would last longer than ones in pencil.

Helen walked round with little Rebecca, checking everything was in place, trying to placate her child who wanted to stop and play with everything.

'No, darling, these aren't for you. Later I'll buy you a small cake and if you're really good, an ice cream.'

'Me likes ice cream. Want it now, Mummy.'

'The man's not here yet, so we have to wait.' They had hired a man to come with his bicycle and cart to offer his wares too. The weather forecast had been for a warm, sunny day, so ice cream would be a welcome addition.

At two o'clock, the gates were opened and the long line of people began to filter in. Helen was delighted to see so many had turned up. It would have been a disappointment if the attendance had been poor, also having a disastrous effect on the men who had worked so hard to put everything together. Instead the place became crowded in a very short time. The coconut stall was doing a roaring trade, the vegetable stall was selling quickly, more goods added from the extra hidden beneath the stall in readiness if business was good, and the ice creams were selling well.

The cook was manning his cake stall which had a vast selection of small cakes as well as sponge cakes, fruit cakes and gingerbread men, which the children loved. On each stall was a charity box, which the customers were putting their small change in and as Helen noticed, some had placed paper money in them too.

There was a small queue waiting to have their portraits done after seeing how well Tommy had drawn the first one, much to the delight of the lady who was first to sit for him.

When James arrived with his horses, everyone looked on with interest and when he dismounted and put Rebecca on Valiant's back and led her around on a lead rein, lots of the children clamoured for a ride too. The three horses were in use all afternoon.

Raffle tickets sold well when the customers saw the prizes. There were bottles of wine, a couple of champagne, boxes of chocolates, bath salts, lavender water and pouches of lavender to put in your drawers, and vouchers for meals at the local pub, plus a star prize of a weekend at one of Cheltenham's best hotels.

Edward was running the raffle and Arthur Hurst had made the journey with his friend, Gerald, so all three trustees were there to see and take part in the day. The press had been invited and photographs were taken around the grounds, which would appear in the local paper's next edition.

When it was time to close, Arthur, with the aid of a microphone that had been set up, gave a speech, thanking everyone for coming, saying how important Richard

Carson House was to the soldiers needing care, and urging everyone there to spread the word of the good work that was being done and the need for help with the donations to allow it to continue.

Then it was time to clear up, with everyone dismantling the stalls. There was very little that remained unsold and so it was deemed a great success. Helen, James and the trustees dined with the men that night to celebrate the work they had all put in and to thank them for their efforts. Then they were given the following day off work as a reward. They all cheered at this and when the contents of the charity boxes had been counted and the sum collected was announced, the cheer was even louder.

Rebecca, who had been allowed to stay up for the dinner had fallen sleep in James's arms. The horses had been taken back to the stables earlier, fed and watered for the night, so the three of them could go straight back to the farmhouse. Everyone was worn out. Edward was playing host to the two other trustees, so Helen and James didn't have to cater for them, and having settled Rebecca, they too climbed into bed.

James gathered Helen into his arms and held her close.

'What a terrific day this has been. My God, those men worked hard to bring it all together. It will give them such a boost. It was such fun out there with all the stalls. People really enjoyed it. I know I did.'

'So did I and Rebecca certainly did, as did all the other children. Your rides proved to be very popular. Perhaps you should think again of opening a riding school, now you are so much better. After all, you've two good assistants to help you.'

He thought for a moment. 'Perhaps in the spring, I'll certainly think seriously about it.' He sighed. 'Who would have thought, when I walked into that hotel so long ago and you joined me at the bar, that this day would happen? Here we are married, with a child. Me, running a business training horses and now you with a nursing home, caring for troops who suffered during the war and who have just produced a day that will be remembered by many for quite a while. It's unbelievable!'

'I know,' she said. 'Sometimes I wonder how it all happened, myself, and it could have been so different. I could have lost you on that operating table. That still haunts me when I think about it.'

'That was then, darling. Now and the future is what is important. We have a daughter to raise in what I hope will be a better world and we have each other, and you with your work will be helping others to enjoy their future too.'

'We have one person to thank for all this, Richard. He saved your life, and by leaving me his money he is the means of helping so many others.'

'That's his legacy, Helen. He would be so proud of you, I know I am.'

'You forget, James, what you've had to endure and have overcome.'

He frowned. 'Let's be honest, darling, it was Brian Dickinson who did that for me. I was deeply depressed when he arrived with poor Valiant who was all but dead on his legs. I was so incensed by the state of him and the cruelty he had suffered that I forgot my own feelings. Brian was the man who unlocked my depression and who set me on the road to recovery. Without his intervention, I've no idea how I would have ended up.'

'Maybe, but you did recover and you learnt to cope with loud noises and confined spaces, to a great degree, but he didn't do that – you did!'

'Well, I owed it to him to do so, didn't I?' He yawned. 'I am really tired, I suggest we get as much sleep as we can before Rebecca wakes in the morning. She was so tired, with a bit of luck, she'll sleep later than usual.' He leant over and kissed Helen. 'Goodnight, darling. I'm so pleased the day went well.'

Helen had just settled when she heard a noise from Rebecca's room and climbed out of bed to go and see what was happening.

Rebecca was asleep, cuddling her favourite toy rabbit, but she was making soft noises as she slept, obviously dreaming. Helen sat on her bed and patted her, making shushing noises, talking softly until the child settled. She sat for a while watching her, thinking of the number of times she'd done this for James during his nightmares. His, of course, had been more violent, but they now happened very rarely.

She got up and, opening the curtain slightly so as not to disturb Rebecca, looked out over the field that was part of the farmhouse. The moon was shining in a clear sky. Nothing moved, it was silent, unlike many a night long ago, when the sound of gunfire filled the air. How lucky they had all been to have come through it. She thought of the men she'd nursed. Of the boy whose face had been so badly burnt, the soldiers returning after losing limbs. How did they cope, she wondered?

Walking softly, she returned to her own room and

looked down at James, now fast asleep, and silently thanked Richard Carson for saving the life of the man she loved, and for leaving her his money, which had allowed her to set up the house in his name. A testament to the great man himself, who had been her mentor and lover. She had no regrets about their relationship. He had told her she'd made him happy and she was glad of that, but now she had found the man with whom she wanted to spend the rest of her life, who had made her life complete, who had given her a daughter. Together they would build a future, helping others to build one too.

Acknowledgements

With love as always to my daughters, Beverley and Maxine.